OATH OF SILENCE: A DARK MAFIA ROMANCE

(DEVIANT DOMS)

JANE HENRY

D1534042

PROLOGUE

ROMEO

Twenty years earlier

A brisk wind kicked the dry, fallen leaves into mini tempests, camouflaging the secret trip to the quarry. Narciso "The Skull" Rossi, the head of the Rossi family and most feared man on the East Coast of America, loved the quarry, and so did his sons. Far from their mother's prying and judgmental eyes, the quarry offered the perfect place to teach them life's most important lessons.

How to hit on a girl.
How to command a room's presence.
How to earn respect from those around you.
How to kill a man who betrays you.

Romeo Rossi, at thirteen years old, was the eldest brother of the six Rossi children. A rule enforcer and a natural-born leader, he occasionally liked to push the envelope.

So when their father went to Tuscany to visit the family home and conduct business overseas, he went to the quarry. Didn't need the prying eyes of his younger siblings to tattle to Mama that Romeo was smoking again.

His father would only roll his eyes and tell him to roll his own damn smokes, but his mother despised the habit—no doubt because it reminded her of her husband's own three-pack-a-day habit—and would punish him severely for such an infraction.

It wasn't fear of punishment that drove Romeo to the quarry, though. In a bustling family of eight, privacy was a precious, rare commodity. And Romeo liked to be alone.

Leaning his back against a tree, Romeo reached into his pocket and drew out the pack of cigarettes. Putting one between his lips, he was returning the pack just as the sound of crunching leaves and twigs told him he'd been followed. His spine stiffened, his hand still on his back pocket. The lone, unlit cigarette still dangled from his lips.

He did a mental inventory of the weapons he had on his person. Rossi family boys never left home without a weapon, even when going to school or church or on a date. Especially a date.

Switchblade in his pocket, thin razor blade in his

wallet, brand-new brass knuckles nestled in the hidden pocket of his jeans. Nothing too flashy, but they'd come in handy if push came to shove.

And the lighter. The lighter could be used if necessary as well.

Never one to cower and wait, Romeo's temper flared. "Who's there?"

No answer.

He flicked the blade open, relishing the reassuring heft of it in his palm and primed his senses, but before he could detect another sound, a loud *crash* sounded behind him. He swung, blade instinctively tucked by his side to hide it in case it was a cop.

"For fuck's sake, Tavi." Ottavio Rossi, Romeo's younger brother and the second eldest brother in the Rossi family, gave Romeo a sheepish grin. Almost as tall as Romeo, Ottavio inherited the Rossi family height but unlike Romeo, had his mother's lithe frame. With a shock of chestnut-brown hair he wore shorter than the others, combined with a thin pair of wire-rimmed glasses, he looked almost as old as Romeo, though he was three years younger.

"Sorry, Rome," he said with a sheepish shrug. "Followed the little brats here." He reached behind him and dragged tiny three-year-old Marialena and five-year-old Mario in front of him.

"I not a brat!" Marialena said, her pretty eyes flashing at both of them.

Mario stomped his foot. "Stop calling me that or I'll tell Mama you're smoking again."

Ottavio rolled his eyes, and Romeo glared.

"You two—"

"Three," came an amused voice to Ottavio's right, and Orlando stepped into the light. "Sorry. I didn't know you guys were here."

"Jesus," Romeo groaned. "I came here to be *alone,* not tagged along by the whole damn family."

"Not the *whole* family," Orlando corrected. "And I could say the same. I came here to read, not to babysit." He rolled his eyes at Marialena, and tucked his worn paperback into his back pocket.

Romeo's lips thinned. He didn't want an audience. He wanted one minute, just *one minute,* where he didn't have to take care of someone for once. One minute where he could just be himself for a little while. One minute where he wasn't Romeo Rossi, the youngest kid in St. Anthony's ninth grade, already wielding more power as the Underboss-to-be in the Family than soldiers under his father's command twice his age.

"Nonna's almost got dinner ready," Orlando said. "Let's go."

"No," Marialena whined. "I wanted to see the co-ree."

"*Quarry,*" Romeo corrected, reaching for her hand. He noted how little, how cold it was, and fanned his fingers to warm her. "And no. It's getting cold, and we need to get home to dinner."

Clouds covered the moon and the quarry was plunged into temporary darkness, when a scream and shout broke out behind them. When the clouds parted, Romeo's eyes met Ottavio's. He picked Marialena up in his arms to keep her from following and shoved her at Orlando, the largest of the bunch and the one most likely to keep the willful three-year-old in place. "Stay here."

The brothers froze. Marialena fussed and pushed at Orlando but he held her tight. "Hush, Lena," he said, using their pet name for her. "Let Rome go see what it is."

Romeo pushed through brambles and branches undeterred, even as his heart smashed against his ribcage. His trusty knife lay tucked in his palm.

"It's Romeo!" someone shouted ahead of him. "Rome! Oh, God. Rome!"

Santo, the Family's best friend and adopted brother, stood in front of a small clearing surrounded by small, bare birch trees, his eyes wide and terrified. "Stay back, Rome."

Romeo froze. "You okay, Santo?"

Santo slowly shook his head from side to side.

Romeo's eyes fell to the ground.

A body.

Sprawled out on the ground behind Santo, partially covered by leaves, and obviously dead.

He swallowed the bile that rose in his throat and used the sternest voice he could muster, the voice that even his most willful younger sibling always obeyed.

"Don't fucking move."

Santo stood stock-still, obeying, as the sound of footsteps came up behind them.

"*No!*" Romeo slammed his palm out as if the very

air would stall his siblings from coming any closer. "No."

He glanced over his shoulder and drew in a breath. "Santo, you stay here. Tavi, come here. Orlando, you take the younger kids back to the house."

"No!" Marialena, who managed to escape Orlando's grip, protested. "No! I stay!"

Romeo swiveled to face her, prepared to toss the toddler over his shoulder and carry her back to the house himself, when Orlando spoke up.

"Come, little Lena. You help Nonna with the table, okay? It's cold out here and Mama will be worried if you ruin your pretty new shoes."

Marialena stared down at her brand-new shoes, pretty patent leather they'd gotten in Boston the day before, and nodded. As the largest of the bunch, Orlando firmly took the younger kids' hands and dragged them back up to the brightly lit road, but not before he gave Romeo a meaningful look. They were not finished, and he would tell him what happened later. Romeo gave him one curt, quick nod.

When they were far enough away, Romeo turned back to Santo. "Step aside, man. Let me see."

Santo obeyed and watched. It wasn't lost on Romeo that Santo was the one who had found the body. Only ten years old himself, he was far wiser than his years and had come to the Family as the resident grifter. He was gifted in swindling, and rarely told the truth.

He was Narciso Rossi's favorite. The one child

unrelated by blood, the only one Romeo's mother, Tosca, would let him corrupt to his heart's content.

Ottavio came up beside Romeo, and the two boys stared at the body. Romeo fell to one knee while Ottavio turned and dry heaved beside him.

"Couple days old," Romeo said in a cold, detached voice that belied the fire that churned in his belly. "Maybe a week."

He stared at the legs, askew and obviously broken, and wondered what torture had hurt the worst. He stared at the fingers, cold and stiff with rigor mortis, and flexed his own fingers as if to defy the thought of death freezing his own limbs. He stared at the leaves that served as a makeshift coffin before their own decay.

Santo nodded. "Smells like ass."

"You shouldn't curse like that," Romeo protested absentmindedly. He cursed like a sailor himself, but felt anyone under the age of thirteen should be held to higher standards of purity.

"Fuck off," Santo muttered. Romeo didn't hear him.

He was too fixated on the bloodied body before him.

"Knife up the back of the skull," Ottavio noted, voicing the brutality that lay before them on the bed of leaves. He didn't offer any other notes.

Both Ottavio and Romeo knew it was their father's signature move, the move that got him nicknamed "The Skull." Romeo was six years old when he caught his father practicing his move in a woodshed on their property.

Have your move, son. That way you leave your mark. That way they know you. They respect you.

But Romeo didn't play games.

He'd never killed a man and never planned to.

There was no need for the Boss to get his hands dirty.

Romeo knelt beside the body and patted the dirty, saggy jeans for identification, but everything'd been taken. There was nothing but the body and the putrid smell of decaying flesh.

Why? Why here? The Rossi family was not sloppy with their hits. Ever.

"We can't call anyone," he said to Ottavio. The only person he would trust would be his father, who was currently in Tuscany and had been for the past week.

"Do you know who it is?"

Santo shook his head. Romeo turned on him sternly. "Why were you here?"

Santo shrugged. "Heard the boys come down, thought I'd hide and scare you all."

Romeo scowled, then turned back to the body.

"What do we do, Rome?" Ottavio asked.

"We fucking leave it," Santo muttered. This time, Romeo didn't tell him to watch his language.

He caught Ottavio's eye, and Ottavio's jaw firmed. He knew as well as Romeo did that if their father had killed this man—and all signs pointed to his guilt—he'd go to jail, and this time, they'd toss away the key.

"No," Ottavio said with decision. "We get rid of the body."

"Tavi," Santo said, kicking a tree stump. "How the hell do we—"

"Not we," Romeo interrupted. "*Us.* You go back up to the house and make sure Orlando's got the little ones under control. Fuck if I want them coming back and seeing this..."

"No way." Santo planted his feet firmly on the ground before him. "You guys might be bigger'n me, but you're not big enough to get rid of the body of a man yourself."

He had a point.

It took two hours, six hands, and five lies to his mother, but when he went to bed that night, the deed was done and his father's truck parked where he'd left it.

He couldn't tell his father, though his gut told him his father well knew.

But why did he leave the body like that?

He couldn't tell his mother. She'd send them all to Italy to boarding school like she'd threatened to for years.

He couldn't tell any of the soldiers or the men he'd grown up around and called uncle or cousin, because who could you trust? And what if his father *had* been the one to commit the murder?

And before they went to bed that night, Romeo made Santo and Ottavio take an oath sworn in blood, his trusty switchblade sealing the promise.

Nothing ever happened.

No one saw the body.

They were smoking by the quarry and went out

for a drive, and they'd take whatever punishment they got without complaint.

"We have oaths," Romeo told them, and he felt the weight of his words as he said them. Oaths that bound. Oaths that silenced. "We'll swear an oath tonight."

Oaths that would one day tear them apart.

CHAPTER ONE

"These violent delights have violent ends." Romeo and Juliet

VITTORIA
Present day

I'm a stranger in a foreign land, and I don't quite know what to make of that yet, but the bar that beckons to me with bright neon lights promises liquid courage and actual food. I pull out my wallet and look at what's left.

Pathetic.

Maybe they need a dishwasher here? Heh.

But I'm getting ahead of myself. I'm *not* planning to relocate to Boston. In fact, I'm planning to spend as little time here as possible. Hell, I wouldn't be here at all if not for the letter that showed up on my doorstep informing me of a meeting tomorrow.

Tell no one, the letter had said, and so I hadn't. It's easy when you have literally no one to tell, not a friend or soul to confide in. But I couldn't ignore the damn thing, either. So I'd jumped in my car in upstate New York this morning and driven east with hardly a dollar to my name.

My stomach growls insistently, suggesting this had not been the wisest choice.

But I'm a survivor. That's what I do. And I'll deal with this just like I've dealt with all the other shit that life's thrown at me. Ashton Bryant will not undo me.

I pull down my visor and flip open the lighted mirror to make myself look presentable. Who knows, maybe I'll luck out and a guy will buy me a drink.

No.

I don't need anything from anyone. I'll buy my own damn drink.

Quick swish of mascara that's nearly dried up. Quick swipe of lip gloss from the edges of the tube. My hair's a hopeless cause, but I quickly tame it under a fabric headband and hope it gives me a whimsical look. I glance down at the button-down top I'm wearing and, with a sigh, unfasten the topmost buttons. I'm not about to whore myself out for money, but a girl could flash a little cleavage for a free drink. And hell, do I need a drink. Maybe two.

The entire six-hour ride here, I thought about

the letter in my bag. I'm done now. I don't want to think about it anymore. That's something I'll revisit later, after I get some food in my belly and a little break before hunkering down in my car for the night. I get out and slam the door.

I freeze, startled when a large, lumbering black SUV pulls into the space beside me with a screech of tires, like a raging bull stopped short. It looks bulletproof and powerful and dwarfs the cars beside it. I flatten myself against my car on instinct so I can observe and watch a second, then a third black car—another SUV, followed by some sleek, expensive-looking car with tinted windows—park beside me, so close I feel the heat of the engine on my legs.

They're either celebrities or drug dealers. Maybe both.

Why here? Why now? I want to be anonymous, and this showy flash of cars and obvious money makes me want to put my car in reverse and leave.

Before I can get my wits about me and head inside, the car doors open, and men start pouring out of it like it's a bachelor party playdate. I don't want them to notice me staring, so I try to pretend I dropped something on the ground and peer at them from my almost-hidden position.

A chill skates down my spine. These are no ordinary men.

I'd guess they range in age from late teens to mid-fifties, but every one of them is well-dressed, well-groomed, and they walk with an air of ownership that's hard to miss. A mere glimpse at them tells me they're strong, powerful, wealthy men with a purpose. Their voices carry through the night air.

"Served too long," one guy says.

"Need to get laid," another offers, cuffing a guy beside him I can't quite see.

"Bet they don't serve Frangelico or Limoncello in the big house," says another.

"Don't tell Ma we came here first, or she'll beat your ass," another warns with a grin. "Party line, we just picked Rome up and he'll be home for dinner tomorrow." I can't really see faces in the dark, only hear their voices and... feel their presence.

I straighten up and slow down my step so I don't look like I'm following them.

I hold my purse closer to my hip and hang back, but one of the much younger guys, probably not much older than early to mid-twenties, holds the door for me. The overhead light illuminates his face as I draw closer. His face is perfectly symmetrical, a born movie star or model, dark hair and mesmerizing eyes that soften when he sees me. He's got a bad boy look about him, though. A modern-day James Dean.

"After you, gorgeous," he says with a grin that would melt the panties off a nun. I feel my cheeks heat, but give him a thankful nod. He's all smooth talk and grace, and in comparison, I feel clumsy and foolish and like I'm *really* out of place.

And yet... it feels nice to be called that.

I smile my thanks, and when I enter, walk as far away from the rowdy group of men as I can. There's something about them that oozes raw, unadulterated alpha male, something about them that's all testosterone and steel. Something about them that intimidates me a little. You don't see guys like this in the tiny town I grew up in in upstate New York, and if you do, they definitely don't pay attention to girls like me.

The room grows quiet when they enter, for such a brief moment of time it's almost as if I imagined it. The bartender stands up straighter, the waitresses shoot one another quick, furtive glances. It's so quick, before I draw in another breath everyone's gone back to the way things were.

Interesting.

I find a vacant booth in the corner of the bar and take a seat. This is a good vantage point. From here, I can hear anything I want, eavesdrop and listen and observe, and hopefully no one but the waitress will know I'm here.

"Sorry, honey." I look up to see a middle-aged woman with graying hair standing by my table. "This one's taken."

I look around the booth. "Taken?"

"Yeah, hon. Bachelorette party coming in a few, all tables from here to the back are reserved."

I look where she points to a small *reserved* sign hanging on the side of the booth that I didn't notice before.

"Oh. Sorry about that. Do you have a booth I could sit in?"

She shakes her head sadly. "Sorry, babe. You'll have to sit at the bar."

"The bar?"

"Yeah. But don't worry, you can order food there."

That's not what I'm worried about. I feel like sitting at the bar might as well put an *available* sign around my neck.

This was a mistake. This was a stupid, stupid mistake. I came here wanting to be anonymous, and to break up the monotony of staying in my car, not to be noticed by anyone.

Shit.

My stomach growls, reminding me that I haven't had anything to eat since last night, and it's now evening. It's fine, I reason. I need to shed a few pounds anyway. What's a little starvation?

I glance at the menu, relieved to see there's a Friday-night special during happy hour. A five-dollar happy hour bar pizza sounds divine right about now.

The bartender wipes down the counter in front of me and smiles. She's young, college-aged or so, her dark blonde hair pulled back in a merciless ponytail. "Can I help you?"

I haven't been to Boston since I was a kid, and I half-expected everyone here to talk with a Boston accent. It surprises me she doesn't. When she raises her eyebrows at me, I find my tongue.

"Yes, please, could I get the pizza and the happy hour margarita?"

She gives me a sad smile. "I'm sorry, happy hour ended half an hour ago." My belly sinks. Damn it.

"Don't worry about it," a man's voice says behind me. "I'll get this one."

I look over my shoulder to see a tall, well-dressed man giving me a smile. He's kinda hot, in a deliberately tousled way. He's probably a year or two older than my twenty-eight years and looks decent enough. "Haven't seen you here before."

"Oh, I'm..." I'm not sure how to respond. I'm starving, I've got hardly any money, and did he just offer to get me a drink or food? It can't hurt, I reason. "Just traveling through town."

And hopefully will be going on my merry way soon. Where to? I have no idea. What next? Same black hole of no idea. Where will the next stage of life bring me?

I ignore the feeling of desperation that threatens to shake my resolve and rattle my nerves. I swallow hard and force a smile. I'm not making any other decisions until tomorrow's meeting.

"Welcome," he says. My stomach chooses that exact minute to growl in the most unladylike way imaginable. I stifle an embarrassed snort, but he only smiles, flashing perfectly white teeth at me. "Hungry?"

I decide I don't trust him. Maybe it's because he's standing too close or his tone is too familiar, or he smells really, really good, but there's something about him that sets my nerves on edge.

"Starving," I admit with a nod. "And thank you, but I'll get my own drink and food."

"Don't mention it," he says with a smile, but his eyes hold an icy edge. "I'm just passing through town, too." He leans in close. His breath smells faintly of whiskey. His knuckles graze my wrist.

"Tomorrow, we'll both go our separate ways and neither will be the wiser. It's on me."

Is he... implying what I think he is? What happens in Boston stays in Boston?

My skin crawls with the implication, as the bartender places my frosty drink on a little napkin in front of me.

I want to leave, but I really, *really* want to eat. Maybe for once in my life I should do something drastic. I'm starving and broke, and he can't make me do anything I don't want him to.

"Oh?" I ask, reaching for my drink. My lips feel parched, my mouth a desert. I take a sip, and it tastes so good, I gulp it. I sigh. "And where's that for you? Tomorrow, that is."

He grins. "Heading to the airport in the morning."

Ah. So he's looking for a one-night stand and a little nightcap. Well, I'm not the girl for that party.

"Where to?" I ask. I'll small talk him until I get my pizza. I'm not the kind of person to do this, but I'm going for broke here.

He gives me a smile I can only describe as predatory. "That's a secret."

"Ah. Well, I hope you have a good trip," I finish lamely.

He sits on the stool beside me. Too close. His knee brushes mine, but it doesn't feel nice. I want to push him away, and have just decided to do exactly that when the waitress slides a plate of steaming, bubbly pizza in front of me.

My mouth waters. I'm so hungry I'm weak.

I take a slice of pizza, and bite into it. "Oh, yum," I say around a mouthful of cheesy, crispy pizza. I push the plate his way. "This is incredible."

He smiles. "Go on. You eat it." He shrugs and lowers his voice. "I'd much rather watch you eat."

Ok, he's creeping me out.

My hand trembles a little when I reach for the second slice. I can't shake the feeling that I'm going to regret eating this next to him and taking any charity from him at all, even though technically I've done nothing wrong. I just don't trust this guy.

Loud laughter comes from where the rich men entered earlier, and I'm not the only one to look their way. A table full of attractive, single women sits to my left, whispering amongst themselves and giggling, and even the bartender's gaze has wandered there a few times. I can't hear exactly what they're saying, but the younger one who held the door for me says something that makes the rest of them bellow with laughter.

They're friends, this group, that much is obvious. Likely brothers, if I'm to assume the similar dashing looks and suave grace have anything to do with genes. But they're tight. They laugh with the air of familiarity and companionship most only dream of.

And for one wild, lonely, crazy minute... I want to be with that group. I want to belong the way they do. I want someone to know me, to really, truly *know* me, to care about me, and to welcome me home.

I blame the long car ride and the uncertainty

ahead of me. I'm too pragmatic for such romantic idealism. I shake my head and take another sip of my drink.

I glance quickly back at the group of well-dressed men.

The man at the center of the group, who seems like he's the focus of tonight's attention, smiles sadly and takes another sip from his drink. His dark hair falls over his forehead, and he shoves it away impatiently, like he doesn't have time to have obscured vision. I couldn't really see him before when they entered because so many of the others were crowded around him, but now... now I can't take my eyes away.

I'm not sure if it's the rugged cut of his jaw covered in dark black stubble, or the way... oh, God, the way he takes up half the table with the breadth of his shoulders. My eyes travel down the muscled column of his neck, and even the expensive fabric of the suit he wears can't hide how large and strong he is. Someone talks to him and he responds. I can't hear the words, but the deep, rough register of his voice makes a heaviness settle between my legs. He's raw, unadulterated, visceral male, and I've never seen anything like him in person.

As I stare, he lifts his head. His eyes beneath heavy dark lashes and brows meet mine, catching my eye from across the room. He holds my gaze, and I can't tear my eyes away. I can't tell the color of his eyes from across the room, but I feel the fire in them hit me straight in the solar plexus.

My lips freeze on the margarita glass. My

heart's beating faster. My fingers wrap around my drink more firmly, as if to anchor myself onto something tangible before I drown. I can't breathe while he holds me in his gaze, as if an electric connection's fused us in this one stolen moment of time.

I turn away first. I have to. It feels like a forfeit.

If I don't stop staring at him, I'll become his. He'll beckon me to him, and I'd walk over there as if hypnotized. I'd give him my very soul if he but crooked a finger.

I stare down at the plate of food, as if coming back to Earth. Everything feels strangely foreign. Even when I take another bite of pizza, it no longer holds the tantalizing appeal it did just moments ago.

"Ahh, Romeo," one of the men says behind me in a thick Italian accent. "You need more than a drink and food tonight, *amico,* eh?"

Romeo. Why do they call him Romeo? Is he known for being a charmer, then?

I'm glad I looked away. I have no use for a charmer. I bet he has a beautiful wife at home. I bet she's waiting for him, in their perfect house with their sweet little children. Well, no, his friend's hinting he needs a woman tonight, so… none of this bodes well.

"Is it good?"

I blink in surprise, and look up at the man sitting next to me. I almost forgot about him. He's determined to make sure that doesn't happen. I almost forgot about everyone but the man across the room who's somehow managed to ignite me with merely a look.

"It's delicious, thank you." He smiles and signals to the bartender. "We'll have another drink."

"Oh, no, thank you," I say with as much grace as I can muster. "After this drink, I really need to go." I shake my head at her. "Just a water, please."

"Don't be silly. Of course you need another drink. What's the rush?"

Ugh, one of *those* men, who thinks he's within his rights to push me. Newp.

What is the rush? All I'm going to do when I'm done here is find a public restroom where I can freshen up for the night, then an abandoned parking lot that's relatively safe where I can park and sleep before the big reveal tomorrow.

"Just water," I insist.

"For now," he says, nursing his own drink on the rocks. "So tell me about yourself. What brings you here?"

I take another slice of pizza, finally feeling relief from the ache of hunger in my belly. The food's revived me a bit, but the alcohol's made me sleepy.

For one brief, hysterical second, I imagine myself telling this skeevy stranger the truth.

I received a letter from an attorney to appear at a stranger's house. I'm here with everything I own in the back of my car. I've got no money because my asshole of an ex swindled me, and now I have to start off on my own, and I'm really hoping for a miraculous turn of events at tomorrow's meeting.

I smile. "Just decided I needed a change of scenery for a while. You?"

He leans over the bar and brushes his thumb over my hand that's curled into a fist. I shiver uncomfortably and tuck my hand in my lap.

"I'm here for a one-night stand," he says in a low voice only I can hear. "I'm told I'm good in bed. I'm safe, I use protection, and I'm a very generous lover." My stomach churns. Well, then. So much for foreplay and subtleties. "Join me tonight?"

"I—I can't do that," I tell him honestly. I have less than zero interest in a one-night stand with a stranger, especially someone who looks at me the way he does. "I do thank you for the pizza and drink."

His smile turns deadly. "Surely you're not telling me no?"

"That's what she said," the bartender says with a cool smile. "And here? We always make sure a lady's *no* is well-respected." She leans across the counter. "Got it?"

He cuts his eyes to her but doesn't respond. The food sits heavily in my stomach. I try fruitlessly to follow it with a solid swig of my drink when ice hits my lips.

I feel as if I'm going to be sick. Did he put something in my drink? No, the bartender's been watching him like a hawk and would've realized it. I imagine it's just my nerves.

I have to get out of here, now.

"Your restroom?" I ask her.

She points to the far corner of the room where a neon *restroom* sign indicates the way.

"Thank you."

I am out of here. I'm gonna find an exit, slip on out, drive far away from this place with its beautiful people and predatory scumbags, and *go.* Somewhere. Anywhere. He said he'd pay for my food, so he can do just that.

My hand shakes when I push open the door to the bathroom, but I quickly glance over my shoulder to make sure the guy at the bar—I don't even know his *name*—isn't watching me. He's looking over his shoulder the other way. I take my chance, and run for the back door with the exit sign.

Something tells me he'll follow me if he sees me. My hand fumbles with the doorknob, but thankfully it's unlocked. I step out into the cool night air, and quickly shut the door behind me.

I make a quick mental inventory of where I am. To one side, large plastic crates are lined to the roof, and further back, a full dumpster stands high and tall. A black cat slinks past me, but other than that, there's not a soul out here. Not one.

My heart sinks when I see the parking lot is a good walk away from here. I keep my head down, my chin tucked onto my chest, and walk so fast I'm nearly running. I don't know why some rando hitting on me at the bar makes me feel so sick to my stomach. It happens all the time, probably literally every night here, and I doubt that anyone in there would even think twice about someone hitting on me.

I might be starting over, I might be starting fresh, but I did not work my ass off for years for nothing. I know who I am, and I will not cower.

Ever.

I take out my keys, my hands trembling. I don't have one of those fancy lock things, just a regular old key, but it gives me a measure of comfort to have it in my hand. I draw in a breath as I turn the corner and walk straight into a wall of man chest.

"There you are."

Fuck. He followed me. Not only did he follow me, he went around so he'd catch me.

I step back, real fear clawing at my belly at the look in his eyes that're no longer hooded. His eyes are narrowed on me, and he's pissed.

"You followed me."

"You left me. You took the drink and food and ran."

"Let me go." My words come out so much weaker than I planned. I open my mouth to scream, but I'm not sure who would hear me back here.

"Let you go?" he asks, stepping even closer, his hands out in front of him as if he's innocent. "No one's holding you here. Why are you acting like I am?" I step to the right, and he deftly blocks me. Step to the left, and he's right in my space.

I gather up my courage. "If you don't get out of my way and let me go to my car, I'm going to hurt you."

Wow, Vittoria. Terrifying.

He takes a step closer and shoves me against the wall. My head cracks against concrete, and a spider skitters down the wall beside me. I stifle a whimper, but before I can move, one of his hands is around my arm and the other around my throat, pinning me in place.

"Were you threatening me?"

I can't speak. My head feels too light, my cheeks too hot, and there's a ringing in my ears that makes me feel like I'm going to pass out.

I shake my head. He's too big. He's too strong. I could kick his nuts but I'd never make it to my car in time. If I scream, who would even hear me?

I gasp when he releases my throat, only to drop his hand to my chest and grope me. I slap at him, but he quickly deflects me.

"I wanted you alone tonight. If you're not gonna give it to me easy, I'll take it. You owe me."

Panic makes me manic. I shove at him, I try to push him, but he's as immovable as concrete. He's heavy, and way too strong for me to fend off.

So this is how it happens, I think wildly to myself. *This is how women get assaulted.*

His fingers grab onto my top and he yanks it, the fabric tearing. I go to scream, but before I do, his hand cracks across my face. The metallic taste of blood fills my mouth.

I scramble to get away, but he yanks me to him. I open my mouth to scream when something's shoved between my teeth. He pushes me onto the concrete facedown and my head bangs with a sickening *thunk.* I push and shove and claw and scream against the gag, but I can't get away.

"Fucking bitch," he growls. "I didn't want to do this the hard way."

I'm going to vomit. I'm going to pass out. I'm overheated and terrified and shaking.

The sound of a cigarette lighter snicks in the darkness. A flame illuminates the shadows of a face about ten feet away.

"The lady said no." A deep, dark, dangerous drawl. "And where I'm from, no means no."

The lit end of a cigarette burns in the night sky, the shadows of a stranger's face and his body leaning casually up against the hood of a car.

A sane person would run, but the asshole who's got me pinned beneath him's hell bent for leather on having his way.

"Get the fuck out of here. This has nothing to do with you."

The stranger's chuckle sends a shiver down my spine. While these two are having their little conversation, I'll find a way to escape.

I wriggle, but he holds me fast with no effort. *Jesus.*

The voice of the man smoking is low, but even I feel the hint of deadly warning imbued in his tone. "Let her up. I'll give you one minute to get the fuck out of here, and we'll pretend like this never happened," the stranger says in warning. He takes another drag of his smoke, and this time the light of the smoke shows me the glimmer of a suit. He's one of them, then. Figures.

"Or what?" the asshole mutters. But he's already backing away from me.

The stranger exhales the smoke. "Or I'll kill you."

My heartbeat spikes.

"The fuck you—"

"You know what we're celebrating tonight, asshole? My release from prison. Served eighteen months for manslaughter and believe me when I tell you, I ain't afraid of goin' back." He shrugs out of his suit coat in a way that's suddenly ominous. "So make me."

The asshole's got a death wish. He lets me go, only to lunge at the man leaning against the car's hood. I scramble to my feet to right myself, but to get to my car I need to run past the two of them. I huddle against the wall, wondering what to do next. Something tells me not to call the police. Maybe the bartender?

The stranger steps out of the light. Is that the man from the bar? The one who arrested me with those mesmerizing eyes? I feel frozen in place now just watching him, his confidence. Menace drips off of him like poison.

He steps casually to the side to avoid the asshole's attack. With effortless ease, he casually grabs my assaulter around the neck and bends him over in his iron grip. The sizzle of smoke and screams of pain tell me he's used his cigarette as a weapon. I cringe and stifle a scream.

I didn't realize when he was with all those other guys *exactly* how big the man in the suit was, but I see now. He makes holding my attacker in his grip look like child's play.

My attacker punches the air and finally connects with my brutal savior. That earns him a savage punch to the gut that makes me wince, followed by another that no doubt breaks ribs. My attacker screams like an injured animal. I choke on a dry sob.

A flash of silver. Oh *God.*

I scream when I realize the bar jerk has a blade in his hand. He slashes, but my scream's warned my rescuer. He easily dodges the blade, then slams his knee into the man's belly.

"You shouldn't have done that," my rescuer says with a growl that makes my hair stand on end. "Stupid motherfucker."

Undeterred, bar guy slashes again with his knife. The man in the suit grabs his wrist. There's an audible *snap* and a howl of pain.

Oh, God. He just... he broke his wrist as if it were a stick. Just... *snap.* I watch in horror as he grabs the knife from the man's hand, and with the expert grace of someone way, *way* too skilled with a knife, slices straight across the asshole's throat. There's a terrible gurgling sound as blood gushes over my attacker's hands, painting him in a sheet of crimson.

Shaking his head, my rescuer shoves him to the ground then steps casually back is if preserving his shoes. It's all so... matter-of-fact.

No. *What? No.*

I cover my mouth in speechless horror.

This isn't happening. No, this isn't happening.

One minute, they're fighting. The next, my protector—my murdering felon ex-con protector—wipes the blade and shoves it into his pocket. He holds my gaze and points at me to stay in place while he whips his phone out of his pocket. I couldn't move if I wanted to.

"Got a situation in the back. Send Leo and Tavi." He steps over the man's body and glares at me. "You alright?" He's walking toward me. I just saw him slice a man's throat. I back up until I hit the wall. I nod dumbly.

I look down at my torn clothing and see, to my surprise, that I'm still okay.

"Yeah," I whisper.

"Good," he says coldly. His voice is raspy like he hasn't spoken in months. He brushes a thumb over my swollen lip gently, so it doesn't hurt. My skin heats. He shakes his head.

"This never happened. If I hear even a whisper on the breeze about this unfortunate turn of events, I promise that whatever this fucker was going to do to you will seem pleasant compared to what *I'll* do. Do you understand?"

I nod so hard I'm dizzy.

He releases me, and I stumble. He reaches for my arm, only to give me a little shove. "Good. Now get the fuck out of here."

———

CHAPTER TWO

"What, drawn, and talk of peace?" ~ *Romeo and Juliet*

ROMEO

Goddammit.

My father always told me my penchant for looking out for pretty girls would one day get me in trouble. And now, he's right. I hate when he's right.

Dio.

Tavi and Leo shake their heads at me when I quickly fill them in. Leo, my dad's youngest brother and one of the highest in rank with us here tonight, looks like he wants to shake some sense into me. If I were younger and not in line to take over as Boss, he'd kick my ass. Tavi, on the other hand, has no such compunctions.

My brothers speak three languages: English, Italian, and Violence.

"For the love of fucking God, Rome," Tavi grumbles, making a fist. His dark brown hair's grown longer since I was in the big house, almost shadowing his eyes from me, but not so much I don't see the way they're narrowed.

"He tried to rape an innocent woman," I mutter. As if I have to explain myself to them. As if my family fucking cares.

"Was she your fucking sister?" Leo mutters.

"No," I say through gritted teeth. "If she was, he'd still be alive so I could cut off his nuts and make him bleed out." If I was feeling generous.

Leo stares at me for a few seconds, then grins at me. He's got my dad's salt-and-pepper hair and the chilling blue-gray eyes my family's known for. If it weren't for his nose that's been broken too many times to count, I'd sometimes think I was staring at a younger version of my father.

Leo cuffs me good-naturedly. "Good to have you back, bro. Go. Get the fuck out of here. Go home. This never happened. We'll get rid of this. Last thing you need—"

"I know, I know." One more reason to go back to prison.

Tavi's already covered the body and pushed it into the shadows, and three men stand guard by the back door.

Leo's right.

"Why a fuckin' knife, Rome?" Tavi asks, as if he's disappointed in me for not using something better.

He's already putting on gloves to dispose of the body. We've got men stationed at every entrance to the back here. No one's getting through the wall of Rossi.

I shrug a shoulder and light another smoke. Mama doesn't like me smoking in the house but damn, I've missed it. I'll quit. But not tonight.

"He pulled it on me, I turned it on him." My brothers know I hate the mess and clumsiness of a blade.

"Why didn't you say so?" Tavi mutters, as he tapes up the body before he slides it into a bag that looks like he's packing up for a hockey match. He does clean-up like some men make their morning coffee: sheer muscle memory and a matter of routine.

"Say what?"

"He fuckin' threatened you. That's a whole other animal, you know that."

I do. I didn't want to get into it, didn't want to have to justify myself. I know I fucked up, but as Underboss I have to stand my ground. I've only been out of prison for hours, and it was my second stint. Three strikes, you're out, and the next time, I ain't coming home.

Not to mention I'm on goddamn probation.

I turn to the sound of an approaching ride. Santo rolls down the window and grins. There's a new scar across his cheek that wasn't there before I left, but he wears the same jaded, arrogant look in his eyes he's had since he was in middle school. "Get in the car, motherfucker," he says affectionately.

"Let's get you home before your mama sends out a search party and the lasagna gets cold." My stomach growls. God, I've missed good food. Good to know wiping off another man's blood hasn't affected my appetite.

Tavi might give me shit about what I did tonight, but no one... *no one*... will ever find out. The oath of silence is an unbreakable oath, no matter what the consequences, and covering up for me's something my brothers might not like but won't ever question.

We're ten minutes from my family home, the iconic home called simply "The Castle," where I grew up north of the city. Though all of us have private apartments or condos in downtown Boston for both business and pleasure, we all grew up in The Castle. And to this day, we all still call it home. It's expected that we show for Sunday dinner, and that we arrive for a meeting my father calls within an hour of him calling it.

The paradox of mob life means that while we're rooted in tradition centuries old, we're practically nomadic—moving as times warrant it, from the North Shore home of the Family to our private places in Boston, or to our family home in Tuscany.

The Castle has made history and the news more times than I can count, but my parents haven't allowed reporters in since my sister's wedding several years ago. They said it was more publicity than they needed and didn't like the reporters' implication that the servants' quarters and basement functioned like dungeons.

They do, though. We just don't like to publicize that fact.

With fourteen bedrooms, eight bathrooms, ten fireplaces and servants' quarters, The Castle is a veritable mansion, worth an estimated twelve million dollars. It also features quirky, historical features such as a turret, a seven-story tower, carved woodwork, and a functioning organ my eldest sister played before she married and moved to Tuscany herself. The ten main living areas include a dining room, library, study, exhibit rooms, a kitchen, and guest bedrooms, not to mention an inner courtyard, southern tower, and a Great Hall.

We've made many memories in this home. Some say we aren't the only ones, that The Castle is haunted. But I don't believe in ghosts.

Demons, on the other hand...

The smell of baked lasagna and fresh bread wafts through the air as we pull up to The Castle. I draw in a breath and let it out slowly, savoring the chill in the air and the wide-open sky above me, like blue velvet studded with rhinestones.

I don't care how old I am or how many houses I own... I like coming home.

I have business to tend to since I went into the slammer, so I won't go to my own private house until later in the week.

Tomorrow's a big day, and everyone—cousins and aunts and uncles and honorary members of the Family—will be at The Castle tonight.

There'll be women here, too. They're guests, but with the understanding that I don't have to sleep alone tonight if I don't want to. And *fuck*, I don't want to.

My mind goes to the curvy brunette pinned to the ground by the motherfucker whose body's growing cold. She was so helpless. So innocent. So fucking beautiful I could almost feel her.

I better never fucking see her again.

When we arrive, the dogs greet me with whines and licks, belying their underlying viciousness. With sleek black and speckled brown fur, the Rottweilers we raise and keep are not here as family pets. They're highly trained and vicious, and never allowed near any of the children. Even my sisters won't touch them. I raised them myself from infancy, so they never bite the hand that feeds them. I scratch behind their ears, pat their heads, then order them back to their place by the door. They obey on command. If only my brothers were trained so well.

"Romeo." My mother stands on the front stoop, unfastening her apron as I walk up the steps. Her typically stern face lights up with a bright smile. To some, my mother's austere, even haughty, but it's only the undercurrent of strength that she can't hide. She's got a sensitive side one doesn't see very often, and a spine of steel. A lesser woman would buckle being wed to a man nicknamed The Skull.

My mother's only learned to be crafty.

She grasps both of my arms and yanks me to her, kissing first my left then my right cheek, then does the same thing a second time before she holds me at arm's length.

My mother was a beauty in her day and even at her age, still turns heads with her golden-brown hair and the large, chestnut-colored eyes my sisters have all inherited. Those eyes are trained on me now, sad and a little concerned, but guarded as usual. One would think she'd have gotten used to her sons serving time by now, but she definitely hasn't.

"How are you, son?"

I kiss her but then gently extricate myself from her hands so I can step around her. The smell of food and the clink of glasses welcome me. My family welcomes brothers home from stints in the big house like a feast for the Prodigal Son.

"Fine," I say over my shoulder. "Famished. Tell me you saved me some food, Mama."

She laughs and comes in behind me as my brothers enter with her. "Enough food for a Rossi army." Knowing how my brothers and I eat, that's saying something.

The main entrance to the house opens to a sitting room to the left and a circular stairway to the right that goes to the second floor. Adjacent to the sitting room there's a reception area and a lobby, followed by a coat room and the entrance to the Great Hall. Beyond the Great Hall lays the dining room and pantry, but for tonight's purposes, we'll dine in the Great Hall.

"Smells divine, Mama," Santo says, greeting my mother with a kiss on each cheek.

She tweaks a lock of his hair. "Made your favorite, you little devil," she says.

He gives her a devilish grin to match his nickname. *"Panzerotti*, Mama?"

She smiles. "Go on," she says with a wave of her hand. "Why don't you see, then?"

The little deep-fried crescent-shaped turnovers are typically prepared for the Carnival season in Italy. Like mini calzones, they're a childhood favorite of ours. Mama and Nonna, who do all of our cooking by hand, make them for special events. Santo can eat them by the bucket.

Tavi comes in behind Santo, bearing huge white pastry boxes no doubt filled with cannoli from his bakery in the North End, and Orlando follows, his arms laden with large bottles of wine. Mario brings up the rear, but all he's brought is a girl on each arm. Typical. I give him a stern look to warn him not to overstep in The Castle, and for God's sake no pantry fucking blow jobs. He nods in deference to me.

No one's missed a beat while I've been gone. It's as if I never left. I'm not sure how I feel about that.

We leave our coats in the small coat room beyond the main reception and head to the Great Hall.

Though The Castle is several hundred years old, still bearing the charm and antique sobriety of a much earlier time, my parents have kept it well-furnished and updated. The original woodwork gleams, decorated simply with Persian rugs my father received as a thank-you gift from the Iranian Prime Minister. Thanks for what, I don't even want to know.

The entire downstairs rooms bear cream-colored walls that accent the varnished hardwood floors, elegant chandeliers in each room, and artwork my father's collected from generous politicians and clients. On a regular business day, my footsteps echo on the wood while I walk through these rooms large enough for a king. But today, The Castle is bustling.

I lose track of how many handshakes and backslaps I get, kisses from the ladies and fist bumps from the men, and a cute little around-the-knee hug from my cousin's four-year-old daughter. Wine flows like a river, and my glass, as if enchanted, never empties. God, it's good to be home.

An hour or so after we arrive, though, I still haven't seen my father.

"Tavi, where's Papa?" I ask. We've eaten appetizers served on little platters from white-gloved staff, gone through dozens of bottles of wine, I've eaten a truckload of pasta and cheeses and Mama's panzerotti, and I still haven't seen my father nor heard his booming voice. It's distinctive.

Tavi's face grows grave.

I draw in a breath and steel myself for whatever he's about to tell me.

Tavi's stern and serious, the most studious in our family. He earned a free ride to Harvard but passed in favor of working with the Family. I'm not sure he ever got over that. When we were kids, he wore glasses, but as a football player they were impractical. I still see him as the studious one among us, even though now he's most known for being undefeated in a fight.

"Last night, Mama and Marialena took a call from Rosa."

Our eldest sister Rosa lives in Tuscany with her husband and their young daughter. She dodged a bullet when it came to an arranged marriage when she fell in love with Anthony Mercadio, a man of prestige and power in Tuscany. Our father allowed the nuptials with the understanding that it would be a mutually beneficial situation.

"Yes?"

He thrusts one hand in his left pocket, his right grasped around a wine glass. "Not good, Rome."

"Tell me."

I stand up straighter. If that son-of-a-bitch hurt my sister, I'll take our private jet and go to Tuscany tonight before I've even unpacked my bags. I never liked my brother-in-law but allowed my sister to marry him against my better judgment. I never trusted him, though. Tavi knows this, which is why he waited until we got home to tell me.

"Now, Romeo, you just got home," Tavi says as if reading my mind. My temperature begins to rise. I polish off my wine and signal for a waiter to take my glass. I need to be sober for this.

"Tavi, he's the fuckin' Underboss," Orlando says, coming up behind me. "Will be Boss any damn day. And needs to know. Fuckin' tell him or I will."

Orlando, the largest and most muscular among us, is our resident heavy. When he walks down a public street, he parts the crowd like Moses parted the Red Sea. But though he can be brutal and vicious, he hates shedding blood and hates causing pain, a decided weakness in our family. Orlando's my father's least favorite, thereby making him a favorite to *me*.

The heaviest eater among us—which is really saying something—Orlando settles his second plate of food on a side table so he can toss the first down before he digs into the second.

Tavi exhales and takes another sip of wine before he tells me.

"Rosa found her husband banging the nanny. She lost it. Cursed him out. Threw shit. He…" he pauses, either trying to get his own anger under control or trying to prepare for mine.

My voice is barely controlled. "Did he hurt her?"

"Tried to. Bodyguard stepped in. Restrained him, called Papa."

"I'll fucking—"

"He's dead, Rome," Tavi says in a low voice. "He's no longer your concern."

I slam my fist on a sideboard table, but no one even looks my way. I smack the exit to the dining room with my palm, relishing the sting of pain. I march past the guards who nod their heads at me, ignore the stare my mother gives me from the kitchen entrance, and stomp past the soldiers taking shots at the bar between the Great Hall and the dining room. Beyond the dining room sits the library and further still, the roughly hewn stones that pave the courtyard. But that's not where I'm going.

I know where he is.

A small, narrow hallway between the dining room and kitchen gives way to a darkened interior and a door you wouldn't see unless you knew it was there. Deeply carved into the wall as if it's an emblem, the door fits flush against the wall. I run my finger along the edge, pull the metal latch forward, then slide my key in the lock and push the door open.

It smells like the recesses of an ancient confessional in here, faintly lingering odors of incense, whiskey, and sin. Here, behind the hidden entryway door, lies the secret wine cellar, a closet furnished with the finest cigars, and a circular war room that hearkens back to days of old. Beyond the war room a small stairway leads to one of several towers, my favorite place to go and hide when I was a child until my father discovered it and made it his own.

And there, sitting amongst papers, smoking his cigar, is my father, flanked by his bodyguards who never leave him even when he sleeps or takes a piss.

He takes a pull from his cigar and lets the smoke out slowly. Small circles rise and spread. He smiles. My father's smile chills one to the bone and is rarely, if ever, provoked by amusement.

"Son."

"Papa."

"Welcome home."

I'm not here for pleasantries. I served time for a crime he committed, because it was my duty as Underboss. I want details, now.

"Tell me about Rosa."

He nods his head. He expected me. He expected the question.

"She can tell you herself."

I school my reaction when he knocks on the door behind him that leads to the war room. A quick rap, and a woman's voice rings through.

"Yes?"

"Come, Rosa. Your brother returns."

The door opens, and Rosa enters. Taller than my mother, Rosa carries herself with the grace of Mama and the confidence of Papa. Our eldest sister is wise beyond her years. She steps into the light, and I blink in surprise when I see one eye's swollen shut.

I step toward her. Gingerly, I brush my thumb across her bruised cheek. I once knocked a man's teeth down his throat because he called my sister a whore. Literally, he choked on his teeth. But this...

"He's already dead, Rome," she says with a small smile. In her eyes is a world of hurt that didn't start with her husband. "Papa saw to that."

I want to hit my father for not leaving the motherfucker for me.

My father lights another cigar.

I sit on a stuffed leather chair in the corner of the room and lean back.

"Does Mama know you're home yet, Rosa?"

She shakes her head. "No. I want you to tell her, brother, will you?" Rosa smiles sadly. "Papa and I had business to discuss first."

I look sharply at him, and for the first time question whether he was the one who gave her the bruises. I wouldn't put it past him.

"I see."

The burnt end of the cigar lights the darkened room, stark red like a devil's pitchfork.

"What business did you have to discuss, then?" As Underboss, there are no questions I'm not allowed to ask.

She looks me in the eye, and I see a deep well of pain there she can't hide. She loved the man. He cheated on her. And now, he's dead. Natalia, her daughter, is a vivacious little five-year-old we chat with regularly.

"You'll recall I was allowed to marry under the condition our family benefit from our alliance."

I nod.

"Papa wanted to ensure his family paid in full."

I look to Papa. "And did they?"

He blows out another ring of smoke. "In full."

I nod. It's only customary for them to pay—in whatever currency necessary—what they promised. I'll follow through on this as well after tomorrow.

I turn to Rosa. "And Natalia?"

"Asleep."

"Soon, son, we'll discuss the next order of business," Papa says. "Tonight, you feast, then we go to bed early. Tomorrow's a big day." My father scowls.

Tomorrow, we have the reading of the will for my mother's father. I missed the wake and funeral but they were able to delay the reading of the will until tomorrow. We aren't concerned much about it. The Rossi family owns ten restaurants in the

North End, and those are only the legal ways we earn money. We have no need for an inheritance, if he even left us anything. My mother, on the other hand, may have more of a vested interest.

I rise, suddenly weary. The days in prison passed like sludge, painfully slow. I was released twelve hours ago, and it already feels as if it's been a full week.

I push myself to my feet and nod my goodnight, but before I leave, I reach for my sister. I pull her to me and wrap my arms around her. She may be older, but I've been bigger than her for years now. The woman's made of steel and gravel, so it's almost surprising how small and vulnerable she feels in my arms.

"Good to have you home, Rosa," I tell her before I leave.

"Same to you, Romeo." She sighs. "Same to you."

I nod to my bodyguard, who's kept quiet watch by the door since my arrival. Would've paid half my fucking inheritance to have him by my side in the big house.

He follows behind me. "Text Mario." It's time I found out who the woman was, the girl who saw me kill tonight. The woman who could get me put away for life if she wanted. "We have some research to do."

———

CHAPTER THREE

"Women may fall when there's no strength in men."
Romeo and Juliet

VITTORIA

"Your name means victory," I whisper to myself as I stare into the rearview mirror. *"Victory."* My mother hated my name. My grandfather was the one who named me, and for some reason my mother went along with it. Likely didn't want to rock the boat. But even though she allowed me to be named Vittoria, she said my name like it was a dirty word.

Vittoria, stated as if it were distasteful.

When I was a teen, they called me Torri, but I didn't like the nickname. I allowed my ex to call me that, against my better judgment, but once I was rid of him, I decided that was it.

I was christened *Vittoria DiSanto,* and that's exactly how I'll die.

I look at myself in the rest stop bathroom mirror and pick an imaginary piece of lint off my fitted white top. This is an occasion I need to dress for. I blink, and the memory of the night before surfaces. When I woke, I almost convince myself it was all a dream, but I know better.

A pool of blood. The threat of rape. One set of vacant eyes, and the ruthless, blue-gray eyes of the man who saved me before he bullied me into fleeing.

Who was he? How did he get rid of the body?

How will I thank him?

It's an odd thought, really, thanking a person for killing someone for you. I'm honestly not sure if that's why I really want to see him again.

I push that all behind me. It never happened. If I tell anyone, something tells me that beautiful angel of death will make me pay. His parting words made it clear he has the ability to administer swift, harsh punishment.

So I stare at myself. And I focus on what comes next.

I need a good haircut, but I can mask the split ends by putting my hair up. I sweep it into a pony-tail then swirl it into a bun I keep in place with bobby pins. I tuck the dried ends into the bun so only glossy hair shows. I'm wearing sensible pearl earrings, and the lightest brush of makeup like the night before.

I'm not sure what awaits me, but I'm at the point where I have nothing to lose.

I've come a long way since the day I found the truth out.

The day I saw my bank accounts and wallet had been emptied, and even the change jar I kept on the mantle in my living room gone, was the day that changed the course of my life forever. I stared, unbelieving, before I fell to my knees.

It was a lie. All of it.

My landlord told me I was six months in arrears on rent, revealing that the money I'd given my boyfriend had never been paid to the landlord at all. When I went to file a report with the police, I was told Ashton Bryant, the man I was prepared to pledge my life to... never existed.

I'd been swindled. Conned. And didn't have a penny to my name to show for it. How can you sue a guy that doesn't technically exist? He was the first man I'd said *I love you* to. I'd been cheated out of everything I owned and everything that mattered to me.

I had charged my phone in the car, so I punch the address into the GPS app, even though I've done this so many times by now I feel as if I know the route by heart.

I'm ten minutes away. Ten minutes to the road that takes me to the next season of my life, the next stage.

Hearing at The Castle, 11 a.m.
Please bring proof of identification.

It should've been a red flag that Ashton systematically cut out every friend I ever had, but at the time, it had felt like he was devoted to me. No one loved me like he did. No one understood me like he did. They were all jealous or toxic or problematic.

In retrospect, he made his moves so no one would thwart his plans.

So I have no one. Nothing but a letter addressed to me and this facade of professionalism I can maintain for a few more hours.

How odd, to get a letter directing me to a castle. I looked up anything I could about the location, and all I could find was a small Wikipedia entry online about the history of The Castle. It's several centuries old and now owned by the Montavio family.

But no Google searches could tell me who they were. All I know is a recent Montavio family death is what prompted the letter sent to me.

Why?

Pictures show a large, stately looking castle nestled deep on the North Shore of Boston in a coastal city called Gloucester in Cape Anne. It seems The Castle was once shown publicly but isn't anymore.

I have no family to ask and Google didn't help, so the only choice I have is to go. What do I have to lose?

Still, I feel as if I'm traveling to a country I've never heard of, and I don't even know the language.

My hands shake on the wheel as I make the drive. It's a bright, sunny, but chilly day here. I wrap my sweater around me as I pull down a long, circular driveway. I stifle a gasp at the sheer magnificence of this castle. I thought maybe the pictures made it look larger than it really is, some sort of a trick of the light or an optical illusion... but they didn't. If anything, they failed to capture the brilliance of it.

I feel as if any moment, a knight bearing a sword and shield or a minstrel carrying an instrument will stride into view. I can almost hear the strings of music on a harp or lyre, almost hear the clash of weapons in a battle on the lawn.

I hope I get to explore this place. It's the stuff of dreams, with its towers and turrets, vines along the roof and walls, gardens that encase the exterior, and large, ornate, stained glass windows at the very top. Bright orange mums bloom in the fall garden amidst vibrant greens, hardy plants and flowers that can withstand the chill of autumn before the frost.

I blink in surprise at how many cars are here. Dozens. There are even parking attendants waiting in uniform by the main door. In the distance, several lithe Rottweilers lay down, chained with heavy black metal links to a sturdy fence.

I'm not the only one here. Am I the only one who doesn't know why?

I don't want to give my keys to one of the attendants. Thanks to Ashton, my entire world sits in the back of this car, and I don't trust them. Where will they park my car? After all I've been through, I trust *no one.*

So I decide to park at the very end of the lot and glance at the time. I have fifteen minutes before the time I was told to come. Is it wrong to be so early? I can walk myself.

The attendants give me a strange look when I wave them off and park, pocketing my keys, but I only smile and wiggle my fingers like a weirdo, then walk in my heels to the front door. A cold wind kicks up leaves around my ankles. I wrap my cardigan tighter around myself.

Typically, a castle's main entrance is shielded by a portcullis—a heavy, vertically closing gate most noticeable in medieval times, though modern-day castles still boast such entrances. The latticed grill made of wood and metal slides down into grooves set within the doorjambs. I look above me and smile to myself when I see the entrance does indeed have a portcullis, but it's been raised. The large, heavy door looks as if it would take three strong men to open it.

Excitement roils in my belly. This is a special place and I'm on the cusp of the unknown. I lift the knocker and let it fall heavily. It makes a satisfying *gong* sound.

The door's opened by a prim and proper young woman in full uniform, one of the Montavio family staff I'd guess. "Hello, may I help you?"

My voice wavers. "Yes, I'm... I'm here because of this."

I show her my letter clumsily. She squints at the page and reads it, her eyes widening as she does.

"Your name, Miss?"

"Vittoria DeSanto." She nods, then gestures for me to stand inside the foyer. I'm uncharacteristically nervous. I'm usually a little more sure of myself, but after everything that's happened…

"Come in, Miss."

I move as if on instinct then realize I'm standing dumbly beside the door.

I'm glad she didn't call me *ma'am.* I'm too young for such formalities. But a house like this seems to beckon ceremony and solemnity.

The chill gives way to a comfortable warmth, likely due at least in part to the fire burning in the fireplace in the sitting room. The elegant main entrance is enough to take my breath away—a cathedral ceiling, hardwood floors so shiny they nearly blind me, heavy, ornate furnishings that have stood the test of time. Sparkling chandeliers gleam above me like twinkling diamonds. I glance at everything quickly, even though I could stand here and take in every intricate detail, from the tapestry decorations to the embroidered drapes, for hours. It would be almost stifling if not for the bright open spaces and cheerful windows that let in light.

Who is the Montavio family? Why have they called me here?

Why?

I've never been one to balk in the face of something new, though, and I'm not going to start now.

The rich scent of coffee and baked goods wafts through the air, and my stomach growls. I had a foil-wrapped granola bar from a gas station hours ago.

"Come this way, please, Miss DeSanto," the woman who greeted me says. She brings me to the reception room to the left of the main entrance. Beyond the room there looks to be a small closet with coats—a coat room?—and further beyond that, a massive hall filled with people. Laughter and voices echo in the huge house. But that's not where she's brought me.

She sees me looking and smiles. "The Family's in the Great Hall, prepared for the reading of the will, Miss. But no one outside the Family's allowed in until summoned by Mr. Rossi. Please, help yourself to something to eat or drink while you wait."

Why does the phrase *the Family* seem to have so much weight in this context?

Wait.

I blink. I blink again.

The will?

Mr. Rossi? I thought this was a Montavio family home...

I have so many questions that need answers.

Before I can respond, the woman leaves. I turn toward the table laden with baked goods and large, steaming, chrome teakettles and carafes.

There's a will?

I look around the room and see half a dozen or so others, but no one looks my way. They're well-dressed and fairly normal-looking people. I surmise that if they're here, they aren't part of the Montavio family, but outsiders just like me.

When I approach the table, my mouth waters.

My mother was barely Italian, mostly in name only, her heritage fully Americanized as a third-generation Sicilian. We never ate good Italian food unless we were in the North End of Boston, but that was so rare I've forgotten everything.

Some pastries I'm not familiar with, but I recognize biscotti, thick slabs of fresh bread, and brioche nestled beside something that looks like a flaky croissant drizzled with chocolate and sprinkled with snowy flecks of powdered sugar. I swallow. Another uniformed waitress or something comes up beside me and smiles.

"Coffee, Miss? Espresso?"

"Yes, please."

She takes a delicate light blue coffee cup and pours dark, fragrant espresso in it, then politely points to small pitchers of milk and cream. I take it with a grateful nod, then pour cream and sugar into it.

I sip. Oh, God, it's divine. Dark and almost bitter, if not for the chocolate undertones. I wish I could take a whole plate of these pastries back with me. I'd eat them for days. For now, I'll eat as much as I can to tide me over to my next meal.

I take the flaky croissant, a buttered slab of bread, and a cookie that's shaped into a figure eight, then find a vacant corner of the room so no one sees me stuff my face. It all smells heavenly. I don't care why I'm here anymore. All I want to do is drown myself in pastry and espresso. I already love the Montavio family, and all they've done is woo me with baked goods and coffee.

Sigh. I'm a woman with simple needs, really.

I eat the bread and cookie quickly, savoring every decadent morsel, then chase them with coffee.

By the time I get to the croissant, I'm full. I glance around the room. No one's close by. I can't let good food like this go to waste. I wrap it in a napkin and tuck it into my bag, then sit up straight like it never happened.

My belly feels pleasantly full, something I haven't felt in so long I almost forgot what it's like.

"Good, isn't it?"

I nearly drop my cup when I see a young woman sitting only inches away from me. She moved like a cat, nearly silently. Oh God, I hope she didn't see me swipe the croissant.

"Delicious."

She smiles and extends her hand to me. Younger than I am by a few years, she's a beauty with thick, dark brown wavy hair that hangs all the way to her waist, heavy brows over luminous blue-gray eyes that look eerily familiar, a delicate Grecian nose, and a small, almost whimsical chin. She wears a red, off-the-shoulder cocktail dress and death-defying heels like she's about to walk a runway.

She extends a well-manicured hand. "How interesting. My horoscope said I'd meet a stranger today and we'd become instant friends."

I blink. "Oh?" How does one respond to that?

She smiles, and though she's friendly, there's something almost ruthless in her toothy grin. And I can't place why she looks so familiar. So very, very familiar. Those eyes… I've definitely seen those eyes before.

"Yup. Mama says horoscopes are bullshit, but whatever. I love them." She takes a sip from her little espresso cup. Looks like she likes it black. She waves her hand at the elaborate buffet. "We don't really eat breakfast, to tell you the truth. But Mama likes to make sure we feed our guests."

I nod. I have so many questions for her I'm not sure where to begin.

"Who are you?" the young woman asks, her head tipped curiously.

"My name's Vittoria."

She smiles. "And I'm Marialena Rossi." She pauses as if to wait for recognition, but when I don't respond, she continues. "And thank you for telling me your name. But you still haven't told me who you *are*."

I don't know how to respond, but I'm fabricating some sort of response when a man in a suit walks into the room.

I... recognize him. I know I do. He was one of the men accompanying the others at the bar last night. Not the one who met me in the alley, the avenging angel, but one of his friends. An older one who sat with him behind me in the bar.

No.

No.

I can't... surely those men had nothing to do with this letter.

Did they?

I'm so stupid. Oh, God, I'm so stupid.

Why did I come here? I don't belong here. They don't know me, and I don't know why I'm here, and this is all a terrible, terrible mistake.

I remember the icy voice of the man who saved me. The chilling tone. His ruthless gaze.

This never happened. If I hear even a whisper on the breeze about this unfortunate turn of events, I promise that whatever this fucker was going to do to you will seem pleasant compared to what I will do.

I shouldn't be here.

I shouldn't be here.

No one told me if there was a penalty for not responding to a letter from an attorney, but at this point, they can't find me. I have no home, no money to my name, and being put in jail now would be a kindness. At least then I'd know where my next meal was coming from.

Now, wait, I tell myself. Just because this is one of the guys from last night, it means nothing. He doesn't know who I am. I don't know who he is. There's only one guy I absolutely, positively, cannot see today, and I don't see *him* anywhere.

I scan the room. I scan the next room.

"You okay?" Marialena asks with concern.

I nod. "Didn't sleep well last night," I say, which isn't a lie. Cars might be good places to sleep in an emergency or maybe for a nap, but no one ever got a solid eight hours in the back seat of a car. "Feel a little off. Sorry."

She smiles and reaches for a black bag sitting by her seat on the floor. Ah. Chanel. Of course.

She unzips it and takes out a little flask. Holds it out to me. "Sip."

"What?"

"*Sip,*" she says more insistently. "Listen, if you're

here for the reading of the will we're probably family anyway. Drink it."

"I'm good."

She blows out a breath, then rolls her eyes. "Look, babe. When we get in there? My father's going to have to give these speeches." She gives me a pointed look. "Maybe even in Italian *and* English," she says, as if to emphasize her point. "Do you have any idea what that's like?"

I grimace.

"Exactly. Just take a swig. It's good stuff, from Tuscany. And unlike the American stuff, won't put hair on your chest." She gives me a wink.

I look over the shoulder of the guy I recognized last night, only to meet another pair of steely blue-gray eyes. Not my avenging angel's, but he's definitely family.

Oh my God.

What have I walked into?

I take her flask and tip my head back.

———

CHAPTER FOUR

"I DEFY YOU, STARS." Romeo and Juliet

ROMEO

I sit to my father's right, a strategic position that allows me a full view of every single person who enters this room. Tavi announced my grandfather's wishes, and I can only imagine the grumblings and rumblings outside this hall right now.

Only immediate family and those expressly invited to attend.

That means that none of the extended family that visited from out of state's allowed to be present at the hearing. I can imagine the fits and the attitudes and all the Italian curse words spewed by my aunts and uncles, cousins and great-aunts, and all the other relatives that came all the way here to hear how Giorgio Montavio will divide his assets.

Nonna, on the other hand, has walked about the house with platters of food she's made herself, encouraging everyone the same way any Italian grandmother would. *"Mangia, mangia!"* She doesn't care about the will. Her inheritance is set in stone. Like many married couples within our family, there was no love lost between her and her husband. She's more concerned that her meatballs and pasta fill our bellies than anything else.

But she's the only one that doesn't care. Tavi almost got into a fight earlier this morning with one of our cousins, and Orlando decided it would be best to have all the cousins meet somewhere other than the Great Hall. That led to a party in the library, which my mother wasn't aware of until someone almost wrecked a chandelier.

The Rossi family likes food, and the Montavio family likes to party. So when the Rossi family meets with the Montavio side of things... let's just say both wine and tempers flow.

My father talks to me in Italian; his low murmur and choice to speak in Italian versus English is intentional, to prevent anyone from eavesdropping. "She needs to go," he says in a harsh whisper. "I want her out of my goddamn house." The "she" being my mother's sister Francesca.

"It's her father's will," I remind him tightly, not wanting to stir up old wounds.

"That she was written out of years ago when she married the fucking Irish," my father mutters. True, but I suppose she can't help but wonder if anything's changed. She also likely came with her sons and daughters, hoping for a piece of the Montavio family pie.

When my grandfather married my mother to Narciso Rossi, he did so to forge an intentional alliance between both Tuscan families. The Montavio family got the shit end of the stick, or at least they'll have you believe that they did.

We got the house. Off they went to Gloucester, against my father's better judgment. Nonna came to live here when my grandfather was put into assisted living.

My father doesn't like my mother's side of the family, but it can't be denied that my parents' union forged the strongest alliance ever known to any Italian mafia family. Between my grandfather's riches here in America and my father's family owning real estate in the North End that rivaled anyone else's, theirs was a match that perfected the art of the alliance.

"Romeo." Cousin Niccolo stands in the doorway, his fists shoved into his pockets. As Boss of the Montavio family, he leads them all. He assumed the throne only months ago, after his own father's death, and now stands as the youngest Boss in America.

I stand and walk to him. Niccolo and I have always gotten along well.

"What is it, brother?"

He claps his hand on my shoulder and his eyes warm at me. He's known for being a particularly ruthless killer but to me he's just cousin Nic.

"I'm not sure what to tell you," I say to him

before I close the door so my father doesn't eavesdrop. "We can't go against Nonno's wishes, and you know that."

"Bullshit," Nic says. "You're the fuckin' Underboss."

"I can't tell you anything new," I say, shaking my head. I can't. It's illegal for me to do so, and anything less than following my grandfather's wishes to the letter of the law means forfeiting something monumental, like the very house my family lives in.

I hear the front doorbell in the distance and the sound of heels clicking to answer it, followed by Mama's most welcoming voice. The lawyer's arrived.

"Go," I tell my cousin. "I'll make sure to tell you anything that happens, and for Christ's sake, Nicco, trust me. I won't let things get fucked up, cousin."

I hear the familiar sound of my mother's heels clicking on the hardwood floors, a sound my brothers and I learned to heed at a very young age. When I got older, I realized she did it on purpose—an alarm, so to speak, to give us warning to hide our smokes or our girls before my father found out. God how I've missed the little things while I was away.

A few moments later, my mom enters the Great Hall. She takes her place by my father.

"Romeo, Narciso. Meet Gerardo Rocco, my father's lawyer."

Gerardo Rocco is an older gentleman who once had red hair, but he's now gone gray and white around the temples. He's taller than my mother but not me, and holds his hand out like we're old friends.

"Pleased to meet you." I notice he greets me before he greets my father. Interesting. There was a time when that'd earn him a beating, but my father's older now. I'm more likely to pour him a fucking shot for giving me preference.

It's time. I'm ready.

"I'm so sorry the others can't be present," Gerardo says. "Your grandfather was very specific with his instructions."

"Right. Let's see it." I take the paper he hands me, squinting at the words. The list is short. Christ it feels good to be back.

Those allowed to be present:

TOSCA ROSSI
  Narciso Rossi
  Rosa Rossi
  Romeo Rossi
  Ottavio Rossi
  Orlando Rossi
  Mario Rossi
  Marialena Rossi
  Tosca Montavio
  Vittoria DeSanto.

"Who the fuck's Vittoria DeSanto?" my father

asks at the same time my mother says, "He left Santo out?"

I don't know why she's surprised. He never did accept Santo as a member of this family.

I look to Gerardo. "Who's Vittoria DeSanto?"

"I'm sorry, Mr. Rossi, but I have no idea. She was listed on the invitations. My office sent her a letter asking her to come to the hearing." He frowns. "Does anyone know if she came?"

Marialena waves her hand. "Oh. Oh! Yes. She's in the sitting room! Pretty woman with kinda crazy auburn hair?"

I frown. Last night I met a pretty woman with crazy auburn hair, but there's no way she's here now. Not after my warning to her.

I don't know why my mind went to her of all the people in the world. Lots of women have crazy auburn hair.

Don't they?

I look to Tavi, but he only shrugs. Orlando's brows are knit together, and even jovial Mario rubs his fingers across the stubble on his jaw. "Not even Leo can come?"

My mother shakes her head. "Remember, boys. My father was explicit in his instructions. Perhaps he wants us to share the news after?"

Does she know something we don't?

"What news, Mama?"

"I mean the details of the will."

I turn to Tavi and Marialena. "You two go to the main room and ask if there's a Vittoria DeSanto. I want to get this started." I'm feeling impatient, irritable.

I turn to Mama. "Mama, do you have any idea what he wanted?"

She sighs. "No idea, son. If I knew, I'd have told you."

Would she? I've always been closer to my father than my mother, due in no small part to my father's animosity toward anyone and anything that threatens his power. Still, I'm not sure if I trust her.

Nonna smiles to herself, her hands clasped on her knee. She speaks hardly any English, but she knows we're perplexed and my father's pissed, and if there's anything that makes her happy, it's knowing my father's angry. She's probably silently fist pumping right about now.

"Sure thing, brother," Marialena says with a smile. "I know who she is." Maybe she's the one that knows something we don't? Why does it seem like everyone's in on a conspiracy tonight?

I'm busying myself with the stack of paperwork the lawyer gives me to look over, when I hear footsteps approaching again. I don't look up when I hear them, but hear my mother stand and walk over to our new guest.

"Well aren't you lovely," she says. "Please, can you tell us how you knew my father?"

"I... I didn't know your father," a woman's voice says, barely more than a mumble. Jesus.

I look up from my paperwork to see who this mumbling woman is and drop my pen on the table with a clatter.

No.

No.

It can't be. There's no fucking way. I rise to my feet just as her eyes meet mine. I open my mouth to berate her, to tell her I'm a man of my word, to remind her that she was told to *never,* ever come near me again, when I realize she's staring at me with the same shocked expression that likely mirrors mine.

Vibrant auburn hair twisted into a thick bun. Large, hazel eyes with thick dark lashes, a slender nose, full lips and a dainty chin. I drop my gaze to the low-cut top she wears. Even her slouchy cardigan doesn't hide her full, voluptuous breasts or ample hips.

"Are you... who are you... how can you..." Her words trail off. I'm aware that every eye in the room's on us. Orlando's body visibly tightens, and Tavi's hand is on his gun.

"Rome..."

I take a step toward her. I can't let anyone know that I've met her before. If my father knew what she knows, she'd be buried in the quarry by midnight.

"Why are you here?" my mother asks, oblivious to the flare of heat between us.

The woman of the night before who witnessed me killing a man with my own bare hands, who has the keys to lock me away with a whistle-blow, stands before me now in rumpled clothing as if she slept in them the night before.

Where was she? I narrow my eyes. Did she spend the night in a man's bed? Did she put these clothes on and smooth out the wrinkles she got from tossing them to the floor, then slide into those shoes so she could come here and fool my family?

Why do I care?

She's no one my grandfather knew, of that I'm sure.

"Where's your ID?" I ask her. My words sound like the crack of an ax, and the people around me jump. Not Vittoria, though. No. She meets my eyes without flinching. Perhaps I've underestimated her.

I stare at her and curse the day I met her. Why does a woman who's so obstinate have to be so damn sexy?

I imagine wrapping that silken hair around my fist, kissing the gentle slope of her neck, holding her against me as if she matters to me. I've never had a woman like her, one that comes without glamour and a high price tag.

And I want her. I fucking *want* her.

Frowning at me, she takes out a large bag and unzips it. She reaches in to take out her wallet and something wrapped in a paper napkin tumbles to the floor. Clumsily she picks it up. Is that food? Did she… steal a croissant? Take from the Family?

Why?

She shoves it back in her bag before I can ask any questions and yanks out an ID. I glare at it, as if somehow the little plastic card with her picture on it will tell me who she really is.

Why she's here.

What she wants from me.

This woman is sitting on a bed of lies, and I mean to untangle those sheets.

I blow out a breath and give it back to her.

"You didn't know my grandfather?" She's lying. She has to be.

She shakes her head and sits down beside Marialena.

I take my place beside my father. "Let's hear it, then," I tell the lawyer. "Tell us why she's here."

"I got a letter," she says, her voice loud and forthright in the small quiet of the room. "It came to my P.O. Box, which is publicly listed while my home address is not, so whoever got it looked me up. It said to arrive here today and when, but didn't tell me anything about a will or why I was coming."

"And where do you come from?" my father asks sternly.

"New York."

My mother and father share a look I can't decipher.

"Do you have anything at all to do with the Montavio family?"

The lawyer clears his throat. "Excuse me, Mr. Rossi, but the instructions here explicitly state we aren't to question the presence of Ms. DeSanto."

Oh, *really.* Nonno had a few tricks up his sleeve.

I discreetly gesture to Tavi. Does he know who she is? He shakes his head. He didn't get anywhere trying to find out her identity, I suppose.

"Go on, then," I tell him. "Let's get to why you're here."

He goes through a list of preliminary readings and protocol that bore me to tears. I want answers.

"The abbreviated version, please," I finally interrupt. "You need to understand, we're all dying of eagerness to find out Ms. DeSanto's place in all this." In other words, tell us before this gets ugly.

I glare at her. The bitch will answer to me for setting me up. I won't let a crime like hers go unpunished.

"As am I," she says, meeting my glare with one of her own. "I came from New York in answer to a letter. I have never heard of any of you before."

Mario lets out a low whistle and winces. "Now you don't have to hurt our feelings." I give him a look that shuts him up.

The lawyer clears his throat. "This is the last will and testament," he begins. My mother wipes away a tear but my Nonna looks forward stoically as he reads the fine print. He goes through assets and property, and none of us are surprised he's bequeathed much to his daughter and little to his wife. Long ago, she came from a line of Castellanos. She has money of her own that she spends lavishly on her grandchildren.

Everyone sits up straighter when he continues. "The remains of my estate will go to the following: fifty percent to my grandchildren and daughter, and fifty percent to Vittoria DeSanto, with conditions."

A vein pulses in my father's temple. My own cheeks heat in indignation. This isn't about the money. My family members are millionaires several times over. This is about loyalty and justice.

The room grows silent. "Ms. DeSanto will inherit one half of the estate under one condition. She must remain in the Montavio family home, herewith known as The Castle, for the entirety of thirty days, during which time it is expected she will marry one of the Rossi men."

Silence reigns in the room for long minutes.

Other families would rage at this. Some might cry or scream or throw things. My family, however, grows deathly quiet. A muscle ticks in my father's jaw. My mother's eyes go wide, and she gently lays her hand atop my father's. He flicks it off angrily.

Vittoria's still. "Excuse me?" she whispers. "Can you... repeat that?" She's either a good actress or this is all news to her.

My fingers itch for a smoke. My lungs ache for relief.

I exhale and stare at her. "This isn't just an eccentric old man's parting wishes. My grandfather insisted on archaic laws, to which the Rossi family's agreed," I tell her. "All of us must be married to maintain our ranks and position."

Her brows furrow. "Ranks? Position?" She shakes her head and tips it to the side. "I don't understand."

Tavi and I share another look. He gently shakes his head from side to side. Maybe she didn't come here with questionable intentions after all. Maybe she truly doesn't know who the fuck we are. I doubt it.

"And if we don't marry, our ranks are forfeit to those who are." I look to the lawyer, who's nervously shuffling papers. My patience is gone. "We will explain this more later, Ms. DeSanto. You'll eat dinner with our family this evening."

"Actually," she begins. "I think it's best if I—"

"Eat dinner with the family," I say more insistently. "Since you'll be living under our roof, you'll obey our rules." She frowns at me but doesn't respond.

"And what if she doesn't stay here the thirty days?" my father asks, a vein pulsing in his forehead. He should see a cardiologist. The man's laced with pulsing veins. I'm sure his blood pressure's off the charts. "What then?"

The lawyer speaks up, shifting uncomfortably. "She forfeits all the money, and her portion goes to charity." He looks through the paperwork. "Though if she stays the full thirty and doesn't marry, she earns a smaller portion of the inheritance."

"How small?" she asks.

"Ten percent."

So if we drive her away from here, she gets nothing, but we don't benefit either. If she stays the full thirty, she gets a good sum of money. If she stays and marries one of us, she's set for fucking life.

Who is she?

My father's eyes narrow to slits. This isn't about the money for him. My father has more money than he knows what to do with.

"What charity?" he asks.

The lawyer flips through papers. "Looks like Santa Albertina's Home for the Blind."

With a roar, my father knocks over a jar of pens. The glass cracks on the floor, sending pens and pencils scattering. No one flinches. We're used to this by now. Mr. Rocco looks at him in surprise, but none of us offers an explanation.

He doesn't know why my father hates the charity, why it's a personal insult to him from my late grandfather. Santa Albertina's was founded by my father's nemesis, a biker family my grandfather attempted an alliance with that fell instead into neutrality, thanks to my mother's marrying my father. I couldn't care less, but this is a personal insult to my father. An act of indulgence for my mother's ex-boyfriend, the only man my father wanted dead whose heart still beats.

Vittoria stands. Her cheeks are flushed pink, making her look prettier than ever, and I fist my hands by my sides. Unless she makes a mistake, she's spending the next month under this roof.

One of us will marry her.

One of us has to.

Goddamn it, that has to be me.

―――――

CHAPTER FIVE

"*My only love, sprung from my only hate.*" Romeo and
Juliet

VITTORIA

I stand in the small room, my cheeks flushing so
hotly I feel faint. This… this can't be happening. It's
like a strange, waking dream where I don't know
why I'm here or what's going on. First, the strange
letter to a *castle* of all places. Then, the odd intro-
duction to this family that I know nothing about.

Are we related?

Then the reading of this will and the archaic
laws of the Family. I don't understand it at all, but I
know for a fact that this isn't going to happen.

I stare at the man who killed in self-protection
last night. Who killed *for me.* Was this all part of
some strange conspiracy?

Why?

How?

I'll have something to talk about when we're alone, no question.

I clear my throat. All eyes come to me, including the furious gaze of the man they call Papa.

I don't like him. He looks as if he'd tear my limbs from my body with his own bare hands and not regret it.

Lovely.

"Ms. DeSanto, you're free to speak," the lawyer reminds me gently, as if telling me I don't have to be given permission.

"I don't know why I'm here," I begin. "I got a letter from an attorney mailed to my P.O. Box. If I ever met Mr. Montavio, I have no recollection."

No one responds. I'm not even sure what I want them to say.

I fumble with my words, which is unlike me. In my profession and in my personal life, I'm articulate, even if it takes me a while to think of what to say next, to formulate my words clearly. I don't jump into things headfirst. I think before I leap. I research and study and look at the big picture before I make a decision, so all of this is completely out of my realm of experience.

"I want to know why I'm here," I explain, "as much as I'm sure you do. And while the idea of staying here is appealing, because it's a lovely home, I'll have to decline the invitation."

The old man with graying hair narrows his eyes on me. "You may not leave, Vittoria." He rolls the "r" in my name like we're in Italy. Like he knows me.

I give him what I hope is a cold smile. "You can't keep me here, Mister…" My voice trails off. I don't know his name.

"Rossi." He says the name as if it should make me recognize him, but I still don't.

I look quickly about the room and note Marialena's eyes, wide with fear, as if I'm walking on thin ice defying this man. Next, I look to the man I met last night. His eyes are narrowed. Focused. Cold.

"We'll discuss this privately, Ms. DeSanto," he says. He crosses his arms over his chest, making the muscles in his suit coat bunch beneath the expensive fabric.

Oh, we will. Yes, we will.

"Despite the unusual… turn of events," the lawyer says, tapping the sheath of papers together nervously, "I trust that you'll sort out whatever details are necessary." He gives me an apologetic look and hands me a small light blue business card with golden lettering. "Please give my office a call if need be."

The older Mr. Rossi growls under his breath. I want to slap him. I take the card. "Thank you."

I turn to them.

"I can't stay here. I don't know you. You don't know me. Whatever personal interest in my… well-being… Mr. Montavio may have had, perhaps he's made a mistake. If I didn't know him, what's my purpose here?"

The old man's eyes snap my way. "You're lying."

My cheeks flush hotter. "I'm not. I've never met him in my life. What makes you think I have?"

"Because Montavio gave fucking *nothing* away. Maybe you were his bastard child."

"Narciso!" The pretty woman with the haunted eyes sitting beside him looks at him in shock. Her voice trails off in rapid Italian, which I don't speak, but I catch the words *impossibile* and *bambina*. Impossible. Child. I'm more likely her daughter than granddaughter.

He lifts a hand to silence her, and she flinches before she clamps her mouth shut, silently fuming.

The older woman also called Tosca, clearly the wife of the deceased, clears her throat. She speaks in broken English, but her meaning is clear enough.

"My husband had no other children but Tosca and Francesca." She waves her hands at her daughter and makes a scissoring motion with her fingers. The youngest of the brothers laughs out loud, ignoring the furious glare from his father.

Montavio was fixed. Infertile.

The older woman looks back at me and speaks in a thick Italian accent. "Old? How old you?"

"Twenty-eight."

She shakes her head. "*Impossibile.*"

"Of course it's impossible," I sputter. "I knew my father! I knew my mother. I have my father's crazy wavy hair and his smile, and my father had nothing to do with any of you!"

The man I met last night eyes me warily and speaks in a low warning tone. "Be careful, Vittoria."

My heart thumps wildly. "Excuse me?"

He merely thins his lips before he speaks, then says curtly, "You heard me."

Be careful of what? *Or* who? Is this some kind of a threat? Uh, excuse me?

Marialena speaks up. "Perhaps she can share my room. It's large enough for the both of us and will give—"

"No," the man—her brother?—says shortly. Marialena scowls but doesn't contradict him.

I don't know who this man is, but I know he's someone with authority here. Maybe even the most authority.

"This is ridiculous," the older man says, slamming his palm on the desk. "Even in death, her goddamn father is trying to ruin everything. *Everything.*"

"Of all the things to complain about…" He turns to her and looks as if he's going to slap her, but one of the sons steps in.

"Mama," he says quietly. Warning, perhaps. She closes her mouth, stands, and walks to the other side of the room and sits beside Marialena and another woman that looks like Marialena's sister.

It's all so strange and unusual. This is no normal family. First, they live in a castle. Second… do they even live anywhere else? Why are grown children like this still at home? Or did they just come here for the reading of the will? Third, it doesn't make sense that I met them all last night and now they have some sort of hold against me I wasn't prepared for.

My head spins, even as the logical part of my brain can't help but piece this all together.

I have nothing, not a penny to my name. Nothing. And here, if I stay for thirty days, I'll have half of the inheritance.

Then it dawns on me with such clarity, I can't believe I didn't think of it before.

I have no idea how much the inheritance is, and that matters. Would I give up my life for a few thousand dollars?

I clear my throat and turn back to the lawyer. "I need to ask."

"Yes?"

"I'm not even considering giving up my life for a small sum of money." I hate that I sound like I'm money-grubbing, but it has to be asked. "I need to know exactly what the stakes are before I make any decision."

"Do you?" the older man at the desk asks. My blood turns cold just looking at the way his fingers tighten around a pen.

"Ah, yes," the lawyer says. "A reasonable question, Ms. DeSanto. The inheritance in question is an estimated twelve million dollars, estimated only because there are investments and the like that will be cashed in upon receipt of the inheritance."

I sit back down involuntarily. I think my knees just buckled.

I slept in my car, ate a gas station granola bar and used a slim bar of soap in a dismal public bathroom to clean up before I came here, every penny

I've ever earned was stolen, and now I'm given the chance to inherit *six million dollars?*

No.

No.

It's like some sort of twisted nightmare or dream, I don't know which one.

"Thank you for your time," the guy I met last night says to the lawyer. "If we're done here, you may leave now." He nods to the door, and the largest brother of the bunch stands and escorts the lawyer out.

The door slams shut, and the room falls into silence. I shake my head at them.

"There are things here that I don't understand."

"There are," the man who saved me says. His voice, a composed, deep baritone, commands immediate attention. "And there are things I understand very well."

I remember his promise to me. I remember what he said he'd do to me if I showed my face again. No one else recognizes me, no one else knows what I witnessed or what we shared. He promised me he'd hurt me if he ever saw me again, and he doesn't look like someone who makes idle promises.

The pastries from earlier sit like stones in my belly.

"Before we make any decisions, some introductions are in order," he continues, the deep, masculine timbre of his voice carrying with it a tone of authority all heed. He nods to his father. "Narciso Rossi, the head of our family and our father. Our mother, Tosca Rossi." He nods to them. I stare before I remember my manners and finally just nod a greeting. He gestures toward his sisters. "My sisters, Marialena and Rosa. You've met Marialena it seems." I nod again, then he points to his brothers. Oh gosh. Why does Rosa look like she has a black eye? I cringe inside to think of how Rosa got that black eye. Did one of them do it to her? Or was it her father? It makes me queasy.

The largest brother who escorted the lawyer to the door gives me a sheepish smile. Though he's a big, muscled guy with tattoos on his knuckles that look like skulls, there's a hidden gentleness to his eyes the others don't share. "Orlando," he says. "My brother." He points to the suave looking one that appears as if he'd smile as he rips my panties off with his teeth. The youngest, I presume. "Mario." I nod again. Then finally he turns to a stern, studious-looking brother. "And Ottavio. We call him Tavi."

I nod but don't say anything. I have to leave.

Don't I?

"And you?" I ask before I can stop myself. My voice is husky as if I haven't spoken in hours. "What's your name?"

He frowns. "You don't know my name?"

"Why would I?"

And why is the whole room staring at us?

A shadow crosses his features, but he doesn't respond at first. His mouth tightens as his brows draw together. Those blue-gray eyes of his look cloudy and angry, and I wonder if he's going to snap. Why would I know his name?

"My name is Romeo."

At another place and time, I might laugh at that, like he was joking.

Romeo, Romeo, wherefore art thou Romeo?

There isn't a trace of humor in his face, not even a hint of amusement.

"This is outrageous," his father fumes, and he pushes himself to his feet. He shakes his fist in a fit of rage. I muse to myself how a man his age can still have temper tantrums. Didn't anyone ever tell him those are for children?

Marialena studies her nails, frowning, one shapely leg draped over the other. Her sister Rosa looks bored, smoothing out invisible wrinkles in her linen skirt. Unlike Marialena with her youthful beauty, Rosa looks tired and weary, but she's no less beautiful.

"Sit, Papa," Romeo says in a voice I can tell most people obey. Romeo gentles his voice. "Please." It seems he isn't the head of this family when it comes to his father. "We can't control what Nonno did, can we?"

The elderly woman that must be Nonna chuckles softly to herself, and Narciso steps over to her.

"You think he won, don't you, old woman?" he says in a dangerous whisper. "You think because he's unnerved me and tried to control this family that he will have the final word, do you?" He continues to lecture her in Italian.

Tosca Rossi is on her feet. "Enough, Narciso," she says to him. "You can take out your anger toward my father on me, but not my mother."

Romeo's voice overshadows them all. "He will take out his anger on *no one.*"

The old man whips his head around to glare at Romeo, who gives him the same steely look I saw in the alley. Narciso mutters under his breath in Italian, and I have a feeling it isn't something for polite company. He turns on his heel and storms out of the room, cursing under his breath the entire time, but before he leaves, he turns and looks straight at me. "You'll fucking marry one of them or you'll deal with me. I'd rather kiss her father's cold, dead balls then give the money to that charity, and he fucking knew it." He stabs his fingers into the air to emphasize each word, then utters words in Italian that make his mother-in-law flinch. "You'll marry, and you'll marry into *this family.*"

Was that supposed to convince me?

The door slams behind him. Seconds later, glass crashes and something heavy clatters to the floor. No one but Romeo moves. He slowly draws in a breath before shooting me another hostile glare.

I blink, not sure of how to respond. Was that a threat?

Alright, these people are crazy. My gaze turns back to the rest of them. Marialena looks amused. Rosa bored. But the brothers... they're all eying me with various degrees of interest except Romeo, who still stares with fury.

No. *No.*

"I won't," I say softly. "It's against the law to coerce someone into marriage."

Tosca laughs quietly to herself and stands. "How very innocent of you, *cara*," she says in a tone touched with sadness. "Perhaps you haven't manipulated your way here." She forces out a mirthless laugh. "How refreshing." She gestures to her daughters. "Come, girls. We have business to tend to, just as your brothers do I'm sure. Romeo will determine where she will stay."

"And what if I don't stay?" I say, feeling angry she'd even assume. Why do they act as if this is a done deal?

Tosca turns to me and gives a weary sigh. "Vittoria, is it?" she says.

I nod. "Yes."

"Vittoria, you will find one thing that we've all found much earlier than you." She smiles sadly. "In our world, choice is only an illusion. You have no choice in this. My husband will kill, literally kill, before he sees a penny of my father's money go to that charity, and my father knew this. It's why my husband's so angry, though admittedly it doesn't take much to do that."

"And if I leave?"

She grimaces. "I wouldn't advise that."

I turn to see Romeo staring straight at me. "We will find you and it will not go well for you." My jaw drops, but no one even blinks.

Who is this violent, threatening family? I shiver uncomfortably.

"But I won't marry you," I whisper.

"Then marry *me*," Mario says. "I'll treat you right, *mia donna*."

I stare at him in disbelief. "Are we really talking about marriage like we would a date for homecoming?"

Rosa laughs. "I wondered," she says as she gets to her feet, "if you had connived your way in here. But, no. You haven't. You don't want to be here anymore than I do."

I don't know if there's a single Rossi I like at this point. Maybe Marialena...

"Clearly," she continues, "you're incredibly innocent. Naïve, even, aren't you?" She turns to Romeo. "She has no idea who we are, brother." She stretches her arms and sighs. "The rest of us should go now and allow our brother to give our houseguest a bit of an education." She winks at me. "Let me know when you're ready to tour the garden. It's my favorite place to be." I wonder why she winks at me. This family is so strange.

"Dinner at six," Romeo says. "Mama, I'll put her on the second floor across from Marialena." Tosca nods.

Romeo turns back to me. "I'll show Vittoria to her room. The rest of you come to dinner promptly." The tone of his voice dismisses everyone from the room.

Before they leave, the large, muscled one who I think they call Orlando—names are blurring at this point—smiles at me. "Welcome," he says. "My family welcomes you."

Sure they do. Right.

Still, I thank him politely. I can be polite, too, even if no one else can.

That leaves the two of us. Me, and the man I once thought an angel, who may choose to make good on his threat at any minute.

I was wrong. I was so wrong.

I stare at him, the large breadth of him. He seems to radiate so much anger, I half expect fire to come out of his nostrils like a dragon. He's frowning at a paper in his hand, before he shakes his head. When his gaze comes to me, I take a step back. There's raw, visceral hatred in his eyes I've never seen before. My stomach turns in knots.

"I told you never to come near me again," he says, pushing himself up from the desk. He looms as he approaches, probably six to ten inches or more taller than I am. I take an involuntary step back.

"I had no idea you were here. I have no idea who you are. I told you the truth. I came here because I got a letter asking me to come."

How could a man named Romeo be so unromantic? I think wildly as he draws nearer. He bares his teeth with a low growl that only magnifies the animalistic vibe.

"You think I'm stupid?"

"And you think I'm lying?" I snap back. He's coming closer to me, so close I can smell the faintest scent of cigar mingled with the masculine scent of pine. I hate cigars. I would never kiss a man who smoked, much less do any more.

"Step back," I warn, which is probably about as effective as telling a wild animal not to attack. If I screamed, I already know that no one in this house will come running. His father might bluster and fume, but Romeo is the true head of this house.

"You saw what I did last night," he says in a furious whisper. "You came here to threaten me. Don't you know that no one threatens the Rossi family?"

My own anger's starting to boil. "Threaten you? Are you that full of yourself that you can't imagine that someone doesn't even know who the hell you *are*? And what have I done to make you think that I threatened you? I've done literally nothing but respond to a letter. And as far as last night, who the hell asked you to intervene? I could've handled it myself." *Like hell.*

His eyes spark at me. I expect him to stand and fume, but apparently he has different plans. When he reaches me, he tugs my hair until it falls loose from the bun. Without prelude or apology, he wraps a hand in my hair—*in my hair*—and drapes it around his fist. My mouth gapes open involuntarily when he yanks my head back, baring my throat to him.

"How dare you," he growls. "How fucking *dare* you come in here and talk to me that way?"

I've had it. I don't care what the consequences are, no asshole's going to manhandle me and act like he's God's Fucking Gift to Women. I go to kick him, but he knows this move. He's been here before. He blocks the kick, swivels, and before I know what's happening I'm pinned up against the wall. His arms are on either side of me, trapping me. The cords of muscles along his neck and arms flex as he holds himself back from hurting me.

I'm not going to win this, I know that now, but I won't go down without a fight, and the first thing I'm gonna do is poke a hole in his inflated ego. "Who asked you to help me last night? Huh? And I have no idea who your grandfather was, nor do I have any concept of why his antiquated notions of *marriage* have anything to do with *me*."

"But you want it," he growls. "You want those millions in your greedy little hands, don't you?"

I laugh in his face. "My greedy little hands? Who the hell wouldn't want six million dollars? You think I'm Mother Teresa?" I shake my head at him. I lower my voice. "If you think you can bully me out of this, think again, Romeo." I lift my arm and slice it in the air, breaking his grip on the wall. He stumbles. "And if you ever fucking put your hands on me again, I'll report you for assault."

He rights himself and shakes his head. "So that's your plan. Come in here, swindle your way to the millions, take it all and go home, but play the victim in the meantime."

My jaw drops open. I have no idea what he's talking about. None. Is he insane? Maybe he is. Maybe he's a narcissist. Wouldn't surprise me with a father named *Narciso* . Maybe he's taught all his damn sons to be full of themselves.

"Believe whatever you want," I say to him, seething, pushing my words through my teeth while my heart slams in my chest with fury. "I know the truth. I've told you the truth. You're the idiot who fails to believe it." The utter *nerve* of him.

He reaches for me again, but I dodge him, duck,

and slip under his arm. I run toward the door. He grabs the back of my hair and yanks me back. I open my mouth to scream, but he clamps his hand on top of my mouth.

"You're done," he whispers in my ear. "This is done. Do you understand me? Go ahead, Vittoria. Call the police. See if they'll come. You're in a place that's off their radar, and that's on purpose." He spins me around and yanks me to him. My heart beats rapidly, involuntarily. I've never been in the presence of anyone that exuded such raw masculine strength without apology. I hate that he's such an asshole. "No more fighting me. I will open that door, and you'll walk alongside me. I'll show you to your room. You'll join us for dinner at six." He shakes his head slowly from side to side like he can't believe this is happening. "My grandfather knew that if you were here for a month, you'd earn every penny of that money. We start now."

I could leave. I could run. I could pretend this never happened. I could shake the dust from this house off my feet and never look back.

But I have a legal right to fight for that money. I need to at least think this over. Are there any stipulations as to how *long* I'm married? Are there any loopholes? I'm not giving up so easily. That's not who I am.

Fine. *Fine.* I can at least play along to get him to release me.

"Let me go," I whisper. "Let me go, and I won't fight you."

He shakes his head from side to side. "That's not

even in question. If you fight me, I'll punish you. If you disobey me, I'll punish you. If you raise your voice, guess what I'll do?"

I refuse to answer him. He laughs, a low, dark chuckle that sets my nerves on edge.

"Come, little Vittoria. Let's get you in your room. Then, we'll go over your rules."

———

CHAPTER SIX

"O WILT thou leave me so unsatisfied?" Romeo and Juliet

ROMEO

That went well… if I was trying to ensure she chooses one of my brothers.

Dio.

She'll be mine. I'll be sure of it.

It's time I take a wife, if I'm going to ensure my place as head of the house. I have the right and privilege of an arranged marriage if I so choose, but this chance… this might be a better option. I've seen the women my father's suggested I marry.

I don't want to marry a mafia princess.

I want Vittoria.

I've never liked anything given to me without a fight.

I bring her to the guest room. She stomps her

feet as if to show me she's not doing this of her own free will, but she could have left. No one's bound her here. Yes, she'd be walking away from a chance at six million dollars, but she seems like a woman of pride.

And maybe she needs this money. I'll know soon enough if she does.

But who doesn't?

I suspect I know what she thinks she'll do. Stay here free of charge with food and a clean house and a room of her own. Put up with us for thirty days. Sulk her way through. Then on day thirty, she leaves and gets the smaller portion of the inheritance.

Or, she'll seduce one of my brothers—probably fuckboy Mario—then take the six mil and screw the marriage.

She won't leave before then. No, she's too tenacious to do something like that, I'm sure of it.

My grandfather was a crazy old man. He had ferrets for pets that had free rein over his house, drove nothing but antique Cadillacs, and smoked hundred-dollar Cubans over breakfast with Limoncello chasers. No love was lost between him and my grandmother, and we all knew it. She came to live with us long before he died, though he visited often. When I grew to adulthood, I wondered if it had more to do with needling my father than anything. My grandfather had a nasty streak, and my father brought out the worst in him.

Who is this woman? That question above all

needs to be answered. I don't know why she's here. And why the fuck was she at that bar last night?

I don't touch her as I bring her to her room. I haven't decided if she's here to blackmail me, but I want it clear, I won't take that lying down. Is she really as innocent as she appears?

I doubt it.

She walks beside me, her face set in anger. It doesn't lessen her beauty at all. If anything, it enhances it.

"You're beautiful when you're angry," I say, feeling my lips curl in amusement. She's like a feisty little kitten with needle-sharp teeth. I could curl her in the palm of my hand to subdue her, and she'd purr for me.

And as we walk, I start to think for once not about her choices… but *mine.*

"Humor me," I say as we walk up the circular staircase that leads to the second floor. "Tell me everything. Where you came from. Why you're here. What you hope to accomplish."

"No."

I'm so surprised by her patent refusal that I don't respond at first.

No one tells me no, but she doesn't know that yet. She'll learn it, though.

I shake my head but don't respond. A response like that will earn her punishment, but we're too new. If I'm going to make this woman my wife, she'll learn soon enough.

So I try another tack.

"If you don't tell me everything, I'll be forced to

make assumptions, Vittoria, and believe me when I tell you, my assumptions won't be in your favor."

"Is that a threat?" she spits out.

I don't respond. She really doesn't know who I am. From the moment I was born, to the very first nanny that wiped my ass and fed me, everyone has known who I am, where I come from, known my family's wealth and power.

And now this woman... she actually doesn't? Our first interaction was her seeing me kill a man that threatened her. I have no idea how she feels about that. Is she scared? Does she think me only a ruthless murderer?

Why do I care what she thinks about me at all?

She gives me a haughty shrug. "I didn't choose to come here."

"Lie. Careful, *bella.* Lies will earn you punishment. No one brought you here in chains, though I'll admit the concept intrigues me." Chains and cuffs, her naked and under my command... Yeah. Yeah, I like that.

A slight rise of her brows shows me she heard that. Felt it, maybe.

She shakes her head. "I have no interest in divulging anything about myself to you."

"So you'll live under my roof and take advantage of my family's hospitality, but you won't tell me a thing about yourself? Excellent. I'll have my men find everything out anyway."

Yet another really well-thought-out threat. Any other woman who dared talk to me this way would've been over my knee by now, but no one's ever had the audacity. I still can't believe the nerve she has. I don't allow anyone to speak to me this way, and she'll learn soon that I won't tolerate it.

At the second floor, she still doesn't speak as we walk down the hall to her room. I don't know why she unnerves me. I'm not used to women treating me this way. I'm not used to *anyone* treating me this way.

This one's special.

I show her to a guest room, one that my mother renovated. With the pointed arched doorways, renovated fireplace, stained glass accent windows and wooden ceiling beams, the Gothic appeal of this room often wows our visitors.

"It's a beautiful room," I say, hands in my pockets. I try to soften my tone.

She merely narrows her eyes. She doesn't trust flirtation. I stifle a chuckle.

Vittoria walks past me and looks around, her eyes wide with surprise. "This is your *guest* room?"

I nod and glance at the time on my watch. "It is. You'll stay here for the remainder of your visit."

"Thank you." She sighs. "Much appreciated, Mr. Rossi. You may leave now," she says, as if dismissing me.

No one dismisses me.

I itch to show her who I am, to remind her that she should be afraid of me. I never should've touched her and let her go. She thinks she can get away with anything she wants.

I decide to give her a warning. "You don't dismiss me, Vittoria. No one does."

She turns to me and shakes her head. God, she's gorgeous, all simple curves and soft, creamy skin, those feisty eyes that dare me to dominate her. I like to imagine what she'd do if I showed her what it's like to submit.

She will.

"Oh?"

I take a step toward her. Maybe it *is* time she learns her place, learns what I expect. If she's to be my wife, the sooner she learns this the better. I watched Leo spoil his pretty Sicilian princess, and I saw how that ended. I saw my father mistreat my mother, and witnessed the demise of their marriage as well. I decided long ago that marriage to me would be the best of both worlds: my wife will obey me, my wife will defer to my authority, and in return I'll take care of her every wish and whim.

"I'm tired," she says, shaking her head. "This has been a long day. I'm only telling you I don't need any more explanations or tours. This room is beautiful," she says with a weary note in her tone. "Everything about this house is simply stunning. But please try to understand that I have *much* to process. So much. I need some time alone."

Maybe I'm going about this all the wrong way. She pissed me off, and I let her know it, but the reality is, I could use this to my advantage. I haven't thought this through.

I need a woman to marry me, to wear my ring, in order to assume my throne. This is non-negotiable, one of my family's rules that's never broken. Both my grandfathers agreed on this one rule, and have carried it forth from generation to generation. I know why. A man with a woman by his side doesn't make the mistakes a single man does. He has a woman to bed, to alleviate his stress, to share the burden of his throne.

He isn't swayed by the wiles of another woman.

In theory, that is. It's all in theory. It's not a secret that my father had multiple partners, that their marriage bed was cold and defiled long before my mother finished having children. My grandfather was no exception.

But that won't be me. I despise infidelity on any level.

I can't force my way onto this woman. I can't command her to marry me. If I try, my brothers could easily step in, marry her, then assume a position of power above mine.

Fucking archaic laws.

My father will not let this woman out of our home without marrying one of us. He'd just as soon chain her in our dungeon and force the marriage then let the legal proceedings allow any of the inheritance to go to his most despised charity.

My grandfather was a conniving son of a bitch.

I'll have this woman researched. I'll see who she is and why she's here. I'll know before the sun sets tonight whether or not she's set me up. And in the meantime... I'll have to start thinking things through more clearly.

I have an opportunity here I can't fucking squander.

"You need a tour of the house," I say in a gentler

tone than I've used with her yet. With... honestly, anyone.

She looks at me in surprise, her eyes narrowing warily.

"Oh?"

"Oh." I run a hand through my hair, my mind racing. She'll think I've got multiple personality disorder if I start sweet-talking her now. We've had our first impressions, and they were utter shit. "I'll have one of my sisters show you around. Make yourself at home. Do you need to go anywhere to pick up your belongings?"

"How do you even know I intend to stay?" she asks. She runs her fingers along her collarbone absentmindedly. A sign of vulnerability.

I'll remember that.

I want to kiss my way down the length of her neck to where her creamy skin softens, giving way to the most perfect set of breasts...

I've never seduced a woman. I've never had to.

I've had women who wanted my money. Made men have their groupies like celebrities, and I've used women to suit my needs. But this woman... she doesn't even know who I really am. Not yet.

I wish I could keep it that way.

By dinnertime, I'll know more about her, but she'll know more about me, too. And what she finds out and how she reacts will be telling.

My phone rings. I glance at the screen and frown. Tavi.

"Excuse me," I say to her, and her eyes narrow

further. She doesn't trust the change in temperature.

"Yeah?"

Tavi's tone is troubled. "You got a minute?"

I look at Vittoria. She's looking around the room in wonder and nervously twisting her fingers at the hem of her top.

"Give me five. We need to talk."

"Oh yeah."

"Where?"

"Dungeon."

Shit. He doesn't want a fucking soul to overhear us.

"I'll be there."

I turn to Vittoria. "Forgive me for what I said earlier, Vittoria."

I like the feel of her name on my lips. I'd like the feel of her body even more.

I run my hand through my hair, feigning nervousness. I don't get nervous. "I've been under a lot of pressure. I thought you were here to spy on me after last night."

She purses her lips and doesn't respond, but wraps her arms around her torso. Finally, she gives me a little nod.

"My father can be a difficult man," I tell her. "Assuming you decide to stay, which I assure you would be the right thing to do, I'll be sure you enjoy your time here."

She rolls her eyes. "You just want me to marry you."

I feel my brows rise just as she bursts into laughter.

"That was the most ridiculous thing ever. I can't even believe this is happening. It's like some sort of a dream or nightmare or a reality TV show." She's laughing with an almost maniacal glee. "I... I just can't believe any of this is... real." She squints at the heavy drapes, the lamps beside her bed imported from Sicily, the thick, vibrant Persian carpet handwoven overseas. My mother's taken great pains to furnish this house with the most luxurious amenities possible.

I smile at her. Actually smile. I'll pretend we just got off on the wrong foot. I nod. "I do. We all do. Your value to us is worth more than you might know."

"More than a crown of glory and six million dollars?"

I smile again, a full-on smile that actually seems to melt a bit of my stony heart. Is she seducing *me*?

"That about sums it up. But a crown to the throne of Rossi and six mil is nothing to sneeze at, *bella*."

She looks away. Maybe she wants to hide the flush of her cheeks when I call her beautiful.

I bow to her as I take my leave. "I'll have staff come and assist you with your belongings."

A knock sounds at the door. "Come in," I say.

The heavy door opens, and Marialena pops her head in. She's changed into jeans and a slouchy sweater, and squeals when she sees Vittoria. "Ohh, they gave you *this* guest room. I love this one. Come with me, Vittoria, and I'll show you around The Castle." She looks to me discreetly, asking for permission. Unlike Vittoria, Marialena knows the hierarchy here.

I nod my approval. "Go. Dinner at six."

Vittoria follows Marialena and lets out a breath.

"Ciao, bella."

———

CHAPTER SEVEN

"Teach me how I should forget to think!" Romeo and Juliet

VITTORIA

"My brothers are going to try to seduce you," Marialena says as she takes me down the carpeted hall. My heels sink into the velvety burgundy carpet, and I wish I'd changed into something a bit more comfortable like her.

I laugh nervously. This family is insane. "Is that right?"

"Of course," she says with a musical laugh. "You heard the terms of that agreement. My grandfather wants them all married so they outrank my father in time. It was part of his plan. But he put this all in place so that if you don't marry one of them, my father will see his archenemies richly rewarded."

She shakes her head. "I miss Nonno. He kept things interesting around here."

"Seems like he still is," I mutter to myself.

We walk down the spiral stairway, like something out of a fairy tale, and my stomach growls with hunger. Dinner at six seems pretty far away.

"Ah, Marialena, you showing our guest the place, eh?" Mario stands at the foot of the stairs with a bouquet of flowers. For one frantic minute, I think they're for me. If these men try competing for my attention... But when I get to the bottom of the stairs he only winks at me and goes on his way.

"Mario has a flavor of the month. No, *day*," she corrects. "The man treats women like they're on a conveyor belt."

"Lovely."

"So don't marry that one. He's fun if you want to go drag racing or if you get stuck somewhere and can't get back by your curfew..." I look at her to see if she's joking. She isn't. I bet she's talking from personal experience. "But he won't be... faithful. It isn't his nature." She frowns but doesn't elaborate. I wonder if fidelity is in the nature of any of the Rossi men?

Why do I care? I'm not marrying them. I learned my lesson about trusting men. I *might* stick it out to the end of the month to get the smaller payout, though... maybe.

Voices rise and fall in distant rooms, but we're the only ones in the main hall. I don't want to start off on the wrong foot. I need to be honest with her. "I'm not sure I'll marry any one of them, Marialena."

She sighs, almost sadly.

"You will. You will see." She pauses and gives me a curious look. "Something tells me… You don't know who we are, do you, Vittoria?" Her eyes focus on me with concern. She isn't the first to suggest that.

I hear Romeo's deep baritone from the other room and look to see him conversing with one of his brothers. Tavi? Orlando? God, I can't keep track. From here, I can watch Romeo unobserved, but I keep my observation brief.

He's taken off his suit coat and rolled up his shirtsleeves. I swallow at the corded muscles of his forearms beneath the crisp white fabric, so utterly masculine my heart flutters. The rich outlines of his shoulders strain against the fabric of his dress shirt, and for one crazy minute I imagine slipping the shirt off and revealing his naked skin. Everything about him is commanding, defiantly masculine, though he carries himself with an almost nonchalant grace. Comfortable in his skin. His dark brown hair has flecks of gold, and curls in a way that'd be almost feminine if not for the cut of his jaw and his ruthlessly cold eyes. The shadow of stubble covers his chin, and I idly wonder what it would feel like against my skin.

I drag my gaze away. An attractive young man who doesn't look like one of the brothers steps through the doorway and sees us. Though his face is unlined and shaven, giving him the appearance of someone younger than Romeo, there's a world-worn weariness about him that's unmistakable.

"Santo, meet Vittoria," Marialena says. "She'll be staying with us for the next thirty days."

A muscle ticks in his jaw. He gives me a look one might give a pesky fly, his lips curved downward in a frown. "I heard."

Marialena sighs and places her hand on his arm. "My grandfather was an eccentric old man, Santo. It wasn't right that he excluded you."

He shrugs her hand off. "Good luck, Vittoria." He curses under his breath. "You'll need it."

He storms out the front door. Yeah, there's all *kinds* in this house, and the only one I like is standing beside me.

"You ever get your Tarot cards read?" Marialena asks.

Oh Lord. "Uh, no."

Her eyes gleam with excitement, and she's going on and on about a friend of hers that does readings and the phases of the moon and horoscopes, but I'm only half-listening. Romeo's having a heated conversation with his brother, and he's looking straight at me.

I recall the feeling of his fingers in my hair, the fear that spiked my pulse before it melted to heat, his apology in the guest room.

If I leave tonight, I'll spend the night in my car.

If I stay, I'll spend the night in a *castle.*

If I leave, I'll get nothing. Not a penny.

If I stay, even if I don't marry any of them, I'll end up with enough money that I can start my life again.

And if I marry one of them…

Nonna passes by me with a knowing smile. I want to ask her what exactly she knows. Ask her what the Montavio family has to do with mine, but she speaks hardly any English and I don't know if she's offering anything new.

I'll ask her, though, even if I have to study Italian to find the answer.

I'll get the answer, and hopefully before Romeo does.

"Vittoria." I blink at the sound of my name in that deep, masculine voice. Romeo's still staring at me from across the room. He beckons to me with his finger. "Come here."

Do I go? I've never obeyed a summons from a man before, and I'm not sure why I'd start now.

"Go," Marialena says furtively. "Just trust me. Please."

I fold my arms on my chest and wait for a beat to pass.

His jaw tightens. "Please."

I don't miss Marialena's gasp.

I walk to him, ignoring the way his brothers laugh. Marialena whispers to me, "Oh yeah. Romeo wants you. I don't know if I ever heard him say please."

When I reach him, he gestures to the older man who accompanied him the night before. "This is Leo, my father's youngest brother. He thinks he might have known your father."

I look at him in surprise. "Did you?"

He nods. "His name was Frances, no? Worked in NYC."

My hope deflates. I shake my head. "I'm sorry, no. My father was Richard Mellow. DeSanto was my mother's maiden name. She took it when my father died."

Romeo frowns. "Why?"

"Why what?"

"Why did she not keep your father's last name after his death?" The concept of a wife not keeping her husband's name seems to bemuse him.

I don't answer at first, because it bothers me that I have no idea. "She was an independent woman," I finish lamely.

"Was? Is your mother no longer with us?"

I shake my head. "She died a few years back in an accident."

"I'm sorry to hear that," Romeo says. It feels like the man standing before me now, with the gentlemanly attitude and sincerity in his voice, is the exact opposite of the man I met yesterday. It's unnerving.

"Thank you," I say awkwardly. I turn to Leo. "I'm sorry you didn't know my father. I'd like answers as to why I was called here just as much as the rest of you." Someone mutters a curse in the corner of the room. It doesn't surprise me to see Narciso Rossi with a glass of wine and a cigar.

Marialena tugs me along with her. "Annnnd back to the tour. Here's the Great Hall," Marialena says in a loud voice with a forced smile. The Great Hall, a regal room with cathedral ceilings and heavy, solid wooden furniture that looks as if it were carved by hand, invites a large gathering. It smells of ancient wood, fresh-baked bread, and roasted garlic. My stomach rumbles. I look around the room and feel my eyes widen at the sight of a massive pipe organ, flags that hang from the ceiling, turrets and a view of the hallways that lead to various other rooms.

"Here we have many of our family's gatherings."

And perhaps they eat turkey legs with their bare hands and drink wine from goblets before they sharpen their swords by the roaring fire?

You don't know who we are, do you?

It seems finding that out is the first order of business.

"Behind us is the coat room," she says, gesturing to the small room I saw this morning not far from the reception room. "We loved to hide there when we were little," she says with a wistful look in her eyes before she smiles and gestures for me to follow her. I marvel at the many rooms, majestic and well-furnished. The house is bustling with people, servants and family, and I imagine some are those still lingering from earlier today.

We walk beyond the Great Hall, its entrance at our back, to what Marialena calls the sun room, a small, quaint room with a huge skylight and large, arched windows that let in so much light my heart seems to lift, even as I feel Romeo's eyes following us. Rocking chairs with hand-sewn quilts make the room look cozy and welcoming. I imagine the women like to gather here while the men conduct business, like an ancient throwback to archaic times that demanded segregation of the genders.

Something about this place makes me feel like we've gone back in time, as if we're no longer solidly living in the twenty-first century. It adds to the unusual feel of this place.

Beyond the sun room sits a large pantry that flanks a formal dining room. The dining room takes my breath away. I stand in awe for a full minute before I follow her again. One wall of the dining room boasts nothing but wine—a full *wall* of glass with nothing but bottles of wine in reds and whites and pinks, bedecked with golden labels, and I realize that the chandelier itself is made of *wine glasses. Whoa.*

"I guess you guys like your wine?"

She smiles. "Romeo used to tell me Mama put it in my bottle when I was a baby to shut me up." Either his mother's insane or he actually has a sense of humor. I file it away on my mental list of notes.

A doorway from the dining room opens to a circular room. When Marialena opens the door, I stifle another gasp. I don't want to seem like a country bumpkin, but I've truly never seen anything like this. When people hear I'm from New York, they think I'm a city dweller. What they don't know is that I'm as far away from the city as possible. I grew up at the foot of the Adirondacks, in a one-bedroom house with well water, a garden, and heated by a woodburning stove. I rarely went into the city, and haven't in ages. I lived a sheltered life until my mother died. I'm shocked to see an actual castle like this right here in the present day.

I stare at the library. Wall upon wall of leather-bound books, plush armchairs, another fireplace with a roaring fire, and a side table with a tea set beckon for me to come and repose.

"Forget the guest room," I mutter. "How about I sleep here?"

She grins.

I've never seen anything like this. It's nothing short of breathtaking.

"Since you'll be here for the next month, I'm sure you'll have time to spend in here. Come, there's so much more to see."

Oddly, the only way out of the library is the way in. We backtrack through the dining room, and my mouth waters to see servants bringing in large tureens of soup and trays of crusty bread.

"Hungry?" she asks.

"Starving."

"Good. We'll come back in a few minutes after the tour and have some lunch."

My belly clenches at the thought of eating with the family, though. She must see the hesitation on my face. "On second thought, let's bring a tray upstairs?"

I nod and sigh in relief. "Please. I need a few minutes."

"It's all a bit much," she murmurs. "But you'll adapt. I can tell you will."

Does she want me here because in her mind I'd be a sister-in-law? Will she be disappointed when I don't choose to marry one of them?

Or does she have another motive as well? I don't really trust any of them.

"Now," she says in a low voice. "This is a good time to give you the tour of the North Wing of the house. We don't typically bring guests there, because it's where we have the staff room, the war room, the kitchen, and a few secret rooms my brothers use for meetings."

Not secret anymore?

"Still," she says. "It's one of the best parts of the house."

We walk past the kitchen, and I imitate the way she walks, with her head held high as if we're not out of place here at all.

"Here," she says with a flourish, tracing the edge of some heavy woodwork with her fingertip. A hidden doorway? My mouth drops open when a door seems to appear as if by magic.

"You sure this isn't Hogwarts?"

She grins. "Magical, isn't it?" The heavy scent of cigar smoke and whiskey permeates the air.

"Ok so this is a man cave to beat all man caves."

Marialena nods. "Ooooh, yeah. You could say that."

It holds a heavy desk, solid chairs, and a table, though no electronics. "It's more of a study, though, isn't it?"

She nods.

My curiosity rises. If she wasn't here, I'd be Googling on my phone as fast as possible.

"Down here's the secret wine cellar. It's not a secret now, but was during an earlier time. No one knew it was here when the Montavio family owned this house, but we discovered it when my parents bought it."

There's a story there. I wonder what it is.

"Interesting. Why a secret wine cellar? I mean, the dining room looks as if your family definitely enjoys their wine."

"Secret passages were built into castles for the wealthy," she explains. "Royalty, aristocrats, and the rich had tunnels and rooms for escape or stealth operations. Rumor has it that my great-great-grandfather had this room built because he continued to import wine during Prohibition."

"Ahh. Sneaky."

She turns a key, and a wooden panel gives way to another doorway. I shake my head. There are any number of secrets built into this house. If the walls could talk…

We hear voices behind us. Looking over my shoulder, she quickly locks the door and replaces the key with a furtive glance. "Let's go. No need to rile up my father any more than he's already been riled up today." She rolls her eyes. "Trust me."

If I never see her father again, I'd be happy. I follow behind her.

We quickly walk back through the kitchen to the dining room and exit down an imperial set of marble stairs that leads to another large, arched doorway. I could sit for hours and take in every detail, from the hunter green ivy that adorns some of the east-facing windows, to the pots of flowering plants gathered on tables, to the stained glass that decorates various windows throughout the house.

"And this, I think you're going to like," she says with a whimsical glint in her eyes. She trots down the stairs and I click behind her in my heels.

We step inside an archway, and I gasp. "No way," I whisper. "Are you kidding me?"

"I was like sixteen years old before I was allowed in this part of the house," she says. I can see why. There's an actual *pool* inside The Castle.

Laughter echoes inside The Castle, deep and masculine. I wonder if he's there.

Why do I care? I look back to the pool.

Shaped like a shield, it's surrounded by an iron fence with a gate that I suspect wouldn't keep out curious toddlers. I don't blame her mother for not wanting children nearby. But for others, this is astounding.

Stone archways let in plenty of natural light, and the potted plants that line the perimeter almost give the courtyard the appearance of being outside. I look up, and up, and up. The ceiling keeps the elements out, but a large skylight lets even more light filter in.

I shake my head. "Do you actually swim here?"

"Of course," she says with a shrug. "The ocean's cold for most of the year, but this is heated." I look beyond the arched windows and see the blue tint of ocean waves far beyond.

"I can't believe you grew up here," I say to her, shaking my head.

"Eh, she hardly grew up here." I startle at the sound of a deep masculine voice behind me. My heartbeat races. Is it...? I look to see Tavi standing behind us with his hands in his pockets.

Why am I disappointed?

Marialena rolls her eyes. "I spent four summers in Italy, yes, but I did spend a lot of time in The Castle, Tavi. Just because you're jealous you didn't get to summer in Tuscany doesn't mean I didn't grow up here."

A muscle ticks in his jaw, but he doesn't reply, other than to say, "Tell your story the way you see it," before he turns to go. "I'll tell mine. Once you're done with the tour, I need to speak with you, Marialena."

She sighs. "We're done for now. I'll be up in a minute." She turns to me. "I can tell you're tired." It's more like overwhelmed, but I only nod. "So let's get you up to your room and fed, and we'll finish the tour later."

Alone in my room, I feel as if I've lived this day four times over. After she sends up a tray and I've eaten, my eyes are heavy. My belly's full of home-made soup, bread, and a tossed salad. I'm sleepy. I can barely begin to even process everything that's happened. I lay on the large four-poster bed and gaze at the ornate furnishings.

I should feel like I don't belong here. I should feel as if I'm a stranger, or a guest, or maybe even a trespasser.

Why don't I?

Why do I feel a strange sense of... belonging?

I wonder where Romeo is. I wonder what he's doing.

I wonder why I care.

I close my eyes, so tired I feel as if I could sleep for hours.

So much to think about. *So much.* My run-in with Romeo and my attacker feels like a lifetime ago.

Who was that man? I slide my phone out of my pocket and try to see if there's anything at all in the news about a missing person, a mysterious death, this family, anything. I find nothing.

How odd. Why can't I find anything about this family? They live in a castle. They're wealthy as fuck.

My eyes heavy, I type in *Rossi family Boston.*

Nothing.

Maybe it's all my imagination. Maybe I just need some sleep.

I walk to the bathroom and find it stocked with the essentials—towels, high-end toiletries. I clean up and decide I need a rest before dinner. I'll need clothes, but I can wait. Maybe even borrow some from the girls.

I lie on the bed and listen. Laughter downstairs. Voices outside my door that rise then fade as footsteps walk past. I close my eyes, listening for the one voice I want to hear but don't.

———

CHAPTER EIGHT

"Love is a smoke made with the fume of sighs." Romeo and Juliet

ROMEO

Tavi and I sit in the dungeon, and at first when he's talking to me, I'm only half-listening. I'm not usually so preoccupied, but this time I can't get Vittoria out of my mind.

It's the first time I've ever truly seen someone as a potential wife. I have to see her that way.

And this changes *everything*.

In the modern day, castle dungeons have been remade to house everything from offices to basements to storage units. Ours, however, is a secret place to meet which still functions the way it's meant to when necessary—a place for captives, punishment, and interrogation. If the walls could speak...

I light up a smoke and sigh into the first drag, my lungs expanding and my tension dissipating. We've been smoking down here since I was a teen. The dank walls and concrete floors seem to swallow the smell of the smoke.

"New York," Tavi's saying. He's frowning at something on his iPad, shaking his head from side to side. "Mother died, all true. I don't have many details about her father, but it looks like her grandfather served in the military at the same time ours did." An Italian-American immigrant, my grandfather served in the Second World War. After the war he opened his first restaurant here in the North End. "Seems like there could be a connection there."

Interesting.

"But here's the strange thing, Rome."

"Yeah?" I watch the tendrils of smoke rise and think of the bonfires we lit in the quarry when we were younger.

"She was pretty well-off. I mean, I wouldn't say she was wealthy. She was firmly established, solid income. Money invested in stocks, lined up with a realtor to buy a house. Then about a month ago, everything just... vanished. Bank accounts wiped clean. I can't even find a record of where she lives. Landlord says she was evicted a few weeks ago."

Motherfucker.

"We have some more research to do."

He nods.

We talk about business, go over our numbers,

but I'm only half-listening, vaguely aware that our restaurants in the North End turned a higher profit than we've ever seen, but I can't focus. My mind's on the woman upstairs, the woman who will change the course of this family's history forever.

I don't know why I'm so damn obsessed with her. I could have just about any woman I want. There are no shortages of arranged marriages I could've orchestrated, but I've passed on every one of them.

Greta Costa, the eldest daughter in Sicily's Costa Family. Beautiful but haughty, she told me over dinner she'd wear my ring and bear my children but only marry with a prenup. Bold for a woman like her, born to defer to the male leaders in her home, and my father didn't trust hers. Celia D'Agostino, middle daughter of my father's best friend. She's only ever been like a sister to me. Cute in a nerdy, bookish way, but she jumps like a little scared bird when I move too quickly. I can't have a skittish, fearful wife. Martina Canto, a leggy blonde born and raised on the South Shore of Boston with a reputation as long and winding as the Charles River. No one could ever prove she blew the entire fuckin' Boston University football team, but the rumors prevailed. Mario warned me to steer clear, and on this one thing, I trust him.

I want a faithful wife, who'll take my name and bear my children. I want a wife with a fucking spine, who doesn't cower from a strong gust of wind but who will defer to me as head of the house and know my word is law. And is it too much to ask that I want to wed a woman I actually *like?* For a man in my position, who was fucking capo before he could grow a beard, I should maybe know better. But I witnessed the demise of my parents' marriage and my grandparents' atrophied relationship, and I want more.

I've got one fucking chance to live on this Earth, and goddamn if I don't want a wife I want to come home to.

My mind goes back to the mane of wild, thick auburn hair I want to wrap my hands in. Those shimmering eyes that shift from brown to green depending on the light, intelligent and thoughtful. I can still see her sprawled on the pavement in the alley behind the bar, still feel the flare of fury at seeing her about to be victimized.

I killed for her once without thinking.

I'd do it again.

In one day, I'm more entranced with this stranger than I've been with women I've known for decades.

"Rome? Earth to Rome. Hello?" Tavi snaps his fingers, a look of concern in his eyes. "You hear a word I said just now?"

I shake my head. "Sorry, no."

He nods, the most patient among us, and blows out a breath. "Admin's got a meeting later in the week to go over where you want us stationed in Tuscany." The top-level management of our family includes my father, the Boss, me, the Underboss, and the consigliere—our advisor, Leo. Our family tradition says we'll swear in our new associates, the men who've risen in rank but haven't become made men yet.

"Made men by the New Year," I say with a nod. As my father's faculties and mental fortitude wane, we need to strengthen the Family. The associates I choose will take the vow of Omertà, one of the most powerful oaths we ever take. The code of honor, loyalty, and silence, the oath all take when sworn into the Family. Not all men with rank in the Family have to be born into rank, but all take the oath that demands loyalty to the brotherhood above love, friends, or country.

Tavi takes notes, and will fill in the rest of our army later.

"You're preoccupied, Rome," he says with a knowing glint in his eyes. "Go into town, bro. Take Mario. He'll hook you up. Spent too much time in the slammer." His jaw clenches before he continues. He knows my last stint was in my father's stead, that I wasn't even guilty of the crimes I was convicted of. Doesn't matter, though. I've got a list of crimes I committed as long as my arm no one knows about.

I shake my head. I can't afford to do that, not now.

Tavi's pacing like an old woman.

"Sit down, Tavi. Jesus."

I sit up straighter in my chair when I hear the sound of pounding footsteps, heels clicking above us and getting louder. Growing up in The Castle, we came to identify every set of footsteps, from Mama's high-heeled clicks to Papa's heavy, foreboding steps that scattered us boys like ants, to Rosa's softer steps and Santo's leisurely stroll.

Whenever we heard Mama coming, we knew to hide our smokes or girls or whatever the case may be. Later, as I grew older, I realized that Mama wore those high heels to warn us of Papa's entrance. She never said anything, but it became a silent understanding between us.

Papa is nearly soundless, but everywhere he walks he can't help but make a sound, whether it's a snarl at a servant, or a cough or wheeze from his three-pack-a-day habit. Now, however, I don't know who it is.

A KNOCK SOUNDS at the door. Tavi cocks his pistol and stands by the door.

"Come in." I look up curiously, surprised to see Rosa enter. I didn't expect her. Tavi puts his gun away but not before she sees it.

"You'd pull a gun on your own sister, Ottavio?" She can't hide the wounded look in her eyes. "Shouldn't have brought you these, then, hmm?" My mouth waters to see she's holding a silver tray of our bakery's famous butter cookies. They've won awards all throughout New England.

"Didn't know it was you," he mutters, clearly repentant because he wants those cookies. "Give those here."

She smiles and hands him the tray of cookies, little pink ones dotted with sprinkles, rich butter cookies enrobed in powdered sugar, little mounds of delicate half-moons with chocolate filling. "Thought you two knew everyone's step?"

I don't respond. She's been gone too long for us to recognize her sound anymore. She's changed too much. I take four cookies and pop them in my mouth one at a time like popcorn. *Fuck*, they're good. Delicately sweetened and rich as sin, our bakers bake them in small, handmade batches and sell them in the North End. They're usually sold out within an hour of opening.

Rosa shakes her head and takes one pretty pink cookie and nibbles it like a mouse. She rarely touches sugar, but likes to indulge in our family favorites when she comes home. The dim light reflects on the fading black and blue around her eye. She's a beautiful woman, and I hate to see her marred like this, but more than anything I hate that anyone struck her.

My hands clench into fists, and a slow simmering rage coils in my stomach. She's seen the doctor, that much is obvious, because her eye looks better than it did yesterday. I still wish I could slice the throat of the motherfucker who did that to her. I'd beat the shit out of him first. I'd beat the shit out of anyone who dared to raise a hand to a woman, but for laying hands on my sister, a sound beating would only be the beginning before I made him die a painful death.

When Marialena was eighteen years old, she went out to a college party with a friend of hers a few years her senior. Most of her friends are older than she is, but that's the way it is in our family.

Raised to grow up fast, we didn't have much use for peers.

Marialena called me in tears, the sound of her desperate voice haunting me to this day. My parents were in Tuscany and she was under my watch.

She'd been assaulted. She'd gone to a party anonymously, without her bodyguard. Said she wanted one night without being a known Rossi. She'd had too much to drink, and a drunk frat boy tried to take advantage of her.

His death made the news.

We're usually more careful, but we wanted to make an impression that time. First time I broke my own damn hand delivering the worst beating I'd ever given a guy. Still hurts when the weather goes to shit where I broke a bone.

I wasn't greedy, though. I let my brothers take turns, too.

Orlando hung his body from the Zakim Bridge overlooking Boston, castrated and bleeding out, and Marialena didn't leave the house for the rest of the summer. When fall came I stationed three guards on her instead of her usual one.

She forgave me, eventually.

"Rosa." She sits beside me. "How are you?"

I try to keep my features calm, along with my voice, but she gives me a sad smile when she sees me staring at her eye.

"There's nothing you can do about it now." She'd sound abrasive if not for the lilt in her voice. I know my older sister too well. The Rossi women learn to keep their poker face on at all times, but they feel, and they feel hard. They may be in circumstances they wouldn't choose, but it doesn't detract from who they are.

When she enters a room, she walks with her head held high, regal as she's always been. She sits beside me and rests her hand on top of mine. She gives me a sad smile. "He left me a lot of money, Romeo."

She doesn't need the money and we both know this.

"He left you a daughter."

Pain flits across her features, and I don't ask questions. We both know it probably would've been better for her if he had left her a son. Women are second-class citizens in my family. I don't like it, but there's not much I can do to change it.

She changes the subject with a bright smile.

"So did you marry her yet?"

I have no idea if Vittoria wants to marry me, but I also don't care. I need that woman to get my throne.

"No." I shake my head at her. She gives me another sad smile.

"We need you to marry her, Romeo. There's no real choice, you know that."

"Who gave you that black eye?"

She looks down. She doesn't want to answer me. But not answering this is answer enough. If it were her dead husband, she'd tell me, because there's nothing I could do to complicate her life any further unless he was alive.

It was my father then.

I slam the table.

"Be better, Romeo." There's steel in Rosa's voice, and her eyes are guarded when she looks at me. "He rules with fear and intimidation, you can do better than that."

I shake my head. "I hate that my hands are tied."

She tips her head to the side and gives me a questioning look. "But are they?"

I look at her in surprise. "Rosa, you of all people should know that forcing someone to get married isn't what I want to do." A lifetime of misery and intimidation isn't what I want at all.

She shakes her head. "You misunderstand me, Romeo. That's not what I'm suggesting. But surely a man of your power and conviction understands enough to know that you have some say in this?"

Tavi watches us both curiously.

I don't want anybody to hint around anymore. I want her to tell me exactly what she's talking about. I want to know exactly what she has in mind.

"Say it, Rosa. What are you telling me?"

"I did my duty as the oldest in this family, Romeo." She holds my gaze. "You are the oldest son. It's your turn.

She knows well enough by now that I'm not going to shirk my duties. "You know that I would do anything for this family."

"Anything?"

"Anything. For fuck's sake, I just served time for a man I hate."

"I know." She sighs. "I'm sorry, Romeo. I

shouldn't put pressure on you. You've done more than your fair share around here."

Tavi rolls his eyes. "Ok, ok. I've had enough of this mutual pity party. What the fuck do you want, Rosa?"

Someone who doesn't know him would think that he's angry, impatient. He's neither. He's concerned. He knows the stakes as well as we do. Rosa is now single, and any day will have to brace for blowback from the death of her husband. Whether or not it goes to actual war will be up to me. Whether or not we throw fuel on the fire is up to Papa. And we all know what's more likely.

"So what are you suggesting?" I say to Rosa. Goddamn if I just want a clear path sometimes.

"Romeo," she says, gentling her voice. "You have so much to offer a woman. Unlike some people we know, you would actually be faithful to your wife." She gives me a look one might give someone slow on the uptake. "Think about it. You're a billionaire. You live in one of the most beautiful places in the country, and you have your choice of where you would raise your family. You have an army of men that's loyal to you."

"Yeah."

"You need to marry her, but I wouldn't recommend by force. Your instincts and mine are right on this. Sometimes an arranged or forced marriage works out, but it's too risky this time. She knows nothing of our life, and won't forgive a thing. She's innocent to who we are." She looks at me keenly, her eyes bright. "For starters, you need to make sure it stays that way."

"Already done," Tavi says to her.

She swallows hard. "I hate that it's come to that, I hate lying." She was always the most honest out of all of us. "But I've come to realize that sometimes the best choice isn't necessarily a lie, but to not share the truth until the time is right."

"I've already done everything I can to make sure that she doesn't find out who we are until she knows a little bit more about what we can offer her."

"If she finds out too much too soon, she'll run. Or worse."

I shake my head. "Might as well tell you."

They both look at me.

I explain what happened last night. Fill them in. Rosa watches in silence. Tavi already knows.

It wasn't my first choice. I have plenty of people that will do it for me, and I hate taking the life of someone else.

"Fuck," Rosa says under her breath. "So she can literally blackmail you?"

I blow out a breath and nod.

"Does Papa know?" I shake my head.

"Keep it that way, too," Rosa says.

"I plan on it. So tell me, Rosa, as a woman. What do you think I should do?"

Any other person in my family might think that I'm giving her shit, but I respect her opinion.

She smiles sadly. "It's easy, Rome. I think you need to make her fall in love with you."

I snort out loud, the idea is so preposterous. "Are you fucking kidding me?"

She shakes her head. "Of course I'm not. It's a lot simpler than you might think."

"If it were that easy, why doesn't every man do it?"

"Lots of reasons, Rome. Ego, ignorance, their egotistical dicks."

I can't help but smile. Fuck I've missed her. "Good to have you back here, Rosa."

She sobers as she continues.

"Wish I could say it was good to be home." She looks at the walls with a frown as if they have ears, as if they'll rat her out. None of us has had an easy life, but I sometimes worry that being the eldest has scarred her permanently.

"Our needs are simpler than you might think, Rome. A woman wants to be valued, cherished even. She wants to be understood. Appreciated."

"Yeah? Thought they wanted more than that," Tavi says with a frown.

"Some, maybe, but if you make a woman feel cherished and valued, you can get away with a lot more bullshit than you think."

I look at her curiously. Her asshole husband didn't give her this. She deserves someone who would. I finally nod.

"How do I make a woman I don't even know feel that way?"

She stands, brushing crumbs and flecks of powdered sugar off her hands.

"Tell you what, Romeo. You do your part and we'll do ours."

I grunt. "Who's this *we*?"

She smiles. "Me and Marialena."

"Oh fucking *great*," I mutter. "You two playing Cupid?" I stifle a groan. This is gonna go over well.

Rosa rolls her eyes and walks to the door, but sobers as she leaves. "You're a smart man, Romeo Rossi. Mama didn't raise a fool." She doesn't say anything about Papa and sighs as she opens the door. "Think about it. You'll figure it out. Oh, and Rome?"

"Mmm?"

"If she doesn't come to dinner, you *don't* have to go all *Beauty and the Beast* on her. Give her some space or she might hate you." I suspect she's talking from personal experience.

"What the fuck is 'all Beauty and the Beast?'"

She rolls her eyes again and she's gone.

I look to Tavi who only shakes his head while he eyes the last chocolate cookie. "Uh. So there's like this scene where Belle doesn't want to come to dinner and the Beast practically breaks her door down demanding she come…"

"So that makes me a *beast*?"

"This surprises you?"

I grunt.

"And you know about the movie how?"

"Watched it with Natalia," he says, referring to Rosa's little girl. He reaches his hand to the platter.

"You eat the last chocolate one and I'll break your fucking fingers," I warn him.

He only smiles. "Go ahead, brother. Eat it. Maybe it'll sweeten your sour-ass disposition." He shoves three more of the pink ones into his mouth before handing me the tray.

I glance at the clock. Dinnertime's coming. I eat the chocolate cookie in one bite.

———

CHAPTER NINE

"Under love's heavy burden I sink." Romeo and Juliet

VITTORIA

I WAKE the next morning to the sound of birds twittering outside my window. I roll over, trying to remember where I am. I'm not on the back seat of my car but in a bed. A gorgeous bed with elegant bedding, and… I sit up and gasp while it all comes back to me with vivid clarity.

I'm in the Rossi Castle.

I don't even know who they are, but one night here means I only have twenty-nine more to go.

I can do this.

"Oh, ew," I mutter to myself when I realize I'm in bed still fully clothed. I cleaned up a bit before I laid down but never even brushed my teeth. *Yuck.*

And I'm starving.

I blink, suddenly remembering Romeo's stern reminder to come down to dinner at six. Will he be angry? Why does the thought of his scowl set my heart to racing?

Is it hot in here?

I throw off the covers, then realize I didn't put those on me. I look to the door. It's unlocked.

Someone came in here. Someone saw me asleep and covered me in a blanket. Huh.

I push myself to my feet, and my stomach growls. I haven't eaten in way too long. My mouth waters at the smell of bacon, coffee, and cinnamon. If yesterday was any indication of the way they feed people here, I'm in for a treat.

I nearly trip over a large brown paper bag by the door, one of those fancy ones with a pink ribbon tied to the handle you might get at a boutique. I look inside and find a stack of clothes with a hand-written note.

You can borrow these until we can get your clothes sorted. Hope you like them! I made Romeo leave you alone last night but it's probably a good idea to come to breakfast. ~M

She made Romeo... leave me alone last night.

How does that work?

I look in the bag to see a small but really nice stack of designer clothes. She's a little thinner and taller than I am, but when I look closer I guess these aren't just hers but maybe her sister's as well. I pull out a pair of black leggings and pale green sweater and a pair of simple white underclothes still in the package.

I feel badly for not going to dinner last night. I wonder if Romeo will be angry with me.

Why do I care?

All I have to do is live here for the next twenty-nine days and I'm free and clear. I'm not marrying the guy. I'm not marrying any of them. But twenty-nine more days with my housing paid for, my food cooked for me, some companionship with his sisters, and a massive paycheck at the end? I'd have to be a fool not to want that.

I quickly change and feel faint with hunger at this point. I don't hear any voices downstairs, but this castle is so solidly built, I don't think that means no one's downstairs.

I find a pair of flats at the bottom of the bag and slide them on. They're a tad too tight and pinch a little, but they'll do.

My head feels heavy, like I'm groggy from too much sleep, then I remember I haven't had any coffee since yesterday morning. There's coffee downstairs, and if yesterday's food is any indication, it'll be the good stuff.

I have to make myself go. No one's going to do this for me. It feels like I'm the new girl on the first day of school, only ten times worse.

"I volunteer as tribute," I mutter to myself.

I check my phone, butterflies erupting in my belly at the knowledge that I have to go downstairs. It isn't the brothers I fear, though, nor really any of them.

Maybe he's busy. Maybe he's somewhere else…

I open the door and almost walk straight into a hard wall of muscle otherwise known as Romeo's chest.

Maybe he's standing right outside this door.

"Hey, sorry about that," Romeo says. My heartbeat spikes at the sound of his voice. There's still a raspy edge that scrapes across my nerves, but there's a thawing to his tone I haven't heard before. When he runs his fingers through his dark, curly hair, he looks almost boyish. "Didn't mean to startle you."

I'm suddenly very wide awake.

"Oh, no, it's fine. Just thought I'd go downstairs for some breakfast." My cheeks heat when I remember that I didn't do what he told me the night before. When I remember how he said he'd treat disobedience. "I… I fell asleep."

He doesn't move to back up. He's so close to me I could reach out and touch him. So close he could slide his hand along my lower back… So close, I note how he smells like spice and pine and all things masculine.

His eyes are sharp and assessing, full of intelligence and something more, something I can't quite figure out. "I know." His jaw tightens, and he puts his hands in his pockets, like he's holding himself back and trying to play nice. "I'll let it go this once."

Or… what? I want to ask him. He'll let it go? I bite down on my lip so I don't snap out a sardonic reply, even as I combat undeniable excitement. He's dangerous, so fucking dangerous, I feel just being in his presence is like toeing the edge of a cliff.

Why do I feel this magnetic attraction to him? Why do I want to take the one step to him? Run my fingers through that silky, tousled hair? Trace the rough edge of his jaw?

I nod. "Thanks." My voice is almost a whisper. A part of me says this is wrong, that I shouldn't have to *thank him* for letting me *get away* with not coming to dinner.

But a part of me's already accepted this. Already accepted him. Maybe the threat of being punished by him did that.

"You look beautiful." He speaks directly, without fanfare. I look down dumbly at the simple leggings and sweater, but before I can reply, he continues. "But I don't like you wearing borrowed clothing. Since you'll be here for the next month, I've had some things ordered for you."

"Thank you?"

I don't know what else to say. Before I can respond, he reaches for me. I stand, enraptured, watching his strong fingers and the palm of his hand as if in slow motion. He cradles the back of my head, and my eyelids flutter closed for a fraction of a second. It feels so good. It feels so right.

"You shouldn't think so little of yourself."

The gentle tone's gone. His voice is back to gravel and concrete, his grip in my hair tightening.

"What makes you think I think so little of myself?" It's hard to stand with my knees wobbling so hard, but he instinctively seems to know this. His free hand finds the small of my back and holds me up.

"I could see it. My compliment made you uncomfortable, didn't it?"

I nod. Whisper, "A little."

His mouth at my ear makes me shiver. "I could do lots of things that would make you squirm, *bella.*" I gasp when he nips my ear. "You're a natural, you know that?"

I shake my head. "Natural? Natural what?"

"Submissive."

Submissive. Oh.

Oh God. That makes him... the dominant one.

"We'd do well together, you know." He kneads the back of my head. "I'd make your body sing, sweetheart." Then his grip tightens to painful, and he tugs my hair. I hold my breath when his lips touch my cheek. "Don't do it again, Vittoria. When I give you a command, you obey."

There's a latent threat in his tone that makes my sex pulse. That makes me want to push him, to defy him, to see what he'd do. My skin burns where he kissed, and I unconsciously lean closer to him.

He releases me, and I nearly stumble, but he steadies me with his hand under my elbow. "You'll come with me to breakfast."

What will his brothers think? I don't answer, my mind buzzing with questions and possibilities.

Voices come from downstairs amidst the clinking of glasses and dishes.

"Rome. Torri." Mario stands at the foot of the spiral staircase and grins.

"Ah, yeah, don't call me that, *Mar*, okay?"

He winces, and Romeo chuckles. Oh God, it's the first time I've heard him laugh, all manly and deep and throaty, and it makes me want to make him laugh again.

Mario holds his hands up. "Oof. Mar. Yeah, I can remember that." I don't miss the way he looks from me to Romeo, then back again. "Papa's in rare form, man," he says under his breath.

Shit.

Romeo nods, then reaches for my hand and pulls me to his side.

"Listen to me, Vittoria," he says in a low voice as the front door opens and Tavi comes in with Orlando. They both jerk their chins at us in greeting but walk past us to the dining room. Orlando's gaze lingers a fraction of a second longer than Tavi's, but neither stay long. Neither tries to get my attention.

They know Romeo wants me.

Will any of them try to marry me, like he will? Do any of them want to ascend the throne as badly as Romeo?

A glass crashes in the dining room, and Romeo says something under his breath in Italian.

"Hundred bucks says that was another food fight." He shakes his head and rolls his eyes. "I'll beat the shit out of them."

Oookay.

In the early morning light, the Great Hall's lit up with brilliant beams of sun reflecting on the glass chandeliers, the flags hanging from the ceiling like a stately garland, but no one's here. We head to the dining room instead.

No one comes to greet us when we enter, but it's as if the whole room pauses for a fraction of a second before they resume their chatter.

Marialena and Rosa look my way.

"Uncle Romeo!" I start when a little ball of pink comes hurtling toward us and tackles Romeo at the knees. He's ready for it, though, bracing and gathering her up in his arms. "Mama said you were here."

Mama? She called him Uncle. Rosa's daughter?

A pretty little thing with the same vivid blue eyes as her mother peers over Romeo's shoulder. The man already had sex appeal written in every cell of his body. *Great.* Now that he's holding a *child,* those massive, muscled arms of his wrapped around the little girl as he smiles at her, my ovaries begin to play a violin.

"Natalia," he says warmly, clearly pleased at seeing her. "Your mama said you were here, but I haven't seen you yet."

She looks over his shoulder at me, her eyes wide in surprise. "Probably because you're dating a princess?"

"A princess?" I say with a laugh. "You're now officially my favorite person here, Natalia. It's nice to meet you. My name is Vittoria."

Romeo sets her down on the floor. "She looks like a princess, doesn't she?"

Oh no he doesn't.

"There you are." A young woman who looks like

she's fresh out of college, her hair in a messy pony-tail and with glasses perched on her nose, reaches us. When she sees Romeo, she stops short. Her brows rise comically high, and she snatches Natalia's hand.

"So sorry, Mr. Rossi," she stammers. "I—I turned my back for one minute, and she was gone." She looks sternly at Natalia. "You were supposed to stay with me. She didn't sleep a wink, sir, and the jet lag has her all hyped up."

"Natalia! Give Uncle Tavi a hug, baby." Tavi grins at her, kneels on one knee, and she throws herself at him.

He looks up at the nanny. "Thank you for watching her last night. I was whipped."

She flushes bright pink and stammers, "Oh, no problem at all, sir. Anything you want."

He's talking to Natalia about the next Disney princess movie they'll watch, and totally misses how the nanny's crushing on him. Romeo notes it, though. He looks to me with a wordless shake of his head. I only shrug.

"Who could blame her?" I whisper to him. "Tavi's hot."

He clenches his teeth. Romeo doesn't like that.

"Romeo," I continue in a whisper, "I'm not hitting on him even though I'm allowed to per that contract." It's a stretch, but I'll go with it. "I'm just telling you, you guys are like hot Italian models, so it's only natural."

"One more word, Vittoria," he warns in a low rumble.

Zing. My mouth's dry. "Yeah?"

Still whispering, he warns me, "Tell me again how hot you find my brothers and you'll find yourself over my knee."

"How's that fair?" I say as my pulse thunders.

A corner of his lips quirks up. "All's fair in love and war, sweetheart."

Tavi's gone to join the rest of the family, and the nanny eyes him wistfully. Natalia pouts, but Romeo winks at her. "Go with your nanny, and later I'll get you a strawberry donut." My heart thumps. I want him to wink at *me.*

Natalia grins, and the nanny whisks her away.

"I want a strawberry donut," I say before I can stop myself. He takes my hand and kisses my fingertips.

"Bella mia, you can have anything you want. I hope you know that."

Well if he isn't pulling out the Italian charm.

Anything I want. Why does he make it sound so tantalizing?

It isn't true, though. If I wed him, I forfeit my freedom.

But what would I gain?

"Give me the fucking muffin." Orlando's glaring at Mario, who's holding a plate with one remaining muffin.

"Listen, man," Mario says. "Oh, look. There's Romeo!" Orlando looks at us instinctively and Mario snatches the muffin and shoves it in his mouth, crumbs flying everywhere. I blink in surprise. When Orlando realizes he was played, he turns back to Mario and lunges. Romeo's had it. He grabs them both by the sleeves and yanks them back to sitting before he whacks both of them, hard, upside of the head. I gasp at the resounding *slap* but no one else even looks.

Orlando glowers, mumbling to himself, and Mario chokes on his muffin, rubbing the back of his head. Romeo gives them both a look that dares them to start it up again.

"*Mamma mia,*" Tosca mutters, shaking her head. She looks at me. "Always like this, Vittoria. I cook three turkeys at Thanksgiving. *Three.* And do they fight over who gets the turkey leg every year? They do. Three times two is *six* and *do they still fight?* All of them with enough money to buy a turkey farm, and yet here we are, breaking my good drinkware over a muffin. Look at them! Do any of them look like they're starving?"

I shake my head. I don't know whether to laugh or run.

"For the love of fucking God," Romeo mutters when a maid passes by with a serving tray. "Who ate all of the breakfast sandwiches?" He scowls, and Tosca gives me a knowing look that says *he's as bad as they are.*

"My brothers really like their food." Rosa stands beside me with a wine glass filled with what looks like a mimosa. "You may have noticed."

"I did." I can't say it doesn't amuse me, though. "I mean, why do they fight over it?"

She frowns. "I know, right? There's always more than enough, but it's like this *thing* with them." She shakes her head and rolls her eyes. "You hungry?"

"Starving."

"Good, let's get you a seat." She looks at Romeo, who's eyeing both of us, and waves him off. "He has to meet with Papa. You come sit with me and Marialena."

I do not have to be asked twice. I haven't had bacon in ages, and this is thick and sprinkled with bits of pepper. The pastries taste like they were just pulled out of the oven, and Rosa hands me a plate with a thick slice of quiche oozing mozzarella she says their Nonna makes by hand. I hardly talk, focused on eating the food, and finally have a bit of an inkling why they fight over it. Everything's homemade and exquisite.

The coffee, like I suspected, is rich and decadent, imported from Italy along with their wines.

"Do you guys actually drink the wine in the wall in the dining room?" I ask Rosa.

"Of course. We refill it from our vineyard in Tuscany."

"Oh, wow. Okay, so that's totally cool."

Marialena smiles. "It's good wine."

"Now listen, Vittoria," Rosa says as she leans in closer to me. "Romeo comes across as a total ass sometimes, I know he does."

"Mhm. You don't say?" I don't deny this, which amuses Marialena. She snorts and giggles, then pats my hand appreciatively.

"But he's a good man."

A good man, is he? I saw him slice a man's throat

without a second thought, and he's demanded I do what he tells me. I don't tell her that but purse my lips closed out of politeness.

"Give him a chance, Vittoria."

I butter a scone, take a bite and swallow before answering. "According to the terms of the contract, I kinda think I should give all of them a chance, don't you think?"

"No, I don't." Romeo's voice is in my ear. He moves like a lethal predator, silent and deadly. My skin prickles with awareness at how close he is, so close he could reach out and wrap me in his arms. "In fact, I—"

Glass explodes above us, the chandelier over the dining room table raining broken shards on top of us. Screams erupt like fireworks. I'm shoved to the floor, under a heavy body. I'm not breathing. Another explosion shatters something right beside us. Romeo flattens himself on top of me, and my head hits the floor.

I feel as if I'm submerged in earth, under a weighted blanket. The sounds around me are muffled, but I can hear panicked screams and shouts, the squeal of tires, followed by Romeo's deep booming voice. I can't quite make out what he says, but everything around us seems to calm. There's no more screaming, anyway.

"Are you all right?" he asks me almost angrily, daring me to be injured, daring me to give him a reason for seeking revenge. I'm reminded of the night he killed for me. He looks as if he wished he had someone in front of him now with a throat ready to slit.

I nod. My head hurts, and I feel bruised and tender, but I'm okay. "I'm fine. You can get off me now."

He doesn't move. Maybe he likes the way I feel underneath him, but he's sort of suffocating me. "Uh, Romeo. Can you let me up?"

Still nothing. Lovely. I have a permanent human weighted blanket on me.

He's barking out commands to various people. "Secure the front door. Tavi!" I can't see much but Tavi bolts past, fast as lightning. I hear more shattering of glass, Tosca screams, then a holler and a shout outside followed by a *bang.*

"Motherfucker," Mario mutters. He's kneeling on one knee beside me, his pistol in hand. "Just fuckin' leapt out that window, didn't he?'

Romeo's still shouting out orders like a drill sergeant. "Get Tavi back up! And take that motherfucker to the dungeon. Where's Papa?"

I'm waiting for sirens, but it's eerily quiet. Too quiet.

"Isn't anyone going to call an ambulance? The police?" Someone nearby laughs softly, but I don't see who. Someone else mutters something I can't quite hear, but the words, "doesn't know who we are" are loud and clear before Romeo growls in Italian and silences him.

Finally, *finally,* he moves off of me, but only so he can wrap an arm around my back like a band. "Stay there. You sure you're alright?"

"Yeah." Why does he want me to stay here?

"Marialena okay?" he asks.

"Yes," she says in an affronted voice. "Who *was* that?"

"Not sure," Romeo says grimly. "But that was only a warning." He blows out a breath but doesn't say anything else. If that was only a warning, does that mean they'll be back?

"Vittoria, I want you seen by the doctor."

"She said she's fine, Rome," Marialena says gently. She gives him a placating look, like she's used to him by now.

It only takes minutes for everything to be righted. No one's hurt, but Tosca cries over the broken stained glass windows, one broken by Tavi when he launched himself outside to catch one of the men that attacked. It seems this wasn't an errand to kill anyone, but to scare them.

Food's cleared and the hall's cleaned almost by magic. Romeo gives orders and instructions, and finds his father's been holed up in his office. When Tavi talks to him about the man he found, Romeo looks at me before speaking in Italian. Tavi looks grim, but nods.

"Vittoria." Romeo stares at me, and jerks a finger at the doorway. "Come with me."

I don't know why I go. I don't know why I follow his command, but something tells me now probably isn't the time to push things. He brings me into a small room with coat hangers and shelving. The coat closet?

"Come here, *bella*." He sits on a chair and beckons me to him.

"Uh. Your family just got shot at and you want to have a little private chat?"

"I don't want to chat, Vittoria." His gaze is implacable, his tone insistent. "Now come here."

I walk slowly to him, not sure what he wants to do.

"But what if they come back?"

"Oh, they'll come back," he says, unconcerned.

"Why aren't you... calling the police or something?"

"We don't need the police." He lowers his voice, and his brows draw together. "Now are you going to do what I tell you or are you going to disobey me? Don't try me, woman."

What?

This is the man who wants to marry me?

I swallow and lick my lips. I don't know the effects of adrenaline, but I feel as if my blood runs through my veins with liquid fire.

"Why no police?"

He narrows his eyes at me and beckons. I go. I'm shaking, and my palms are all sweaty, but I go. It's warm in here and smells faintly of mothballs and wool. The shiny, hardwood floor muffles my footsteps.

When I reach him, he tugs me onto one of his knees.

"I want to inspect you."

The deep rumble of his voice goes straight between my thighs, and I pull them together.

"Inspect me?"

"Yeah, *bella.* Inspect you. I want to be sure you're not injured."

I'm obviously not injured, so it seems to me he's just using this as an excuse to get handsy with me, but okay then.

"My sisters and mother have guards on them," he says in explanation. "Natalia was secured in the upstairs guest room. Papa is fine, as are my men."

His men. Who has men?

"Now I need to be sure my future wife is alright."

"Oh, no, you don't," I say, shaking my head at him. "Nuh uh. I did not agree to that."

He doesn't respond, but slips his hands around the hem of my sweater and lifts it, exposing a strip of creamy skin at my belly. "So far, you look unharmed." His calloused thumbs grip my waist, his fingers coming to rest on my hips. "Top off."

It feels like an erotic dance of two steps forward, sidestep, one step back. I shrug out of my top, and he continues his perusal of me.

"Ah, baby," he says sadly. "There's a scrape on your shoulder."

Bending, he brushes his lips over a red mark that looks like a scrape. The soft caress of his kiss makes me warm all over.

When he spins me around, his brow is furrowed as if in concern. He kisses so many little scrapes and bruises, I feel as if he's made half of them up, but when he comes to an angry gash on my left shoulder, he hisses out a curse and takes out his phone.

"He still conscious?"

He listens.

"Good. Leave him for me." The phone clatters to the floor at his feet.

Wait. Oh my God. He wants to punish the man who attacked us... because I'm hurt?

Why do I like that?

Do I?

He maneuvers me like I'm a mannequin and he's my master. I'm pliant as he spins me to face him and eyes my bra-clad breasts.

"Off with the bra, Vittoria." The low sound of his voice makes my nipples peak.

"What?" I mean, my *breasts* didn't get injured...

A sharp spank to my ass has me coming up on my toes and hissing out a breath. "Romeo!"

"Take. Off. Your. Bra."

He hasn't moved his hand from my ass yet.

Here, hidden in the coat closet, he's casually stripping me under the facade of making sure I'm okay, and I feel more turned on than I've been in my *life.*

I want to know. I want to see what happens if I disobey him, if I push him back. If I'm going to marry this man, I need to be able to push.

Why did my mind just go there?

I grasp the back of my bra, my hands trembling. I want to do this. I'm alone in a closet with a dangerous man who's a stranger to me but possibly my future husband. I know without question he knows his way around a woman's body, and his words from earlier echo in my mind like a mantra.

Natural.

Submissive.

Natural submissive...

I hold his gaze and choose blatant disobedience. I bite my lip. "Make me."

With a primal growl, he reaches for me, yanks the bra, and tears it off me like it's made of tissue paper. I gasp when my breasts swing free, the fabric falling to the floor. He glides his rough hands up my body and drags me to him.

"You'll regret that," he warns, then yanks me to him. His mouth clamps onto my nipple and his teeth bite down. My back arches, but when I go to scream, his mouth on mine silences me. The kiss is chastening, a physical rebuke of my daring to defy him. I whimper when he bites my lip, and on instinct sink onto his knee. I close my eyes, drowning in sensation, then scream silently into his mouth when he twists my other bared nipple.

I've never been corrected like *this* before. His hand on my ass squeezes. I yelp. He lifts me up, tips me over, and I'm staring at the floor with my belly on his knee.

"Romeo!" My hand flails out as if to steady myself, but he only shakes his head.

"I mean what I say, Vittoria." He reaches above him, grabs something I can't see, then settles me onto his lap. He shifts and something snaps in his hand. "I told you I meant what I say. I warned you."

He lifts his arm and searing pain explodes in a line of fire across my ass. I'm too stunned to scream. My legs scissor when he smacks me again. My naked breasts rub against the rough fabric of his pants, but he leaves my bottoms on. He spanks me again, and again, until I'm panting and, to my shock, squirming in arousal.

"Touch yourself," he whispers in my ear. "Slide your fingers to your pussy and touch yourself."

I'm over his knee getting spanked, so I quickly reason it's not a great time to defy him again, and I'm dying for some relief. I quickly shove my fingers down my pants, wriggling to adjust myself, and groan when I finger my wet pussy.

One hand pushes on my lower back, holding me in place as I stroke, then another smack flares across my ass. My clit throbs, and my movements become more hurried, more insistent.

"Lose the pants," he says in a hoarse whisper. "Fucking now."

He's tipped me up and is pulling them off even as I tug them down, and they quickly fall to the floor. He tosses me back over his lap.

"Touch yourself, but don't you dare fucking come without permission."

This time, I don't give any thought to obeying him. I do exactly what he says, fingering myself while he rubs something hard and unyielding across the back of my thighs. I hardly feel it this time when he gives me another sharp flick with whatever he's holding. I'm engulfed in sensation, throbbing for release, as he continues my punishment. Every smack of pain heightens my arousal, until I'm pulsing with need, on the edge of coming.

"On your knees, Vittoria." Whatever he's holding

clatters to the floor. I wriggle off his lap and fall to my knees.

"I want to watch your eyes when you come." His fingers wrap around my throat and flex. "Come, baby. Get yourself off for me." The first spasm of pleasure jolts me. "*Fuck,*" he groans. "I want that dirty, greedy little cunt for myself." My cheeks heat with his dirty talk, but I couldn't stop myself now if I wanted to. I stroke with frantic movements, whimpering. He grips my throat to the point I can barely breathe, and I shatter.

"Oh God," I groan, my orgasm wrecking me. "Oh *God.*"

"Come again, baby. Make that greedy little cunt happy. Work that pussy, Vittoria." He squeezes my neck, and my vision blurs, my head too hot, but I do what he says until I slump, my face on his knee.

Slowly, he releases my neck and begins to stroke my hair.

"Good girl," he says, as he drags his rough fingers through my hair. "Christ, that was the most beautiful thing I've ever seen."

I can't talk. I can't move. My ass is on fire, and he just made me bring myself to climax twice while he watched. My breasts are bared, my jeans around my ankles. I blink, as if waking from a dream.

"Get dressed, *bella,*" he whispers, as he rights me. "But hand me those panties."

I stand with his help, still shaking. He takes the panties from my outstretched hand, shoves them to his nose, and inhales with a groan. Oh, God. My sex pulses just from watching him. With a labored sigh, he shoves them into his pocket, then drags me over to him. I stand between his knees, still dazed from what just happened. My eyes catch something broken and shattered on the floor. A hanger? He snapped the curved end off the hanger and whipped me with the flat.

"Did you really just whip me with a hanger?"

His lips curve up darkly. "I'd hardly call that a whipping. I spanked you to orgasm." He pulls a lock of my hair. "You complaining?"

I swallow and don't respond.

Am I?

"Go with my sisters. They're taking you shopping. You have no budget."

I blink, then blink again.

"Tomorrow, I want to see what you bought." He frowns, looking in the distance. "Today, I'll deal with the people who attacked us. I've got business to do and probably won't be home tonight."

Why does that make my heart sink into my shoes?

I swallow and nod. I don't want to leave him. He's hard as nails. He's a goddamn beast, but I don't like being apart from him.

I was in danger the other night, and he killed my attacker. Today I was in danger again, and he flattened me under his body, prepared to take a bullet for me.

When I'm with him, I'm safe... from anything and everything but him.

————

CHAPTER TEN

"ONE FIRE BURNS out another's burning,
One pain is lessen'd by another's anguish."
Romeo and Juliet

ROMEO

ORLANDO DOES HIS WORK WELL. By the time we're done interrogating, we've got a bloody pulp of a man crying like a baby on the dungeon floor, begging for us to end it. We know where he's come from and we know why. Took all goddamn day before he stopped breathing.

Blowback from a trade gone sour last month. Easily dealt with. No one comes straight at our house like that, though. Restaurants, maybe. Cars, definitely. But straight to The Castle takes fucking balls.

Marialena calls me around dinnertime.

"Jesus, Rome, twelve texts? Are you insane?"

"You were supposed to fill me in at lunchtime."

"We had no cell phone connection, and need I remind you we have *six bodyguards* with us?" She blows out a breath on the phone and mumbles something to the side I don't catch.

"What was that, you little brat?" I play with a knife on my desk, scratching a geometric design on the leather portion of the calendar.

"Oh, nothing," she says sweetly. "Just said we'll be home by bedtime, don't wait up."

She laughs at my growl, then her voice lowers to a whisper. "Okay, Rome, listen. We did our best, but she's definitely catching onto something."

"Yeah?"

"Yeah."

"Should've ordered online." God. I didn't like the thought of her being here when we did our work on the guy that attacked us today. No easier way to scare her off than to somehow figure out we're torturing, beating, and eventually killing someone. She saw me kill once, and that was enough.

I hang up with Marialena, then I get a call from Tuscany I need to answer, and quickly get distracted. We've got business trades coming in from overseas, and my capo that's in charge of loan-sharking makes a killing this time of year. Meet with him, then Papa, but Papa only wants to bitch about the goddamn will again.

I want to see Vittoria. I want to do what Rosa said… somehow.

But it's two more days before I finally get to see her again. I wake up at the crack of dawn with a raging hard-on. Jerked myself off with her panties wrapped around my cock the first night, the second night with nothing but my fist. But every time I do, it only makes me want her more.

Fuck.

Fuck.

I meet with Tavi in the dungeon to plan some shit I don't want anyone to hear, payback for some bullshit in the North End near the restaurants over the weekend.

"How's she doing?" I ask him.

He shrugs. "Settling in, I guess, but I think she's starting to figure out who we are."

"Yeah?"

It was only a matter of time. I hoped that between her needs being met and the promise of an inheritance, she might take it with a grain of salt.

I hear Marialena's rapid, frantic footfalls before she knocks. Tavi and I are already on our feet when she reaches the door.

The heavy door to the dungeon creaks open, and her clear voice yells down the stairs. "Rome! You down there?"

"Yeah?"

"Get up here! She's trying to leave and Papa knows. Hurry, Rome! He'll hurt her!"

I don't need any more details. My father's a ruthless monster who can't be trusted. Maybe I'm no better, but I have reasons for keeping my future wife safe and unharmed.

I take the steep steps two at a time, and follow Marialena to the main entrance. I'm aware of Mama and Rosa sitting in the reception room, and Santo standing in the doorway watching me. His lip curls.

"She tried to escape, Rome," he calls after me. "Go, Romeo! Go catch your fuckin' Juliet."

Douchebag.

When Marialena sees I'm behind her, she runs as the sound of a high-pitched scream pierces the quiet.

Shit.

I throw open the heavy entryway door to see my Vittoria behind the wheel of an older Volvo. My father stands in front of the car, his Glock in hand. His bodyguards stand on either side of him like a fortress.

Papa's hand shakes. Goddamned idiot. If he kills her, we're all fucked.

She ain't going anywhere, but if he hurts her, I'll take this throne by force.

Son of a bitch.

"Papa." I try to keep my furious voice in check. "Stand off."

His finger shakes on the trigger. "She isn't fucking leaving."

I run down the front steps that lead to the house. Vittoria looks at me, then quickly back to my father.

I nod my head at him. "She isn't, Papa. I'll see to it. But if you shoot her, Nonno wins and you know it."

He growls. "I wouldn't shoot to kill."

Bile roils in my stomach at the vision of Vittoria,

crying in pain because Papa shot to incapacitate. My father's theory is, why use ropes or restraints when you can subdue someone with bullets and pain?

I can't keep my fury out of my tone. "Papa, put the fucking gun down."

He moves his enraged gaze to me. "The Underboss doesn't give the Boss commands." He spits on the ground, but spittle stays on his lips, dripping like melted candle wax. He's lost his fucking mind. Maybe lost it years ago and hid it well.

I've had it.

That's fucking *it*.

I'll marry her before the sun sets tonight for this. I have to. It's my only choice.

I look over my shoulder at Tavi and speak under my breath. "Call Father Richard. I want him in the library at eight o'clock tonight."

My feet hit the pavement.

"Vittoria!" I shout. "Get out of the car. *Now!*"

She shakes her head. Tears are streaming down her face. She's terrified. I don't fucking blame her.

"Vittoria." I'm not sure how much she can hear through the window, so I raise my voice even louder than before. "Turn the car off!"

My wife will learn to do what she's goddamn told.

She shakes her head again. Her face is bright pink and tear-stained, her hands on the wheel in a grip so deathly tight her knuckles whiten. If she hits the gas, my father will shoot, but maybe not if she throws him off first.

Without thinking, I draw my own gun from the harness, cock the pistol, and shoot. The bullet slices through her rear tire with a *pop.* I shoot the front tire, the only other one in my line of vision, each bullet hitting exactly where I mean it to. I empty the cartridge, tearing the tires to shreds. In seconds, the car sinks to the ground like a deflated lawn decoration.

Vittoria's covered her head with her arms.

"Now she won't get away."

My father frowns at me.

"Papa. Gun away, please. You won't solve anything this way."

This will be the last fucking day I use the world *please* with him.

He snarls like an angry dog, his lip curling, but while he utters every Italian curse word known to man, he finally puts his gun away.

"Get her in the fuckin' house," he growls at me. "Before I hurt her."

"I'll get her in the house," I tell him, my own anger lashing out. "But you'll keep your hands off her." I take a deep breath and gentle my voice. It might work to play nice until I secure her as my wife. "Let me deal with her, Papa. It's been a long day. You won't get anywhere with this one making threats."

"Not a threat, Romeo," he growls.

And I'm fucking done with his nonsense. I've had it with the power he wields over this family with the weight of an anvil. I'm over his tyrannical ways, and I make the decision right then and there that this throne will be mine *tonight.*

I open the car door and grab Vittoria by the arm.

"Hey!" she protests, but I ignore her, yank her out of the car, then swing her straight up over my shoulder. If she doesn't get her ass in the house, my father will be at her, and I'll have to hurt him.

That could complicate things.

"Let me go!" she screams. "Put me *down.*"

Ah. So cute. "No."

I ignore her and march toward the house. My men and servants flee, vacating my path.

"I just saved your fucking life," I say over my shoulder in a low voice. "He'd have killed you."

She stills. She doesn't protest anymore as I carry her in.

"Then put me down," she says in a more subdued voice. "I can walk, Romeo." She sighs. "Please."

She's shaking like a scared little kitten. I hate that he did that to her.

I'm the only one who will make her shake, and I'll fucking enjoy it.

I shake my head and continue to walk with her over my shoulder. "No. If he sees you're getting your way, I'm afraid he'll come after you again. I'll put you down when we get inside."

She doesn't say another word of protest. My mind reels with what I have to do next, what has to happen. I need witnesses, a dress, a ring…

Marialena stares from the side. "He's at it again, is he?"

I don't respond. I'm used to her rhetorical questions. She mutters and curses as I walk past her, but when I reach the first landing, I slide Vittoria down so her feet hit the carpet. She's lost her shoes along the way.

Why does that make me feel sympathy toward her? I shouldn't feel anything at all. This is a business transaction, no more, no less.

"I want you in my room. We'll talk in private there." It's one of the only rooms in the house that has no surveillance access. The only room in the house where everything I own is at my disposal.

"Oh, how nice," she says, shaking her head. "The head of the crime family will take me to bed, will he?"

"Vittoria," I warn. My temper's reached maximum capacity. I will absolutely take her to bed, but I won't be taunted or disrespected.

"What?" she snaps. "You think I don't know who you are? Huh? Why do you think I tried to leave?" Still, she walks by my side and doesn't try to run again, but she's no fool. She knows my father's nearby.

Ahhh. So that's why she left. She knows who the Rossi family is now. It was only a matter of time.

"Be quiet," I say as evenly as I can. "This is a conversation we'll have between the two of us in private."

She laughs mirthlessly. "Oh, that's *rich*. So what are you? Boss-in-training? A made man? Hmm?"

"Not now," I say, and this is my last warning. "Do you not care at all that I just saved your life?"

"Saved my life from your insane father? Ha! You people are mad. Ridiculous. Fucking certifiable!"

I narrow my eyes at her and reach for her hand. "No future wife of mine will use language like that or disrespect the Family."

She blinks and freezes, as if stunned by what I just said.

"Excuse me?"

"You heard me."

She shakes her head from side to side. I hate the way her tear-stained eyes break my heart. I'm not given to sympathy, and I can't start now.

"First of all," she begins, but I've had enough. I grip her arm and tug her along faster.

"First of all," I repeat, interrupting her. "We're done talking. I said no more. Say one more word, Vittoria, and the way we have this conversation is with you over my knee and your pants around your ankles. Am I clear?" And this time, it won't be foreplay and she won't fucking come.

Her jaw drops open as if to protest, but she must see the determination in my eyes. I'm not bluffing. Her eyes darken, but she finally nods.

Good girl.

I open the door to my room and lead her in behind me. I place her behind me and go to turn the key in the lock. I don't breathe freely until I see my men stationed just outside the door.

I'll find a reason to send my father to Tuscany. I need him out of here while I do what I have to.

She has no idea how close of a call that was. She

doesn't know how "insane" my father truly is. She hasn't seen what I've seen.

I wish none of us ever had.

Now that I have her alone, I'll explain everything. I turn to face her and open my mouth to speak, but before I do, she wheels around and slaps my face with all her might. Her fingers connect with my cheek. Pain explodes across my skin, and I actually take a step back. Jesus. Didn't know the girl had it in her. Didn't expect that.

"You," she fumes. "You! You lied to me. You didn't tell me who you are! You probably sent your father after me. You probably sent him just so you could be the one that saved me from him, didn't you? You're sick! You're criminals! And if you think that I'm going to stay here—"

I grab her wrist and restrain her by bringing her arm behind her back. She winces, but I'm careful not to hurt her. Fury stampedes across my chest like wild stallions. I take a deep breath to calm myself.

I'll punish her for that, but I don't want to hurt her.

I restrain her against my chest and drag her into my living room. I sit heavily on a leather armchair and yank her across my knees. My dick's already hard at the prospect of punishing her.

"I warned you, Vittoria. I told you to stop. You won't ever raise your hand to me."

The first slap of my hand across her ass to subdue her makes me painfully hard.

I quickly bare her ass. I spank her hard, my handprint blooming against her virgin skin.

She screams and kicks and fights with all her might, but I ignore her protests as I deliver one rapid smack after another. I'd bet money she'd never been spanked before she met me. She needs to be tamed.

My dick throbs while I slam my palm across her ass, over and over again, giving her the spanking she's earned.

Finally, when her gorgeous ass is rosy red and she's screamed herself hoarse, she slumps over my lap, sobbing.

I'm not angry any more, but I keep my voice stern. "Will you raise your hand to me again?"

She shakes her head from side to side. I rest my hand on her fiery hot, bare ass, my cock aching.

"And I won't hear a curse word from you again, will I?"

She shakes her head. Tears splash on the floor in front of her. She's really, truly sobbing.

I've punished women before. I've dominated them, but it's always been in the context of sex. This was… something different.

I lift her in my arms and tuck her against me. At first, she protests, pushing against my chest, but I wrap my arms around her like a blanket, holding her tightly against me. I don't let her up.

"Let me go," she sobs. "I want to go home. You're all evil. Every one of you."

Not gonna deny that.

"Shh," I say, rocking her against me. Somehow knowing that this woman will be my wife, flesh of my own flesh and bone of my bone, makes me feel differently toward her. "You earned that spanking. I saved your life and you slapped my face in thanksgiving?"

Finally, *finally,* she rests her head on my chest. "I don't even know what to think," she says, her voice wobbly. "I don't understand any of this. I don't understand what's going on at all."

"I know. I'll explain everything."

"Everything?"

She looks up at me, and every ounce of anger's gone. She looks… lost.

I can't help myself. I place a finger under her chin and hold her gaze to mine.

"Everything, Vittoria. All of it. But no more fighting me. No more hitting me." I bend and brush my lips against hers. She gasps, but her mouth parts. I make it a gentle, chaste kiss, but it takes all my effort not to deepen it. My mouth at her ear, I whisper, "No more running away." I take a wild leap, remembering what Tavi told me. "Where even would you go?"

She doesn't respond at first.

"Tell me the truth, Vittoria. Where?"

She shakes her head. "Anywhere but here," she whispers. "This place is cursed."

"Yeah, probably. I'm pretty confident the wine cellar's haunted, and the first floor guest room's no walk in the park either."

She blinks up at me. "Are you serious?"

I smile at her. Her hair's damp with exertion and tears. I smooth it away. I've never had a woman inspire anything tender in me at all. I wonder what it is about her.

"Yeah, but you don't have to worry about those either."

"Why not?"

I shrug. "I'm not afraid of ghosts. I'll make sure they leave you alone, too."

She stiffens, as if suddenly realizing she just got a spanking and she's letting the asshole who spanked her comfort her. "May I get off your lap, please?"

"No."

Still, she doesn't protest. We'll talk with her here, just like this, her bared and punished ass on my knee to remind her who she's talking to.

"Vittoria," I say, adjusting her so we both sit comfortably in the chair. "Let's start at the beginning."

———

CHAPTER ELEVEN

"For I ne'er saw true beauty till this night." Romeo and Juliet

VITTORIA

I knew something was off.

I stayed here for days, eating their food, getting to know the sisters, living in the lap of luxury.

At first, my searches online brought up nothing, but I had my suspicions. When I went shopping with the girls, people whispered when they saw us. And I've noticed that *all* of the men have the same tattoos on their right forearms.

I asked Rosa and Marialena, who only gave me evasive answers. I decided I needed to dig more.

I opened an incognito browser on my phone, wondering if somehow my basic search functions were blocked…

And my search online terrified me.

Hit after hit after hit. I couldn't believe I'd never heard of them. I couldn't believe my search of information on The Castle brought up nothing before this.

Maybe that was intentional? Had someone purposefully blocked access to information about the Rossis?

Rossi Family

Head Crime Family of the North Shore

Ruthless Crime Family

The Untouchable Family

I suspected several things, but this? This goes *beyond*.

Why did no one have any information on this house associated with the Montavios? If I'd seen anything at all that led me to *crime family* I never would've come to this cursed house to begin with.

I read until the thought of staying here one more minute terrified me.

I didn't think my escape would be easy, but I didn't expect it would go as poorly as it did.

It seemed the Rossi family was the most infamous family of gangsters or organized crime or... *mafia...* whatever you want to call them, that the North Shore had ever seen. They behaved with near impunity, doing whatever they wanted whenever they wanted to.

Or so it seemed.

So it seemed.

I read until my stomach rolled. I remembered the blood of the night of my attack, the way he killed as if it didn't even faze him. Just... *swipe. Slump. Gush. Done.*

Then I lost the contents of my lunch in the pretty white guest room toilet.

As soon as I got my act together, I gathered what little I had, and I made my escape.

Only I didn't think of it like that. I thought I was just... leaving. I didn't know I was under any *obligation* to be here. I knew that if I left, and didn't fulfill my end of the inheritance agreement, I wouldn't get the money.

But who cared about six million dollars? Or any of it? No amount of money was worth actually losing everything else that mattered. None.

I tried to be quiet about it, though. Thought it better than to cause an issue. I did consider the fact that crazy-ass Rossi senior wouldn't like it if I left...

I didn't know he was watching me.

I made it as far as putting my key in the ignition before I realized what was happening. Romeo's father and his horde of huge, beefy men surrounded my car before I could even begin to drive.

And now... I'm still sitting on Romeo's lap, my ass bared. My cheeks heat when I realize this.

"Can we please talk with me fully dressed?" I put as much dignity into my tone as I can, but it doesn't seem to work.

His jaw tightens, as does his grip on me. "No."

"*Romeo.*"

I half expect him to make me call him Mr. Rossi or *Sir*, like this is some twisted version of a BDSM role-play thing, but he doesn't. In fact, his eyes seem to soften a bit when I call him by name.

"Please," I try in a softer voice.

His voice is obdurate with a gentle edge when he replies, "I said no, Vittoria, and you'll learn that I mean what I say."

I open my mouth to protest, but realize he isn't joking. I mean, the man just spanked me. I don't know what world this is, but in *this* world, his word is law. I don't agree with that, but I also don't know if now's the time to start questioning things when I'm at a decided disadvantage.

"I don't even know you, and yet you take liberties."

He shakes his head. "All that matters is you'll be my wife, and the sooner you learn your place the better."

All that matters to *him.* There are two of us here.

I stare at him, half expecting him to follow this with a laugh or a wink or *something* to indicate he isn't... serious. When he doesn't, I decide this is probably where we need to start.

"Tell me, then," I say, as if humoring him. "What does it mean to be your wife?"

His eyes warm at that. God, the guy's hot. How can I let the guy who just *punished me* seem hot? I can't help it, though. It's like natural female instinct or something, as if being dominated by a man in authority's inherently erotic. But there was nothing consensual or playful about that. I have a hard time understanding why I'm attracted to him despite his domineering personality, but... how could anyone *not* find him attractive? I'd have to be dead.

Those compelling blue-gray eyes, the firm masculine features, the confident set of his shoulders and his inherent strength make me want to know more about who he is. What drives him. What made him the man he is today.

Earlier he was clean-shaven, but now he wears a five o'clock shadow that only makes him look more rugged. The set of his chin suggests an inflexible will. *So that makes two of us.*

"If you were my wife," he says, his voice growing husky as if the very concept arouses him, "I'd take care of you." My belly warms at that. I like that. Who wouldn't? But the knowing look in his eye tells me he expected that, he worded things just so to please me.

Doesn't mean he's insincere, though. I'm not surprised. He killed a man who tried to rape me. Protecting members of the female of the species might be part of his DNA. Some guys are just like that.

He's mafia.

I try to reconcile *mafia* with the man sitting here with me now, dressed in impeccable clothing, the air about him something between aristocratic and nefarious. Maybe both.

"Every need, and I mean *every* need, would be met." He lets the words settle. My mind doesn't go where a normal person's would—riches and cars, jewels and clothing, designer handbags and exotic vacations spent at resorts. No. I envision myself naked, my head thrown back in utter ecstasy, while he wrenches orgasm after orgasm from my body.

Every need would be met.

A little voice inside my head whispers, *Yes. That need, too.*

"Okay," I say with a forced air of nonchalance. "You're obviously wealthy and if I were married to you I'd be wealthy as well, so that's almost a given."

A wicked curve of his lips tells me he doesn't buy my nonchalance.

Does he know I'm dirt broke? Does he know I spent more nights than I care to admit stretched out in the back of my car for a makeshift bed, and brushed my teeth in fast food parking lots?

Something tells me if he doesn't, he soon will. I squirm uncomfortably on his lap.

"Go on," I say, my own voice husky now. "Something tells me there's more to it." I clear my throat. "Isn't there?"

"You'd be safe with me," he says quietly, rubbing his hand down the length of my back almost soothingly. "No one would hurt you."

"Except you," I whisper.

He doesn't answer. "People would know you're my wife, and no one would ever try to take advantage of you again." He pauses as if he's said too much.

Does he know what happened to me? This soon? How could he?

No, I decide. It's just an idiomatic expression.

"Everything from the clothes you wear to the food you eat would be provided."

Provided? Or chosen?

"You'd have a ready family here, as well."

A rush of blood in my ears thunders so hard, I'm momentarily deafened.

Family. I've been without family for so long, even the concept of this crazy family is at least a little bit appealing.

They can't be all bad, I reason.

No. I stop myself from the mental gymnastics of defending them. They are not the family I need.

Marialena, though... and Rosa.. little Natalia, crazy Nonna, and jovial Mario... I shake my head as if to clear my mind, but all I can think about is how nice it would be to be safe, protected, cared for, and accepted just as I am.

It isn't real, though. Like a house made of gingerbread, it would dissolve with the first storm, crumbling to the ground. It isn't real, and it's luring me to meet my demise.

"Do you live here?" I ask. I want to change the subject, but I also just want to know.

"Among other places, yes."

I'm stalling, but I have so many questions that need answers.

"Where else do you live?"

"I own a condo in Boston and a home in Tuscany, though all of us have primary residences here at The Castle as well."

I nod. Makes sense. A man of his stature and privilege won't exactly be bringing women home to Mama here. He'd take a woman to his fancy condo to seduce her, fuck her... why does that thought make my belly twist uncomfortably?

"So what's the catch?"

He adjusts me so I'm closer to his chest, and I'm suddenly so tired I want to curl right up here and go to sleep. I don't, though. I hold myself aloof, apart from him, my back ramrod straight.

"The catch?"

"Yeah. What's in it for me? Let's say I do this. I'm rich, I've got clothes and cars and shoes and hot sex with my hot husband. What's the catch?" I can't keep the sardonic tone out of my voice.

His fingers skate up my back to my neck and tighten at the very base of it. He flexes, and I shiver. "You'd obey me, Vittoria."

I guessed as much, seeing as I just got spanked. I nod.

"You're one of those guys, then."

"Those guys?"

"You like... control. You want to be in charge."

"I didn't know there was a category of guys like us." If he's amused, he hides it well. His eyes spark with something like anger, but I'm not quite sure.

"Some men prefer to be... modern. On equal footing. And some believe it's their way or the highway," he says.

His fingers on the back of my neck soothe, stroke, and flex. It's oddly erotic.

"And some," he says almost thoughtfully, "like absolute control. My wife will take my name. My wife will speak with respect and not out of turn. My wife will wear the clothes I choose, eat the foods I choose, and do what she's told."

"I see." I tense under the stroke of his fingers on my neck. "Why?"

"Why?"

I nod, swallowing the lump in my throat. He's so matter-of-fact about the utter control he'd have over his future wife it's unnerving. I cringe.

"Why do you choose to have such control over your wife? Why not choose a more modern approach?"

His eyes darken, and the slow downward curl of his lips stokes fire in my belly. I'm not sure why.

"That's a conversation for another day, Vittoria. For now, you and I will get ready."

He slides me off his lap, the rough fabric of his pants scraping against my ass. I quickly right myself. Voices sound in the hallway, women's and men's voices, and the unmistakable voice of Narciso Rossi. I don't realize I take a step closer to Romeo until he clasps my hand. I blink in surprise.

"You shot out my tires," I whisper, as if waking from a dream and remembering this man is no friend of mine.

He nods. "My father would've hurt you, possibly killed you. Ensuring you wouldn't run was more of a safety measure for you than anything."

An interesting way of looking at things.

He glances at his phone, still scowling, those full lips of his making my heart do crazy, wild flips. I imagine what it would be like to feel those lips on me again. What it would be liked to be kissed by him, not just a brief brush of lips, but more. I wonder what it would be like to be pinned beneath him as he took me, or on my knees while he took me from behind. Being around him makes every erotic fantasy I've ever had resurface because something tells me there's nothing Romeo wouldn't do.

"Now, *bella*," he says in a gentler tone. "Please get ready for this evening. The priest is coming from the church, and you and I will take our vows."

"Excuse me?"

He turns to the door as his phone rings. He answers it on the second ring and holds a finger up for me to be patient.

Take our vows?

Just like that? He thinks this is some sort of a business transaction? That I'm *marrying* him?

Oh no. Uh uh. I don't think so. A part of me wants to flee again, but I've already seen firsthand that's likely not a very good idea.

A brisk wind kicks up through a window that's cracked to let fresh air in. I shiver and wrap my cardigan more tightly around me and look at his room, but I don't see anything but me, at the altar, dressed in white.

No.

Romeo's speaking in heated Italian, gesturing with his hands. He won't be happy when I tell him I'm not marrying him, but I'm not so hard up I will let myself be forced into something like this.

He hangs up the phone and shakes his head. "Motherfucker," he mutters under his breath. "Mama and the girls will be up with your dress. Let them help you. We don't have much time, but they're confident they can get you ready in time." He glances at his wristwatch and curses again. "Two hours."

"Ah, yeah. About that? I'm not getting married to you, Romeo."

I watch as his spine stiffens and he grips his phone more tightly. "Excuse me?"

"I can't even believe you're serious right now. You... just assumed that for six million dollars I'd take your ring and that was that?" My heart beats faster and my palms feel damp. This is the strangest conversation I've ever had.

His eyes flash at me, making him look even more dangerous than ever.

"You think this is about the money?" he asks.

Six million dollars on the line? Why wouldn't it be?

With a shrug of his shoulders that's anything but casual, he continues. "This has nothing to do with money, Vittoria. The money's only secondary. My family has more money invested than most small countries, and we do not need my grandfather's money. No." He shakes his head. "This is about power and those that wield it."

I am so over these games and his assumptions. "And... what does that have to do with *me*? So you boys like to play high-stakes games? Got it. You want to be like... the most powerful Underboss that ever lived? Got that too. Maybe you need to earn the next ranking of made man or... or something, but I won't be the one to get you there, Romeo. Nope. Not me."

"Vittoria." He gives me what he probably thinks is a warning glance. I sidestep in case he gets ideas.

My temper's ignited, but I don't bother to hide it. I'm fired up now, and there's no turning back.

"You think I'm that easy, too? That you'll put a ring on my finger and I'd be all, *yes, Romeo, whatever you say, Romeo.* That I wouldn't have an *issue* with being under your *absolute rule* like a slave?"

"Ah, *slave,*" he says in a low voice that belies the fury in his face. His nostrils flare, and his cheeks heat with color. "I like the sound of that."

"Of course you do!" I want to slap his face, but I remember what happened the last time I did *that,* and don't wish to find myself over his lap again. "Well look again, Romeo, because I'm no goddamn Juliet."

"You're *goddamn* right you're no Juliet." His jaw clenches along with his fists, as if he's barely controlling his rage. "If you were mine, I'd whip you for your insolence and language."

My jaw slackens. Not exactly convincing me to say *I do.*

He can go fuck himself.

"My father's Boss of the Rossi family," he says, his jaw tight. "With a wife, I take his throne. If you were mine, he couldn't touch you."

I feel as if I've been doused with cold water. So being his wife wouldn't be just about Chanel bags and Louboutins.

His father couldn't touch me.

"And if I don't do this?"

His lip curls, and he bares his teeth. "I couldn't stop him."

I shake my head. "I don't need…"

"You can defend yourself?" he growls, stepping right into my space. He grabs my shoulders and gives me a shake. My teeth rattle, and I try to pull away, but he's got me tight. The man's an inferno, my arms are on fire where he's grasped me. "Can you, Vittoria? Tonight, here in this room, when the lights go out and everyone's in bed? And he comes to you to punish you for humiliating him." His voice thickens with anger and frustration, and even though his tone lowers, I hear every word as if he's shouting them. "He'll force himself on you. Rape you. Humiliate you. Hurt you."

The mental vision this invokes makes me physically ill.

"You'd let him do that?" Why wouldn't he? Does he owe me his protection?

I stifle a scream when he grips my hair so tightly it burns. Tears prick my eyes. "*Let* him? He'd find a fucking way. Do you know what his nickname is?"

I shake my head. Of course I don't.

"The Skull," he says with a look of disgust. "Do you know why?"

I shake my head again. My stomach clenches, and I want to be sick.

"Because his signature move when he murders someone is a knife up the back of the skull. A modern-day scalping. He doesn't care who the fuck you are. He'd make you pay for what you did today."

I'm sick with nausea.

"All I did was try to leave!"

Is there no way out? Am I trapped?

"That isn't how he'll see it. You tried to humiliate him. If you left, his enemy wins and he'd rather see you dead."

"If I die, he loses, too." But it's a last-ditch effort, a weak retort. I know he's right, and the knowledge makes me nauseous.

He laughs mirthlessly. "Don't you see? Punishing you sends a message to anyone else who might cross him." His beautiful, terrible face contorts with disgust. "His favorite thing to do."

I stare into the eyes of a man raised by a monster and wonder.

How much of a monster is he?

———

CHAPTER TWELVE

"It is an honor I dream not of." Juliet, on marriage, Romeo and Juliet

ROMEO

IN MY WORLD, marriage is only a convenience. We don't marry for love. Rarely, anyway. Anytime anyone does, it doesn't end well. Fucking look at my sister and where that brought her.

My parents married for convenience, my grandparents the same, and I've known from a very young age that any modern-day principles about love and equality and shit like that were not for me.

But now... now, as I look into Vittoria's eyes, I see fear, among a myriad of other emotions. She's afraid. She's intimidated. She's intrigued.

And she's fucking turned on.

I don't know her past, but I'll make it mine to know, because any wife of mine will be mine fully.

"Tell me, *bella*," I say, intentionally gentling my voice. I'm not used to using a gentle tone. I command an army, and have rarely had any use for bullshit like civilities.

She eyes me warily, as if she doesn't trust me. Good girl. She shouldn't.

"Yes?" Her back's ramrod straight, as if she wants to physically tell me that she won't give in to me quite yet.

She will.

"We looked into your past. You were doing well for yourself. You had a steady job, you were looking to get a home."

A flicker of pain so brief I almost miss it flits across her face, so quickly I wonder if I imagined it.

"Of course you did," she says, but without a trace of anger. She expected this. Probably tried to do the same for me. "And you want to know."

I nod. Waiting.

She tosses her head. A gentle floral scent wafts in the air, and a deep longing for a deeper taste of her than I've had curls low in my gut. I want this woman. I want her more than I've ever wanted a woman before, and it's not lost on me that it's probably because I can't have her as easily as I'd like.

She might go along with things. She might even marry me. But she won't give herself to me unless I've earned it.

She gives me a haughty look, her nose in the air. "So what is it you want to know, sir?"

She tosses the *sir* at me like she'd say *cur,* like it's a crumb, but I swallow it whole. I'll have this woman for my own, and not just by name.

"Ahh," I whisper. "I like that." In a split second I imagine doing that now, carrying her to the bed and working her body to climax until she screams herself hoarse. I want to pin her down and ravage her. But no. My betrothed won't be seduced so easily. I have to admit... I like that.

So I take my time. I bring her close to me, and I run my thumb along the small of her back, noting how her spine softens, and she moves a little closer to me. Probably doesn't even know she does.

"Like what?" she says, lowering her voice.

"I like it when you call me sir."

"Right. Of course."

I feel a corner of my lips tip up, like I'm flirting with a smile. Jesus, I haven't smiled in so long I almost forgot what it felt like. "You've got a mouth on you."

She shrugs one petite shoulder. "I do."

I trace my thumb along the fullest part of her lower lip. To my surprise, the seductive pink tip of her tongue darts out and licks my thumb before she stifles a groan. Her eyes widen, as if she surprised even herself.

Fuck.

I shake my head from side to side, *tsking.* "What would I do with a mouth like that?" I gently guide her lips open. She suckles my finger, her eyes never leaving mine. The tension of her mouth makes my cock hard. With a soft *pop,* she releases me. I stifle a groan.

Who's the one in charge here?

I'm mesmerized by her lips, so full and pink and slightly dampened. I imagine what it'd be like to have those lips on my body, wrapped around my cock...

"I don't know, sir," she says, her gaze growing wicked. "Something tells me you'd do something, wouldn't you? Maybe... lots of things with my mouth."

"Are you flirting with me?" My voice is thick with arousal.

"Maybe."

"Seducing me?"

Her tantalizing smile makes my pulse throb. A gentle breeze from the open window flutters her hair. Her scent's making me *wild.*

I lean in closer and draw her to me with my hand on her lower back. Our breath mingles. So close, I can see the tiniest dots of freckles along her nose. I want to kiss each one of them. I'm jealous of the sun's rays that brought those freckles to her face, the rays that touched her skin before I did. I'm jealous of anything and anyone that knew her first.

My hand's curled around the back of her neck. I imagine she's mine, that I own her, her every breath belongs to me, her body christened by me and me alone. I imagine we don't have a marriage of convenience but something... deeper. Compelling. *Passionate.*

I've never wanted someone or something more

in my entire life. I grasp the back of her head and pull her to me, then slide my hands along the side of her face to frame it. Her lips are slightly parted, her breath shallow and eager. Her hands come to rest on my forearms. I lick her lower lip, and she moans. I've never wanted to kiss a woman so badly in my life.

My forehead touches hers. I'm panting like I've just run a race. I can hear the sound of her swallowing, the slow drag of her tongue along her lips.

"Romeo," she whispers.

I nod, incapable of speaking. She's got me captivated.

"Let's say we… we marry."

I blink at a sudden vision of Vittoria dressed in white, my band around her finger while we take our vows. I'm not a romantic man, but goddamn if I don't want that. I nod again.

"What if we… what if something happens? How long do we *stay* married? Do people in your family…"

I don't let her finish. My fingers tighten in her hair so I have her full attention. I hold her gaze. "Forever, Vittoria. There is no divorce in my family. We marry for life until death do us part."

We're in this room surrounded by antiques that stand the test of time. My family may not marry for love, but my family does not believe in divorce.

She frowns and shakes her head. "I can't do it, Romeo," she finally says. "I can't allow myself to be married to someone I don't know."

I want to shake her again. I want to punish her

again. I want to slam her onto this bed and make her mine irrevocably.

"Why not?" I speak through gritted teeth, keeping myself calm with great effort.

She only shakes her head and looks away. "Let's go back to our conversation. Please ask the question you were going to. You need to know."

She'll wait, then. She doesn't want to talk of this.

"Fine. Tell me. Where did your money go?"

She nods, drawing in a breath then releasing it slowly. She's prepared to answer. "I was with a man who swindled me."

"Excuse me?" It's hard for me to understand what she's saying. With a man who swindled her?

"I thought I was in love," she says simply, frankly. I like that she doesn't cloak her words in hidden promises and flowers. "I fell in love with a man named Ashton Bryant. At least, I thought I did. We were going to get married." She breaks eye contact and looks over my shoulder. I've learned to read body language. She's in pain over the memory. I'll kill him.

He touched her. He hurt her. I'll fucking *end* him.

"No, we had no ring and no date, and I suppose that should've been an indicator, huh?" She sighs. "But we... well, he just put it off, you know?"

"No. I don't know. Sounds like a fucking douche."

I watch as her face softens and her eyes dance like rays of moonbeams. "You wouldn't, would you? You want to marry a woman you just met to secure your crown, don't you? The concept of pretending to be in love or putting off a marriage is foreign to you, isn't it?"

I nod. "Of course."

A corner of her lips quirks up, revealing a dimple. I stare, mesmerized, and she continues to talk. She's got the tiniest little freckle at the corner of her mouth.

"He wouldn't marry me. I should've known it was a warning sign. A red flag, I guess." She sighs and swallows. It pains her to talk of it.

He'll suffer before he dies. Slowly.

"One day I woke up, and everything was gone. And I mean… *everything.* The car. My purse. My credit cards. The cash in my wallet. He even took some of the gifts he bought me. Jewelry…"

"Son of a bitch," I curse. "What a fuckin' cowardly thing to do."

"Ohhh, yeah. The guy hadn't even paid the rent as he said he would."

"He was supposed to be paying the rent? And he didn't?" She must hear something in my tone, because she pauses before she continues, then blows out a breath.

"Well… I gave him half and he was supposed to pay, but he took my money and never paid a thing. Cleaned me out."

I pinch the bridge of my nose. "You were going to *split* the rent?"

"Romeo, do you have any idea how things work outside in the real world? Where humans are autonomous and not threatened by dangerous hitmen? Where people don't actually *own* weapons?"

I shake my head. "No."

She gives the most adorable, most unladylike little snort. "You don't lie, do you?"

"Also, no." I shrug. "You might not always like what I say, but you'll always trust what I say."

"Okay, I already *rarely* like what you have to say."

I take that as a personal challenge. I do what I've been holding myself back from doing. I bend and kiss the little freckle then lick the place I kissed.

Her head tips back with a moan that begs for more. "I'll teach you to love what I say," I whisper in her ear as her fingers scrabble for purchase, anchoring around my neck. I lift her and walk to the couch, then lower her body, stretching her back against the velvety cushions. I drape her legs around my torso. "If I whispered in your ear how I owned you, how your pussy belonged to me, and how I planned on worshipping that pussy until your body ignites, would you like what I said then?"

"I don't know," she whispers with a wicked little grin. "We should maybe test that out…"

"Naughty girl. Someone needs to go back over my lap for a spanking."

"No! No, I… ohh." She can't hide the little moan she releases when my hands knead her breasts, my thumbs flicking over her pebbled nipples. She holds my gaze and whispers, *"Fuck."*

I reach for her top and slide my fingers under it before I grasp her breast and tweak her nipple. Her back arches and she gasps. "Romeo!"

"What did I tell you about that language? Hmm?" I give her another punishing tweak.

"*Fu* —" she bites her lip. "Not to swear. Got it."

"Good girl." I bend my head to her chest and kiss her abused nipple, drag the silky fabric of her bra down and gently lap the puckered skin. Her mouth hangs open, and her eyes flutter closed.

"You'd like what I said, Vittoria. Wouldn't you? If I whispered in your ear how beautiful you were?" I kiss the top of one breast, then the other, then up her neck to her chin. "I'd teach you to love when I talked to you."

"Something tells me," she says, panting, "that I'd learn to love a lot of things."

I kiss along her jaw until I reach her lips, and before I kiss her again, whisper, "You would, *bella.*"

I don't know what pushes her over the edge. I don't know what pulls the curtain down on the magical moment between us, but one moment she's putty in my hands, and the next, she's shaking her head.

"I can't, Romeo. I can't do it. I can't just... agree to spend the rest of my life with someone I don't know. I don't care how much money I get. I don't care if it means my safety and protection. I don't know you. You don't know me." She values her self-worth and independence more than material possessions. I get that. She tips her head to the side. "Isn't there anything we can do about that?"

I meet her gaze and smile. There's something about her so simple, so unencumbered with lies or pretentions, it's as if she's melting the coldness that surrounds my heart.

I have to keep her from my father. I have to protect her from what could happen.

But I won't take her by force. It could take years to repair the damage done by a forced marriage and I could do irreparable damage in the process.

And yet, I have to have her. There is no other choice.

She looks at me pleadingly. Beseechingly. She doesn't speak while I think this through, and I'm momentarily grateful. Every family member of mine pushes and pushes until they get an answer, but she gives me space to think.

"Stay in my bed, then," I say with a final nod. "For tonight, stay with me. I can't promise you the protection my ring would give you, but if you're in my bed he can't get to you."

She eyes me warily. "Is that a pickup line?"

"Absolutely."

She bites her lip, and my cock hardens. "Let's do it."

———

CHAPTER THIRTEEN

"LOVE IS HEAVY AND LIGHT, bright and dark, hot and cold, sick and healthy, asleep and awake- its everything except what it is!" Romeo and Juliet

VITTORIA

A BELL RINGS DOWNSTAIRS. I sit up, still pinned beneath him. Every inch of my body's on fire, and the proposal he just made hasn't helped.

Stay in my bed.

How could I sleep next to a man who oozes masculinity through his pores?

If I spend the night in his bed, something tells me I won't ever be the same again. How can I spend the night in his bed and not fall for him?

And how could I be falling for a man like him?

I have to change the subject. I have to clear my

head. I have to go… talk to Marialena or something.

"What's that bell?" I ask. Why does my voice sound all breathless? I have to gain back some measure of control.

He sighs. "Dinner bell. We eat in thirty minutes." He looks down on me with a mixture of sadness and desire in his eyes before he kisses my cheek and releases me. He stands. "We'll get you to your room and prepare for dinner. Everything you need should be there."

"Everything I need?"

He nods, running his fingers through his hair, then adjusts his pants so his hard-on doesn't show. For some reason, that makes me laugh.

"What?" he asks, scowling. Hell, even his scowl's hot.

"Nothing," I say, biting my lip to stop myself from laughing, but he only wags a finger at me.

"Liar."

"I suppose you'd punish me for that, too?"

"Oh, you could count on that," he says, crossing the room while he takes his phone out. My heart thumps, and I remind myself who he is, that he's dangerous and can't be trusted. He killed a man in front of me.

For me.

He wants to marry me.

So his father doesn't kill me.

This is so complicated my head hurts.

"Come, let's go," he says, reaching for my hand. "I'll take you to your room."

I'm curious if he'll escort me now that he

believes I'm no longer safe here.

"Romeo, is your father literally so deranged that he'd seek me out and—"

"Yes," he says through clenched teeth.

"So why do you let him? I don't understand why you don't just…" I hunt for the right words. "Usurp the throne or something?" Those were not the right words. Or maybe they were?

Outside the window, the sun's begun to set, a warm orange glow touching the horizon, painting the beauty of the ocean in shades of pink and purple.

He exhales and shakes his head. "Not here, Vittoria." He eyes the walls as if they have ears, a clear reminder of the danger I'm in. As we head to the door, he says in a whisper, "Let's just say my father has as many friends as he does enemies."

Ahh. He couldn't do anything about his father without repercussions. I suppose it couldn't be as easy as I'd thought it would be.

When we open the door, The Castle's alive. Marialena's at the foot of the spiral staircase chatting animatedly with Mario, and Tosca stands beside them, holding a flute of champagne. I realize with a bit of a start that they're all dressed formally. Mario has a freaking *tux* on, and Tosca's wearing something that looks like it was sewn together with diamonds.

The front door opens, and a team of people wearing casual sweats and jeans carries in huge bouquets of roses and carnations, lilies and daisies, and large armfuls of calla lilies.

I stop at the top of the stairs, panicked. Someone's playing music on the piano, and everyone who walks by the foot of the stairs looks like they're heading to a ball.

"Uh, Romeo…"

"Yes?" He laces his fingers through mine as he walks with me to my room.

"They haven't seem to have gotten the memo that we're not getting married tonight."

He looks down at the crowd of people, the fancy dress, the flowers, and finally nods. "Looks like it."

I have to walk quickly to keep up with his long strides. My room is at the furthest end of the hallway.

"Well, aren't you going to do anything about that? Maybe… clarify things?"

He frowns. "No." He doesn't slow his stride.

I stifle a groan as we walk to my bedroom. Four large, armed men flank either side of me and follow behind us.

"Who are they?" I whisper.

"Your bodyguards," he whispers back.

Oh. Bodyguards. I like *that.*

"Can't they keep… him… away?"

His eyes widen before he shakes his head. "No."

This family is maddening.

He opens the door to my room with a little key card, pushes the door inward, then tugs me in.

I gasp.

A large rack of clothes stands next to the four-poster bed, gorgeous, luxurious items the likes of which I've never seen before. Boxes of shoes sit beside them, and on the dresser there's a black velvet jewelry box, opened, laden with sparkling diamonds. Oh, God. I've bought plenty with his sisters, but nothing like *this.*

At the very front, on display, hangs a silky white wedding gown fit for a queen. My heartbeat spikes. That's for me. That stunning, designer dress with satin and ruffles and lace that probably cost a mint, is *mine.*

"Turn away!" I say in a panic.

He turns his head to look at me as if I've sprouted a second head. "What?"

"You can't see the wedding dress."

Why are we still talking about a wedding?

"I thought we weren't getting married," he says, his brow furrowing.

"I didn't say never. I said not yet."

I actually find it sort of amusing when he growls at that and grumbles to himself in Italian.

"What does that mean? I don't speak Italian."

"Good thing you don't," is all he says. "Look, you don't have to wear the wedding dress. Put it away for another day and choose something nice for tonight."

I nod. "Oh, right. Okay then."

I sidle up to the large volume of clothes and touch the silky, decadent fabrics. These are *high-end.* Some are studded with jewels, and still others wrapped in the finest sequins.

"Okay, so you moved fast," I mutter to him.

"My sisters have contacts in every major retail store from here to Canada."

"Shocking."

He reaches a hand out to touch the delicate ivory satin. "Are you sure?"

I don't have to ask him what he means, what he wants me to confirm. I'm not marrying him tonight, end of story. I put as much conviction into my tone as I can. *"Yes."*

"Fine." I can tell he's holding himself back. The king of the underworld doesn't like not getting his way, but we both know it's only temporary. He'll get his way... eventually. The intensity in his lowered voice holds my thoughts captive. "For tonight, if I can't have you in the white, I want you wearing the pale blue one."

I look to see which one he likes. It's a light, baby blue off-the-shoulder fitted gown with a white lace appliqué and a low V-cut neckline. It's stunning.

"Whoa. Gorgeous." I need to push, need to tug a little. I bite my lower lip and shake my head. "But I'd like the pink one." He yanks a lock of my hair. "Ow! Hey! What?" Didn't expect *that.*

"I think you forgot something."

"Uh..."

"I pick out what you wear." He raises his brows as if to remind me, a subtle warning. But I'm holding my own here.

"Right, if we're *married*, which we aren't." I try to meet his fierce gaze, but it doesn't work. He only glares right back, kicks the door shut behind us, and before I know what's happening, pins me against the door. His hand traps my throat with a gentle flex that tells me he's holding himself back.

Romeo isn't used to not getting his way.

"I let you agree not to marry me... yet," he says with quiet emphasis. "I even agreed to protect you, even though you aren't my wife... yet, so my father doesn't hurt you. But make no mistake, Vittoria." He yanks my head back, baring my throat, and I moan when his tongue slides along my naked skin. His voice is a low growl, dangerous and possessive, reigniting the inferno he created within me. He reaches one hand to my ass and squeezes the still-tender flesh. I squeal. "I didn't know it then and neither did you, but you were mine from the moment I killed for you."

My mouth is dry, my vision blurry. I'm either dazzled or afraid or turned on. Maybe all three.

"Oh, is that how it works?" I try to keep my tone teasing, but the words falter on my lips when he draws even closer. My chest is pressed up against his, my breath heaving.

His eyes warm. "Wear the blue one, Vittoria. I demand it. If you come downstairs tonight in anything but what I ask for, I'll punish you."

That sends a little zing straight between my legs. Ah. Maybe that's what it is, then. I don't just need to push him for the sake of my own free will and self-respect. I crave the erotic sensation of danger.

"Do you get off on punishing people?"

His cock's rock hard as he pushes against me, the heavy ridge turning my own limbs to jelly.

"No, baby," he whispers in my ear. My skin's feverish, and my clothes feel too tight, too heavy. "Not *people*. Only you." He nips my earlobe. "Wear."

A heated lap of tongue to skin. "The blue." Another searing lick. "Dress. Disobey me and see what happens."

Is that an invitation?

The warning tone spikes my pulse. I'm panting, on *fire*. I know we're just starting out, and I have no idea what will happen next, but I know that I can't just blindly obey him. I won't just blindly do what he says. But the knowing glint in his eyes tells me maybe, just maybe, he doesn't want my blind obedience.

He'll demand my submission, but I'll make him earn my trust.

"Got it," I say, holding his gaze.

I am *not* wearing that dress.

The voices downstairs have reached an alarming pitch. How many are here tonight? "I'll go now. I'll tell them tonight isn't our wedding, but we'll celebrate our engagement. Now *that* you can agree to."

I swallow. "And what will that afford me?"

"A measure of protection. My father won't touch you, he wouldn't dare." He clenches his jaw. "And my brothers won't hit on you."

I look down at my fingers, so small they could belong to a child. I've always had tiny hands. "No ring, though."

"I'll take care of it."

Of course he will. Probably owns a jeweler's or something. Diamond mine in Russia.

When he lets me go, I stumble a little. I didn't realize I was leaning on him. He steadies me with a gentle hand to my elbow.

"Get ready. I'll send Marialena up to help you with whatever you need. And remember, *Vittoria.*" His voice rings with command. "The blue one."

Turns out his hand on my elbow gives him a little assistance so he can swing me around to deliver a parting crack to the ass that makes me hiss in a breath.

When he leaves, the room feels cooler. I fight a wave of disappointment. Or is it fear?

I remind myself those guards are right outside my door. They might not be able to stop Narciso Rossi, but they'd buy me some time…

I turn to the rack of clothes. They're probably worth hundreds of thousands of dollars, if not more. I stare at the glimmering fabric, the luxurious softness and brilliance of gems and sequins. Is this what it's like to be rich? Is this even what I want? I think back to the nights stretched out on the back seat of my car, of the zeroes in my bank account, and heave a labored sigh. These clothes are *gorgeous.*

I hear voices in the hall, then a gentle knock.

"Babe, it's me. Let me in."

Marialena. I open the door, holding a dress. "I think pink's my color, don't you?"

She grins. "He wants another one, doesn't he?"

"How'd you know?"

One of the stoic bodyguards lets his eyes rove over her before the door shuts behind her with a bang.

She shrugs. "Eh, he's a bossy guy. Was ordering his nannies around before he could speak full sentences. Now, babe." She gentles her voice. "You have to understand. Romeo comes across as a hard-ass."

I snort. "No way. Really?"

She rolls her eyes as she extricates the dress from my hands and lays it on the bed.

"They all do, well, except *maybe* Orlando but even he has his moments."

"You mean the one with those fuck—" I stop myself. He doesn't like swearing. Why do I care? "The one with *skulls* tattooed across his knuckles?"

"The very same," she says. She walks to the closet on death-defying heels.

"How do you *do* that?"

"Do what?"

"Walk on, like, stilettos."

She waves a hand in the air. "It's all practice. I'll teach you."

"I think I like flats."

She grins at me. "Girl, I'll hook you up. Cinderella had a Fairy Godmother. You, my friend, have Marialena." She winks at me, then glances at her phone. "Oof. Fifteen minutes." She turns to face me like I'm a problem that needs fixing. "We've got some work to do."

Precisely fourteen minutes later, we leave the room in utter shambles and walk downstairs. She holds my hand to help me with the heels, and I almost bail on her. These are what she calls "strappy wedges," and she says they're the easiest ones to walk in. I'm not so sure about that.

She's fixed my hair and slapped on makeup and

zipped up my dress before spritzing me with perfume that smells like it was bottled in the clouds of heaven. When I look in the mirror, I don't recognize myself.

I look… elegant. Refined.

Worth it.

The music plays on as we walk downstairs. Butterflies take flight in my belly. Narciso will be down here. They all will.

There are a lot more people than I anticipated. I look around for a familiar face, and see a few— Rosa, and Mario. They're speaking quietly in a corner of the room. Why do they all allow someone like him to do what he does?

I look from left to right, and don't see him anywhere. Tavi sits at a bar that's alongside one wall in the Great Hall, nursing a shot. Marialena takes my hand. "Come, let's get a drink."

Where's Romeo?

My hands feel cold and clammy, and briefly, I consider running back upstairs and changing. Wearing what he asked me to. Not openly defying him. Maybe it will be nice to see those blue-gray eyes of his light up with pleasure and approval, and not—

"Ah, *bella mia.*" I gasp at the firm grip of fingers on my arm, a low voice in my ear, and as soon as my heartbeat spikes, my belly warms because I recognize Romeo's clean, masculine scent. "You forgot something, didn't you?"

Marialena's a few steps ahead of me, at the bar. She turns to me and quickly notes Romeo's hand on my arm. Rolling her eyes, she snaps her fingers at me.

"You want a drink?"

Romeo shakes his head. "She's all set."

No way. I need a drink. "Romeo, I do want—" Something stops me from defying him right here, in front of all these people. I know he wouldn't like it, and I don't know if talking back to him in the possible presence of Narciso is a good idea.

"Tell *me* what you want," he says. "What's your drink, Vittoria?"

My lips feel suddenly parched and dry. I run my tongue along them. "Surprise me." My voice sounds husky and flirtatious.

Who am I? Here, under this roof, dressed in luxury clothing, in the presence of this family, I feel almost as if I've become someone else. Like the gown itself transformed me.

What if I step outside and find that all that glitters isn't gold.

As Romeo heads to the bar, everyone in front of him parts, giving him a wide berth. I wonder if that should scare me. Is it respect? Or fear? Or both?

He tugs me along. All eyes in the room are on me, and I'm not sure I like it. Not sure I don't, though.

The bartender, a stocky man with a shaved head, smiles at Romeo.

"What can I get you, sir?"

I feel a strange sense of jealousy. *I'm* the one that calls him sir.

Where did that come from?

"A glass of house Merlot, please." The bartender looks to me, then looks at Romeo's hand on my arm. "And for the lady?"

"Just the one glass of Merlot, please."

I watch as the bartender pours a generous drink into something that looks like I could bathe in. Romeo nods his head in thanks, then turns to me.

"Don't we have to tip him?" I whisper.

"Babe," he says with a twinkle in his eyes. "He works for me."

Of course. My cheeks flush. Romeo takes a sip, then hands it to me.

"Take a sip," he says quietly, so only I hear. "Drink from the very same place I sipped just now, Vittoria." There's a firm insistence to his tone that isn't like his request for a certain dress. He isn't playing. This time, I don't ignore him.

I sip, my lips touching where his did. It's slightly tangy, rich and sweet, and I feel it warm straight down my throat to the tips of my toes. When I hand the wineglass back to Romeo, I see cold eyes staring at me from across the room.

I reach for Romeo's hand. "He's here," I whisper.

"Who, *bella*?"

"Your father."

"Of course he is. Just trust me." Romeo tucks my arm through his and holds me to him. Then he lifts his glass and clears his throat. "I'd like to propose a toast." The room goes quiet as all eyes come to us. "For me and my future bride."

———

CHAPTER FOURTEEN

"DID my heart love till now? forswear it, sight!" Romeo and Juliet

ROMEO

I HAVEN'T SEEN my father this furious since Rosa's wedding, and that's saying something. He gave himself an actual stroke, and we had to find a doctor in Tuscany to tend to him. He spent ten days in the hospital.

But goddamn, I've had it with his bullying. I'm so fucking ready to take this throne and this crown to end the tyranny he's had over this family for decades, I'm half convinced forcing marriage on Vittoria's the right decision.

I don't know what she's thinking, what she's feeling, and if I'm honest, considering how another person outside this family feels is not something I usually concern myself with. But fuck if she isn't making my job harder.

Tavi walks up to us, another drink in hand. "If looks could fuckin' kill, brother," he says with a look halfway between a grimace and a smile.

"Tell me about it." I take another sip of wine, then hand it back to Vittoria. She sips where I did. Tavi nods slowly.

Rossi family tradition is steeped in superstition; stories passed down through the generations are told since infancy. Lips that touch the same wine glass are destined to be joined again. It's a small gesture, but it can't hurt.

Orlando joins us next, already half toasted. The top buttons of his shirt are open, and he's lost the tie and cummerbund. They weren't sure there'd be a wedding tonight and weren't surprised when I told them not yet, but if I know my brothers, they're here for the food anyway.

A waiter walks by with a tray of canapés. Orlando takes the entire tray and thanks him. "I'll take this off your hands," he says, piling three of them on top of the other before shoving them in his mouth.

"Oh, what are those?" Vittoria asks, running her tongue along her lips. My dick tightens. Fuck, I need this woman.

"Peach and prosciutto canapés," Orlando says, holding the tray closer to himself as if to warn her not to touch them. My brothers don't share women or food.

"Douchebag, leave some for me," Mario says with a scowl. "I fucking love canapés."

"Go get your own," Orlando snaps.

"Boys, boys," Marialena says, observing us from a few feet away. "You do know Mama ordered enough food for a wedding celebration, don't you?"

"As if that makes a goddamn difference," Tavi mutters with a scowl of his own. He reaches for one of the canapés, and Orlando smacks his hand away fiercely.

"You son of a—"

"*Stop.*" They look at me. I shake my head, half ready to shake some sense into both of them. "Jesus, you two are like fuckin' kids. Behave yourselves or I'll knock your heads together." Tavi flips Orlando off, and Orlando shoves three more canapés into his mouth. With a growl of disapproval, I hand Vittoria the glass of wine, which is kinda like a "bro, hold my beer" move, and head toward them. They scatter like rabbits, the empty tray clattering to the floor.

Marialena rolls her eyes as she walks over to us, joined by her petite redheaded friend Sassy.

"Hey, Sass." She's been Marialena's friend so long she's almost like a sister around here. I don't even remember her real name. She's been Sassy forever. "When'd you get here?"

"Oh, about an hour ago. Marialena said there was a wedding, and I wanted to come. I've done nothing but study for like three months straight and I'm so ready for a party." She sips a drink herself, as Orlando comes over with another tray, this one laden with small plastic flutes holding shrimp cock-tail. Ballsy.

Orlando sees Sassy. His nostrils flare, and he scowls. "What's that in your glass?" he asks.

Sassy flushes harder and hotter than any girl I've ever seen. Her cheeks match her hair.

"What's it to you?" she snaps. He narrows his eyes at her, reaches for her shot and plucks it straight out of her hand, then slides it on his tray.

"You two ought to know better," he says, shaking his head at Marialena and Sassy.

"Romeo!" Sassy says. "Tell him to give my drink back."

"Show me your I.D. that says you're twenty-one, and I'll tell him to give you your drink back."

"Et tu, Brute? Rome, are you kidding me?" Mari-alena upends the rest of her drink, but I turn to the bartender, point to Marialena, and shake my head *no*. Marialena stomps off after giving me a furious glare. Sassy follows, still flushing madly.

Vittoria sips her wine and watches. She seems amused, and observes every interaction I have with the people here. There are over fifty soldiers in the Family, and all know she's my future wife. When they look our way, they incline their heads out of respect. Some shake her hand, still others kiss her cheek.

"Pleased to meet you," Leo says. He takes Vitto-ria's hand and kisses it, but quickly releases her when he catches my eye. Leo's a classic flirt and he better watch his fucking step.

"Careful, Rome," he says, shaking his head. "Your father's restless, and you know what that means."

I do. When he gets in these moods, one of two things happens: he takes another woman to bed, or someone dies. I'm not sure how many more mistresses my mother can take before she loses her mind.

I reach for Vittoria's wine glass and take another sip, as my father stands. He clears his throat. He's lost so much respect as Don of the Family, it's only out of force of habit everyone looks his way.

Many of the men watch me, to take my lead. I stand up taller and look at my father. If I want the men to respect me as Don, I'll have to show respect to my father, even if the only reason I show it is because of his role.

"Good evening," he says. *"Grazie per essere venuto."*

Leo looks to me. When my father lapses from English into Italian, he's usually wasted. I tense, waiting to hear what he'll say.

"Romeo." Vittoria winces. I release her hand. I didn't realize I was holding onto her that tightly. Leo looks from me to her, then to my father again. I put my arm around her shoulders.

"You should marry him, sweetheart," Leo says in a whisper. "You have no idea how much easier this will go for you if you do."

Vittoria lifts her chin defiantly. She's got a stubborn streak a mile wide, and I will enjoy every fucking minute of taming that. "Thank you," she says. "I've noted your unsolicited input."

Leo's brows raise slightly before he bellows with laughter. "Ah, Rome. You need a feisty one. Keep you on your toes, eh?" He gives me a wink. I pinch Vittoria's ass.

"Hey!"

I tuck her against my side. Even with her heels, she's several inches shorter than I am, and fits in the crook of my arm like she was designed for me. "You think I didn't notice what you're wearing, beautiful? Hmm?" She bites her lip and gives me a coy look that makes my dick hard. I lean in, tangling my fingers in the hair at the nape of her neck, and whisper in her ear. "You're already in trouble for defying me."

"Rome," Leo says in a warning tone. He clears his throat. I look up to see my father staring me down, his face set in stone.

He looks from me to Vittoria. "Something to say, son?" he asks.

No fucking way he'll upbraid me in front of my future soldiers, my family, and my future wife. I force a wide grin and take the wineglass from Vittoria. Being mafia Boss means knowing when to wield power, when to wield authority, and when to suck up. "To the health of the Boss," I say. The sound of clinking glasses drowns out my father's growl. I catch my mother's eye from across the room. It isn't often she's fearful, but both of us know Papa's in a dangerous place.

I turn to Vittoria. "Have you changed your mind, Vittoria?" I ask. "We have a priest here tonight. Say the word, and we'll take our vows right here, right now."

Panic sweeps across her face. "Romeo," she whispers. "No. I'm not ready."

I look back to my father. I don't trust him. Something's different tonight. Something about my grandfather's wishes and the will have put him in a dangerous headspace.

Tavi walks to my father, his arm around a pretty waitress dressed in a frilly white apron. He says something in my father's ear. My father scowls, then nods, and a few minutes later, takes the waitress with him as he leaves.

"Jesus," I mutter. Vittoria's eyes are sad, and her lips turned down. I look to where her gaze lingers and see my mother sitting by a window. She sighs, turns, and stares out at the moonlit sky.

Vittoria shakes her head. "You make your own rules," she whispers. "You don't follow the rules of others. Tell me the truth, Romeo."

I nod. "I told you, I don't lie, Vittoria."

"Then tell me this," she whispers.

I lace her fingers through mine. "Yes?"

"How will you keep me safe from him? I know you want to marry me, but if you do…. even if we wed right here, tonight, how would you stop him from coming after me?"

"He wouldn't," I say, but I'm not sure I'm as convinced as I was earlier. There's a ruthless gleam in his eyes I haven't seen before.

"And tell me this. You said you'd never lie. You

said that marriage is forever in your family. Would you take another woman?"

"Never. The day my father did was the day he lost my respect."

She shakes her head and sighs. "I'd like another glass of wine."

Mario walks up to us with a tray of drinks. "And one for the sweet," he says with a flirtatious grin.

"Mario, you flirt with Vittoria, I'll cut off your dick and serve it in your fuckin' cocktail skewered on a toothpick."

He splays his hand across his chest in mock offense. "I'm your brother!"

Vittoria shakes her head.

Mario clears his throat. "You two ain't tyin' the knot tonight?" he asks, an uncharacteristic look of concern on his face.

Vittoria answers for us. "No."

"That would—"

She rolls her eyes. "Be a mistake. I know, I know, I've heard it from, like, every other tux-wearing guy tonight, okay?"

Mario chuckles. "Got yourself a firecracker, Rome." He sighs and sobers. "But I'm not joking, Vittoria."

"Dad's got someone," I tell him, as discreetly as I can. We don't speak of his mistresses out loud if we can help it.

Mario frowns. "You think that's enough to keep him in check for now?"

"Don't know." God, I need a smoke. "I'm stepping out. Vittoria." I take her hand.

"Yes?"

"I need a smoke. Come with me."

I take her to the war room, far away from the prying eyes of our guests and the concerns of my family and food-shoving brothers, past the sun room and courtyard, past the dining room and pantry. Here, it's cooler and quieter. She holds my hand and walks with me slowly.

"You okay?" I look over my shoulder to see her wobbling.

"It's these heels," she says. "Ugh, I don't know how your sisters do it. Marialena said they'd be the easiest ones to walk in."

"Lose 'em."

She blinks and looks up to me, and my heart does a little stutter in my chest. Her eyes are like twinkling stars, her cheeks faintly flushed, and a wisp of a curl hits her forehead. "Lose them?"

She's so unlike any other woman I've met. So unpretentious and… honest.

"Just take them off."

"But these floors are sort of… well, cold, and I—"

I face her. "Lose them."

She gives me a curious look before she steps out of them and breathes a sigh of relief. "Oh God, that's so much better. Romeo!"

She gasps when I pick her up and swing her into my arms. We're only paces away from the war room.

"Shh," I whisper in her ear. I hear something. We step behind one of the large columns. I set her down but hold her close to my chest and shake my head to quiet her. It's so dark here, we're completely hidden.

"What is it?" she whispers, but I put my finger to her lips. She nips me. I pinch her ass and she giggles against my shoulder, but a moment later she freezes when the war room door opens.

"Fuckin' millions." A man's deep voice, husky and angry. I squint through the dark and recognize the nose that's been broken three times. Santo.

"Tell me about it." A woman's voice. I peer through the dark and see Rosa. She's brushing off her dress and looking from side to side.

What the hell?

Are they talking about the money? Vittoria's inheritance?

And why are those two alone?

We wait until the sound of their footsteps fade.

"What was that all about?"

"No idea."

I pick her up again and carry her into the room.

"I seriously can walk," she says.

"I know." I like holding her. I like the feel of her up against my chest. I like the way her head sort of falls against my shoulder, like she's sleepy, or she... trusts me.

I nestle her into an overstuffed chair and kick back in a chair of my own, taking a pack of smokes out of my pocket. I light one up.

"If we're getting married, you have to quit, though."

"Have to," I repeat. An interesting concept,

someone telling me what to do. "That's absolutely not how marriage with me works, babe."

"Figured as much, but thought it was worth a shot. So of course I can't make you quit, but I won't kiss you if you smell like an ashtray."

She makes me laugh. Goddamn. I've never thought of quitting in all these years, but this woman just might tempt me. I take in a drag and hold it, feeling the nicotine calm me. I let out a breath and sigh. "You want some?"

"Nicotine or weed?" she says, eying me curiously.

That makes me chuckle. God, I haven't laughed in so long I feel rusty. "You ever seen a joint, babe?"

"Well, yes," she says, but she's obviously lying. "I mean, of course."

"You ever *smell* a joint?"

"Also yes," she says haughtily. She crosses her arms over her chest and leans back. "I'm not a total noob."

"Noob? What the fuck is a noob?"

"Like… newbie? You know?" No, I don't know. "I just mean I know some stuff."

Fucking adorable.

"Here," I say, handing her the lit smoke. "Take a drag."

"Uh uh, *gross,* no way."

"They're good. All the way from Italy."

She wrinkles up her nose. "Smokes, no. Wine, yes. I think it's cool you guys actually *drink* the wine in the dining room."

"Now will you marry me?"

"Still no."

I sigh and take another drag from my cigarette. "I could make you, you know." The words linger in the air with an obvious threat. For me, a temptation. Somehow, with Vittoria the words no longer have the appeal they once did.

She nods, and doesn't speak at first, watching the smoke dissipate. The war room's old, the ceiling so high the walls seem to absorb the smoke. It's why I come here when I want to smoke and why my father smokes cigars. When she finally speaks, her voice has softened to an almost sad tone. "There are a lot of things you could make me do, Romeo," she finally says.

I hold her gaze and beckon to her. "Come here."

I see the struggle in her eyes, the question as to whether or not she should obey me. I love that.

She's stunning as she walks over to me in the silky dress that hugs every curvy inch of her, until she stands right where I do. I push off from the desk, take her hand, and lead her to the trapdoor to the basement. She doesn't show any surprise.

"You've been here before?"

"Marialena gave me a tour, but we didn't actually go down." I can feel her pulse quickening where my fingers grasp her wrist as I open the small trapdoor and we head to the wine cellar in the basement. When I get to the bottom of the stairs, I flick a light. A soft yellow glow illuminates the room. I toss my cigarette to the floor and grind it out with my heel.

"If you quit smoking, I'll kiss you," she finally says.

"You'd kiss me if I didn't."

"No," she says with a toss of her head. "I'd let *you* kiss *me*. I said if you quit, *I'll* kiss *you*."

Ah. Her appeal is devastating, like I'm wrapped in an intangible warmth, light and heat and a spark of something more.

"I enjoyed my last smoke, goddammit."

Her smile's worth it.

"Here," I tell her. I stick a small key in the palm of her hand and close her fingers around it. "Look at this room. Note the location. No one but you has the key to the cellar. If you need to… if anything happens and I can't be with you, can't protect you, you get to this basement and lock the door. Stay here and I'll find you."

Her eyes widen as she looks around the room. "There's no way out, though, is there?" The room's windowless, the only way out the way we came in.

"None. But once you're in, no one else can get to you but me."

Finally, she nods, and she can't stifle a yawn.

"Alright, clear enough." I lace my fingers through hers. "Let's get you to bed." I hand her the clunky heels.

She suddenly looks very, very awake.

———

CHAPTER FIFTEEN

"*AND WHERE TWO raging fires meet together, they do consume the thing that feeds their fury.*"~*Romeo and Juliet*

VITTORIA

HIS NEARNESS MAKES my head spin, my belly plummet, and my palms all sweaty. Part of his plan, probably.

"Is your body temp like a hundred degrees?" I ask, then suddenly wish I hadn't when he looks at me with a twinkle in his eye. That's all I need is for him to make his eyes all magical. They're already mesmerizing with their blue-gray allure, and now that they're smiling, I'd hand over my panties... if I were wearing any.

"Maybe. Why'd you ask that?"

"You're just... like, physically *hot,* it's like I'm standing next to an inferno." He smirks at me, and I feel the need to backtrack. "I don't mean you're hot as in *handsome* or anything."

"You don't find me attractive?"

"I, well I—I didn't say *that.*" His chuckle makes my nipples harden. "I just mean I... well, it's like flames just radiate off your skin or something."

Why did I open my mouth?

He shrugs as we make our way back to the war room. "I'll keep that in mind. No need for clothes in bed, then."

I don't reply. I can't, because I've somehow lost the ability to speak.

I'm not so naïve that I think he's going to put me to bed and go sleep on the couch or something. He's been hitting on me full throttle, and even though I know the plot to get me into his bed is ostensibly for my safety, I know he has a vested interest. There are many other methods he could've used to keep me safe.

Maybe he wants me.

We return, albeit reluctantly, to the guests, but Romeo sighs.

"I want out of here, babe," he says in a low voice to me, as if reading my mind. "Half a dozen fuckin' men wanna chew my ear off, but I'm done. Whisper something in my ear."

I blink in surprise, but he nods and bends his head toward me as if I asked him for his attention. I feel the eyes of those around us fixated on me. My cheeks heat. I lean in and whisper in his ear, "I have no idea what to say."

He smiles and nods, then leans in to whisper back, "You did perfect, babe."

It's too much. All of it, too much. His flirtation, the elaborate display of wealth, the promise of an inheritance and his undying protection. A place to live, the fear of what that means, and the knowledge that the choice to marry Romeo's irrevocable.

In the far corner of the room I see a man dressed in clerical black. He's young, wears wire-rimmed glasses, and he's eying me curiously.

Romeo said he called a priest...

What does he know? Would he extricate me if I asked him?

Is there anyone who wields power over this family?

Romeo's obviously pretending whatever I said to him is urgent, as we've increased our pace. He takes the stairs two at a time, but he seems impatient with me walking in my clunky heels that I'd put back on, so halfway up, he swings me into his arms again.

I feel all tingly and excited, and a dull ache settles between my thighs.

I wonder what he'll do when he gets me upstairs. Will anyone come between the two of us?

I feel as if I've lived a full week this day, like every moment's lasted longer than the one before. I've experienced such a wide range of emotions, too, from fear to elation to arousal and terror. And the day isn't even over yet.

Romeo's phone rings. He sets me down to

answer it, sliding his phone to his ear and taking my hand in his other without missing a stride.

"Yeah?" He scowls. "What do you mean? I fucking told you to watch him." His lips thin, and I can feel the vibration of his anger just from holding his hand. "Fine. Do what you have to. Tell Tavi and Orlando too, and tomorrow, morning meeting. You, me, *office*." I don't know who he's talking to, but I would not want to be them right about now. His verbal lashing alone could flay me.

His father, maybe? He's gone. They lost him.

His thinned lips confirm my suspicion as, cursing under his breath, he pushes the heavy wooden door open for me. The Castle's so big even the sound of the door slamming's quickly muffled.

No one would hear me if I screamed. I tuck the heavy metal key into my bra, a reminder that I have a place to hide if I need to, safe from everyone but him.

What if I need to run from him?

"Stay right there. Do not move." This time, I don't dare to disobey. He opens his suit coat, slides a gun out of a holster, and cocks it. My heartbeat races while he sweeps his room, checking even the closets, the shower, and the ledge outside his window before he comes back to me.

With a sigh, he stalks over to a side table, grabs a hefty bottle, and sloshes a few fingers of whiskey into a glass.

I don't ask for any. Not sure I want another drink. Something tells me I want to be fully aware for what happens next.

I watch him and don't try to pretend I'm not raking him over from head to toe. If he's going to be my husband, I reason I have an excuse.

Moonlight from outside illuminates his features. Cold blue-gray eyes and high cheekbones, his full lips pressed together in anger.

He turns away from me and stares out the window to the ocean lapping on the shore.

"Romeo," I finally say, not liking the brooding silence between us. He doesn't turn to look at me but tips his head back and finishes the drink, then pours himself another. He's the most powerful man I've ever met in person. But now, for this one brief sliver of time, he looks... weary.

I make my way to an overstuffed chair and sink into it. It's soft and luxurious, and I could fall asleep right here. I kick off those stupid shoes, nearly sighing in relief when my feet sink into the cushy carpet. After a moment of watching him, I need to close the distance between us. I rise and walk to him wordlessly on bare feet. He doesn't speak. Doesn't move. Just stares out the window at the ocean below the window and occasionally takes another sip.

Without my heels, I only come to his shoulders. My whole body fits within his, as if he's been drawn around me. Gently, I lift my fingers to his shoulders. I don't know why. I've never touched a man like this before, and I'm not sure why I feel the need with him now. His shoulders tense beneath my fingers, the taut muscles making my own muscles ache in sympathy. Gently, I begin to knead. I can't reach as high as I'd like, but I do well enough. He sighs, and the slightest bit of tension eases from his shoulders.

He takes another sip.

"Your father?"

He nods. His voice is resigned when he talks to me, the tone husky. "Yeah. Thought Tavi was tracking him. Tavi assigned Santo to the job. Santo's car was attacked, he drove off the road." I gasp. "He's fine. Car's fucking totaled. Papa knew I was having him tagged, and he blew it off."

I nod. "Is he that unpredictable?"

He shakes his head. "Babe, you have no idea."

I don't speak for long minutes, just continue massaging his shoulders, then his back, until his body begins to sag under my touch.

"You'll find him. He hasn't gone far."

"How do you know that?"

"The man's name means *narcissist*. He's the Don. Here, he gets all the attention he wants. Of course he'll be back."

He seems to be processing this, for he doesn't respond at first, but finally turns to face me.

"Thank you."

I don't ask him for what. I only nod and swallow, because the predatory look in his eyes scares me. His eyes darken when he brings the glass to my lips.

"Sip, *bella*. I want to watch you swallow."

Holding his gaze, I obey. I part my lips, and he tips the glass up to them. The whiskey's warm and potent, burning my nostrils and tongue, but the sweet undertones make my tastebuds sing. It's delicious but powerful, like a liquid spell. His eyes on my throat make my pulse quicken. He watches, mesmerized.

His hoarse whisper fractures the silence. "What dress did I tell you to wear tonight, Vittoria?"

Shit. I almost forgot about that. I lift my chin and stare at him defiantly.

I begin to tremble as I remember his earlier admonition.

If you come downstairs tonight in anything but what I ask for, I'll punish you.

I hold his gaze so he doesn't think I'm wimping out. I don't want him to know he terrifies me.

"You said to wear the blue one, but I didn't like the blue one."

It's a lie. I love the blue one.

His eyes glow as if lit with a savage flame. "Did I ask you if you liked it?"

Every word feels like the flick of a whip. I flinch as if struck. I shake my head from side to side. "Well, no, but I…"

"But you what?" The icy tone sends a shiver down my spine. "You thought it smart to disobey me?"

Disobey.

It feels like an almost archaic word, like he's the king of this castle and I'm one of his servants.

Maybe he is.

Maybe I am.

I swallow and try to gather up my courage. I'll need it. "Yes. I did. You don't have the right to tell me what to do."

One of his brows quirks up.

Right thing to say? Or wrong thing to say?

"Who told you that?"

My mouth feels dry, my lips parched. "I did."

His phone buzzes. He takes it out of his pocket and hits a button. "I'm busy."

He listens for a minute, then nods. "Spread the word. No one call me unless it's an emergency, and I mean like the motherfuckin' zombie apocalypse."

He silences his phone and slips it onto the sideboard next to the squat bottle of whiskey, his eyes on me the entire time.

"Take off that fuckin' dress."

I've made it this far without dying. I can go a little further.

Biting my lip, I slide it off my shoulder, but find I can't reach the zipper. I try, but my arm's too short. This is a two-person job. In the distance, the waves crash on the shore, but it's the only sound I hear. His room must be soundproofed, or far enough away from everyone and everything that no noise can be heard.

That means no one will hear me, either.

I shiver.

"You can't get the dress off, can you?" I thought his voice was deep before, but now it seems like he gargles with gravel, every word laced with a threat. I stifle a flinch.

"Marialena helped me put it on."

He grabs me roughly and yanks me to him. I jump when he slides a knife out of his pocket and flicks it open. A gleaming silver blade glints in the moonlight. My pulse soars.

"Romeo…"

He reaches for me, pins me to his chest, and slices the thin fabric at my shoulder. The dress slouches down one side. "That's *sir* to you."

He holds me against him with chilling ease, one arm flexed over me while he makes ribbons of the dress with his knife.

Slash.

Slash.

Slash.

I gasp and blink with every slice of the blade, expecting the nick of the knife at any minute, but he never touches me. It's so sharp, even the thickest straps of the dress disintegrate as the blade cleaves through them. The fabric, still warm from my body, pools at my feet like discarded lingerie.

"I don't like defiance."

"I think you do."

The glint in his eyes smacks of danger. I see, for the first time, how he's nearly risen to the status of Don. I've seen the way the men downstairs defer to him, how they grant him respect tinged with fear. I've seen the way he commands, with confidence and skill, how every servant does his bidding. He's as comfortable in his role as leader as a duck is in water, a natural.

Defiance doesn't go well with him.

"You don't fear me yet, *bella mia,* do you?"

It isn't true. I'm fucking terrified. My mouth's so dry I can't respond.

His lips pursed, he reaches for my hair and grasps it between his fingers. I gasp when he tugs my head back. "I asked you a question."

"You scare me," I whisper. "You definitely scare me."

"Then tell me. If I scare you, why did you choose to disobey me?"

I don't know. I try to shake my head, but moving too quickly brings sparking pain to my scalp, and something tells me we've only just begun.

"I… I don't know," I tell him truthfully.

Everything he's said thus far seems almost like a taunt, a push and pull, a sort of dance with his dominance and my reluctant submission. But now when he speaks, I feel the sincerity of his words down to my toes.

"You belong to me, Vittoria DeSanto," he says, the slightest edge of an accent coloring his words. "And if you belong to me, it is up to me to protect you. It is up to me to ensure your safety and wellbeing." He drags me closer to him so I can see his perfectly straight white teeth, the downward slope of his lips. "Obedience isn't optional. If you don't do what I demand, I cannot protect you. If I have to even question your compliance, I can't protect you. If I think even for a moment that you're undermining me, you cannot wear my ring." He tugs my head again, the pain unbearable. Tears prick my eyes. "Do you understand me?"

Maybe this wasn't a joke. Maybe he's deadly serious. He might get off on this, but it doesn't detract from his sincerity.

I try to nod but can't with my hair in his grip. "Yes," I whisper. "I get it."

"Do you, Vittoria?"

"I do."

He brings his mouth to my ear, the deep rasp tickling me. "Go to the bed." I hold my breath with his commands, the visual of what he's asking me to do bringing a flush of heat to my cheeks. "Lie on your back. Feet flat on the mattress. Knees in the air. Lace your fingers behind your head and stay in that exact position."

I shiver, and I don't know why. I've never done this with anyone else before. I... don't even know what *this* is, but I know this is no missionary sex we're about to have. I've walked straight into the punishment zone, and what happens next is up to him. I've made my choice. I know that now.

He makes store-bought handcuffs and hot pink floggers look like child's play. This... *this* is where real control comes in. My first taste of real dominance.

Earlier I thought about leaving. I thought about escaping and getting the fuck out of Dodge because of who he is and what his family stands for. But now... now that we're on the cusp of something I've never experienced before, I'm compelled. I've never been so scared in my life, but I wouldn't leave now if the door was wide open.

I need to see. I need to know.

So I obey. Like a lamb led to slaughter, I obey.

My knees shake as he watches me climb onto the bed and position myself as he tells me. Back down.

My feet on either side of me. This position was intentional, as my knees fall open and expose... everything. And with his eyes on me, I lace my fingers behind my head like he told me, shaking.

He eyes me hungrily as he reaches for his tie. I watch his large, strong fingers nimbly unfasten it, then tug. The silky black fabric slides off his neck, and he wraps it into a ball before he places it on the side table next to his drink.

Next, the suit coat. It's so large it'd be a tent on me, but he takes it off with effortless ease and hangs it on a chair, never breaking eye contact with me. The waves crash on the shore behind him, and my breathing becomes labored. The heat of his stare roves down my body, nestling between my thighs.

"You're gorgeous, Vittoria. A fucking master-piece." I shiver. "Are you cold?"

I shake my head.

"Nervous?"

"A little."

Lie. I'm frozen in fear.

My eyes are riveted on his fingers once more, now unfastening his cuff. He rolls up his sleeve. I stare at the tanned skin, stark against the snow-white shirt, dotted with dark hair, his veins visible. On the underside of his left arm, I see ink. A rose? I want to see it, all of it.

Then, the second sleeve follows the first. I let my eyes rove over him. The crisp white shirt lies flat against his belly, his pants slung low on his hips. I haven't seen him naked yet, but hell do I want to. I can feel the power of his harnessed strength even from here, and I've witnessed how strong he is. He can pick me up without getting winded, do the stairs two at a time.

His fingers, thick and rough, nestle on his hips, as he takes in all of me.

I'm slightly embarrassed because it's been damn hard getting a good shave in with my current nonexistent living conditions. I got a one-day-only pass to a local gym recently and took full advantage of their facilities, but I only had a cheap drugstore razor.

With a scowl, he pours another glass of whiskey, grabs his folded tie, then walks over to me.

I'm vulnerable and at his mercy as he walks to me with whiskey and tie in hand. I don't know why it feels so erotic, everything from the smell of the liquor and his cologne to the scent of my own arousal, musky and sweet. I've been naked in front of guys before. Hell, I was engaged to be married. But this time, I feel stripped of a lot more than my clothes. I feel naked in a way I never have. I'm vulnerable. Completely at his mercy.

The whiskey glass clinks as he sets it on the bedside table, and I jump.

"If you're so skittish, you shouldn't have disobeyed me," he says matter-of-factly. "You got a spanking earlier, but it seems you didn't remember that?"

My voice is hoarse. "I remember."

"Oh?" he asks, unraveling the wound tie. "Fascinating." The words hang in the air like the ticking of a clock in a noiseless room.

Tick.

Tock.

When he leans over me, his scent grows stronger. My mouth waters. I want to touch him. Taste him. The silky tie tightens around my wrists. I gasp when I realize he's bound them together and tied them to the headboard. Not sure what I thought he was doing with that tie, but I don't have a lot of experience with this sort of thing.

Something tells me that's not gonna last.

I gasp when something cool hits my shoulder. I look down to see droplets of whiskey on my naked skin. He braces himself on either side of me, bends his mouth to my shoulder and laps at the little beads, the carnal feel of his tongue on my naked skin making me shiver in anticipation.

I watch as he dips his finger in the liquor and flicks it across my breasts, like little liquid freckles. My wrists strain against the bonds as he licks each one, the flat of his tongue dragging across my skin like an erotic massage. I swallow, my mouth dry, when he dips his finger in his whiskey and paints it across my lips.

"I'd have a smoke," he says with that raspy, guttural tone, "but I want you to kiss me."

Even now, when he holds full control and power over me, when he could hurt me so easily it's comical, he gives me this. This one taste of autonomy.

His hands on either side of me, he braces himself above me. I briefly wonder what strength he needs to hold himself like that over me. "Kiss me, Vittoria."

He bends his mouth to mine. My eyes flutter closed. With my wrists tied above me and my body splayed out before him, every sense is heightened and aware.

I need him. Oh, God, I want him so badly I nearly cry.

I lift my head as far as I can go, and I kiss him.

The rough feel of his lips mingles with the fiery whiskey. I lick his tongue, inhaling his masculine groan. If my wrists weren't bound, my fingers would be buried in his hair and my legs wrapped around his body. As it is, my body pulses with desire, every breath and heartbeat making my core ache with need. I want him. All of him. And he's barely touched me.

Too soon, he pulls away. "You kiss like a fucking goddess," he growls in my ear. "Fucking *goddess.*"

"Thank you." I feel shy and a little flattered.

Kneeling beside me, he drags his fingers down my thighs, one knuckle gliding over my sex. "Such a perfect little pussy you have."

"Thank you," I repeat, the flush returning to my cheeks. He says wicked, dirty things as if he's talking about the weather, and somehow the nonchalance of it all turns me on. Apparently there's nothing he could say that wouldn't flatter me right about now. I swallow hard.

"I want to shave you."

I blink, blood pounding in my ears. "What?"

"Shave you. I want to shave you."

I didn't notice him taking out his blade, the same

one that he used to shred my dress. He flicks it open. He isn't... there's no *way...*

"I'd make it good for you, sweetheart," he whispers. Instead, he raises it to my head and, with the gentlest flick of his wrist, he slices a tiny curl of hair. It falls to my breast, and he blows it away. My skin erupts into goosebumps. "Which means I can't do it tonight." He shakes his head sadly, as if he's disappointed.

"Why not?" I ask, even though I really don't know if I actually *want* him to *shave* me.

I watch as he sobers, the teasing glint in his eyes gone. His voice drops to a lower register, and he grabs my chin between his fingers. "Because tonight, you're being punished for your disobedience."

He pushes off the bed and walks away, leaving me breathless and trembling. Earlier today, he dragged me over his knee for a spanking. What devilry does he have in mind now?

———

CHAPTER SIXTEEN

"Wisely and slow; they stumble that run fast." Romeo and Juliet

VITTORIA

I LOSE track of how many times he kisses me, his teeth grazing my skin as often as his lips, until my flesh feels fevered and chafed. Bracing himself on either side of me, he blows out a warm breath, and my nipples stand at attention.

He told me he'd punish me. He wasn't lying. The throb of need with no relief in sight, heavy between my thighs, is all I can think about.

We share one shot after another, as he drips the whiskey on my tongue with the pad of his finger. I lick and suckle. He paints the whiskey on my lips and suckles it off. My head feels lighter, my mouth dry. And still, I crave more.

When he dips his mouth to my thigh, my hips jerk.

"Ah, *bella mia,*" he says with a shake of his head. "I'll never reward your disobedience."

This whole time, I didn't really know how he meant to punish me. The spanking over his lap earlier seemed like a good starting place, but maybe he knows a part of me liked that. But when his tongue parts the seam of my pussy, realization dawns on me with blinding clarity.

"Romeo," I plead, at the first swirl of his tongue on my clit. "Oh, fuck."

The slap to my thigh is instant and corrective, but sends a jolt of heat straight to my core. "Language."

I nod. He rewards my compliance with another swipe of his tongue. I scream when his teeth graze the tender flesh, only to ask forgiveness with another perfect lick. He holds my hips between his hands, his calloused palms rough on my naked skin, while he eats me out like a starving man who found manna in the desert. I close my eyes and moan.

I savor the erotic pulse of his tongue between my legs, his hot breath on my thighs as he lifts my hips higher. The first spasm of pleasure makes me jerk my hips. He drops me to the bed.

He wouldn't tease and not let me come, he *wouldn't.*

"Romeo…"

Nooo.

"Give me one good reason I should let you come."

"Because you're trying to convince me to marry you and maybe I want this more than I want money."

Desperate much?

Do I?

"But you're willful and defiant. I can't have a disobedient wife." I can't tell in the dim light if he's smiling or not.

He clucks his tongue as he pushes up from the bed. He knows what he's doing. If my wrists weren't bound, I'd finish what he started.

In a haze, I watch as he unfastens his belt, the clink of metal ominous in the quiet room. Is he going to fuck me, then? Take me right here, while I'm bound and panting and so wet I'm almost embarrassed?

But he doesn't reach for his fly. He removes his belt, tucks the buckle in his palm, and wraps it around his fist.

Uh oh.

Shaking his head, he walks around the bed. "If you think I'd let you come after you broke a direct command, we have some work to do."

I nod. Maybe agreeing with him now will get me what I need. "We do."

Do we? What am I agreeing to? Damn near anything to get his mouth back on me.

Without warning, he flicks his wrist and the tail of his belt snaps against my breast. I arch and gasp, and before I can recover, he lashes my right breast. My skin throbs. My pussy *aches.*

"But you've punished me," I whisper, already knowing that he hasn't punished me enough, not to his satisfaction.

"I've begun your punishment, yes."

Fuck.

I try another tactic. "Maybe you should just… put me over your lap again."

"You liked that."

Did I?

"It hurt!" Another whip of his belt makes me scream.

A casual shrug of his shoulder tells me he doesn't care. Tiny welts rise along my skin, but the pain quickly melds into heat. The thrumming need of my pussy only heightens.

"It should hurt." The harsh tone of his voice pulses between my thighs, pulsing in tune to the steady lash of his belt on my thighs, my hips, and across my breasts. My ass aches with the memory of another punishment.

"And what if I obey you?" I'm panting. If he breathes on my pussy, I'll come. Every ounce of blood in my body seems concentrated between my thighs.

"If you obey me, *bella*, I'll make you the happiest woman on Earth." It's an exaggeration, it has to be, and yet, maybe I believe him.

He doesn't even know me. How could he know how to make me happy? How does he know what I want?

Bending down, for one perfect moment, he presses his thumb between my thighs, and my hips rise. Heat throttles my ability to speak. I want him so badly it's painful.

He knows one thing I want, anyway.

He bends down, leaning against his forearm. Small beads of sweat dot his forehead. He hasn't put that much physical effort into whipping me, and he doesn't need to. I'm half his size, naked, and restrained. He's the king of the castle, fully dressed, and wielding a wicked leather belt along with a devilish tongue. *Gawd.*

"Okay, alright," I breathe, captivated by the power he holds, mesmerized by the promise of pleasure, greedy for so much more.

He walks over to me with a wicked glint in his eye. Is he going to take his, then? I let my eyes rove over the thick ridge in his pants. His lips are pressed into a tight, firm line, as if concerned that if he allows himself to speak, he's going to say something he regrets. The bed sags when he sits beside me.

I don't realize I'm crying until he brushes his thumb across my cheek. "If you don't like being punished, you'll remember to obey."

Is that why I'm crying? I want to claw my way out of my own skin.

He pulls my head back and bares his teeth. "You'll fucking obey."

I nod. I've seen what happens when I disobey. I wouldn't say I fear it, but a part of me wonders what it would be like to gain his pleasure, to please him. To obey him. Would it feel nice?

He tips me to the side and slams his palm against my ass so hard I scream. "Don't try me, Vittoria."

"Okay!" I nod. A part of this was playing, but he's not playing now. There's steel in his tone and undeniable authority in his eyes when he flips me onto my back again.

"Spread your legs." The rough tone of his voice makes my nipples harden, and my body quickly remembers where this was going, what it wants, how badly I want him. Heat and warmth pool between my legs. My knees part, granting him access.

I groan when he rubs his stubbled cheek along the damp inside of my thighs. He suckles the skin and releases it, over and over, leaving tiny pink circles on my inner thighs. My clit throbs. I want his tongue *there. Right there.*

One stroke of his tongue and I'm on the cusp of exploding.

"Will you obey me?"

I nod frantically, my fingers forming into fists with the frustration of not being able to touch him, to reach him, to stroke his hair between my fingers while he licks me. He grasps my breasts and strokes my nipples while he drags his tongue over my throbbing sex. His words are hot and insistent against my body.

"Will you take your punishment when you disobey?"

Again, a frantic nod. Yes, yes, I'll take my punishment in whatever sick version of dom and sub he wants to play, because *I need him.* I need him so badly I could cry.

"Tell me." He suckles my clit while he thrusts two fingers in me. "Tell me you're mine." He pumps. I close my eyes at the sensation. His voice becomes insistent, angry. "Tell me you'll marry me. Tell me no other man will ever touch what's mine, Vittoria." He pumps so hard, he sends spasms through my body. I whimper.

He's manipulating me, and I don't care. I might feel differently in the morning, when I'm sober and sane, but tonight, *I don't care.*

My mind races, trying to fuse logic to logic.

Romeo Rossi is the head of this family, and if I give him what he wants, he'll solidify that role. He thrives as leader, the natural order of things aligning with the universe.

I don't know him, and yet he wants me to marry him. Marriage in this family may be convenience, a box to check off. There's no love lost between any of them, I know this already.

Marriage to him means putting myself in danger, but I'm already there. I'm already under his father's watchful eye. I'm penniless because I was swindled, and it's because of me a man's dead.

I nod. "I'm yours." I don't know what it means. I don't know what he'll demand of me. But in my sex-addled mind, it's the only choice. "Yes. I'm yours."

"Good girl," he breathes, and with another stroke of his fingers on my clit, a delicious shudder warms my body, and the first spasm of ecstasy ripples through me. His touch is electric, and my response is so swift it's almost violent. I close my eyes against the power of my climax, swimming in euphoria.

I come so hard and so long I'm breathless, the muscles in my body tense. I fall to the bed as the aftershocks ripple through me. My breathing comes in gasps. I open my eyes, coming back to Earth.

Slowly, gently, he strokes his fingers through my hair, smoothing it off my forehead and neatly behind my back. I feel the weight of it as his finger traces my hairline.

"Tonight, we played. But your punishment was real." He reaches for the silk tie and unfastens my wrists. "I don't enjoy watching you come to the edge of pleasure like this and leaving you hanging."

I swallow, as he rubs the cinched part of my wrists to get the blood flowing again. "Don't you?"

He shakes his head. "I have almost everything I want, Vittoria. Almost. Wealth. Fame. Respect. Power." He leans in close to me. He bends and kisses my cheek. "All I need is you."

———

CHAPTER SEVENTEEN

"DID my heart love till now? forswear it, sight! For I ne'er saw true beauty till this night." Romeo and Juliet

Romeo

I've never slept with a woman in my bed. So that's another first.

Letting a woman get to me... that is a first, too.

I climb in beside Vittoria. She's already half asleep, her arm tossed over her head on the pillow. I never saw a woman come so hard. Fucking rewarding.

But I won't fuck her. Not tonight.

I lay beside her for hours while she sleeps, staring at the canopy above my bed that hides the ceiling that's so far up it fades into darkness. I have to think. Plan. Plot.

I'm used to not sleeping. My father's been Don in name only for a while now. As acting Don, the weight of the Family comes on my shoulders, so it's not unusual for me to be woken from sleep or to go to bed when the sun's beginning to rise. Tonight's no exception.

Narciso Rossi's been pushed over the edge. I don't trust him. And we still don't know why Vittoria's even here, why her name was in my grandfather's will to begin with.

Why her?

I finally strip off my clothes and curl up next to her. Dead asleep, she nestles closer. I inhale and hold her to me. I breathe in and out. So this is why people share a bed. I never knew. There's a comfort in having her here tucked in my arms, my breathing matching hers.

I'm turning everything over in my mind when I finally fall asleep.

I wake before my alarm to the insistent buzzing of my phone. I look over quickly to see Vittoria still fast asleep beside me.

On instinct, I check to see if she's breathing. Things that matter don't last in my world. I don't want to lose her. But she's breathing as softly as a sleeping baby.

I push myself out of bed and walk to the sitting area, phone in hand.

Orlando.

I answer the phone. "Yeah?" I whisper, still not wanting to wake her.

"Fuckin' problem, Rome."

"Spill."

Santo was run off the road last night, we know this, while my father went missing. "It's Mama."

Fuck.

My mother goes on drinking binges when my father takes another woman. One would think she'd be used to it by now. Fidelity isn't part of the Rossi family code. She isn't, though.

"What about her?"

"She's missing, Rome."

I stand up straighter. Mama doesn't even leave the house to get groceries. What few friends she has come here to The Castle to eat lunch with her. Papa doesn't like her traveling, so the only time she ever leaves the house is when she goes to Tuscany with him.

I look over at the bed to see Vittoria still asleep even through my conversation. I grab a faded pair of jeans from the back of the chair and tug them on. I rapidly get dressed with my phone tucked under my chin, listening while he fills me in.

She went to bed before anyone else did, Marialena saw her go up. Then this morning, Rosa went up with Natalia because Natalia wanted to see her Nonna. She was gone.

"Did she take anything?"

"Not that we noticed."

Fuck. My heart beats faster as I think about my father's desperation. Maybe he won't come after me. Maybe he'll off Mama so he can take another wife. Not unheard of in the circles we run in.

He wants a wife but doesn't want her. Divorce ain't an option.

I scowl at the bed where Vittoria still lies. If she were mine, I'd have the power to oust him. I could pull every made man this side of the ocean out of jobs to hunt him down and punish him for what he's done. I'd have the power to change anything.

Without that bond, my hands are tied.

We live in an ancient castle, still bound by ancient laws. Stupid *fucking* archaic laws.

I could make her. I fucking could, and I know it. I've threatened it. How much would she resent me?

I've given her every possible option I could think of, tantalized her with everything that could be hers.

But that's not what she needs. She doesn't want money or status or any of the riches I could promise her.

What does she want?

She needs time.

It's the one thing I can't give her.

Fuck.

I hang up the phone with a promise I'll be down. She stirs on the bed and looks over at me. A twinkle lights her beautiful eyes.

"They should put men in jeans and white T-shirts on the cover of men's magazines," she says as she tucks her hands under her chin.

"I'm not an expert, but I think they do."

"Oh," she says with a smile. "I should check them out." She sobers when I don't respond. "Something the matter?"

I tell her. She sits up straighter in bed. "Oh, God, Romeo. Would he hurt her?"

"If you have to ask that question, you really haven't fully grasped what he's capable of, Vittoria."

"Fu—" she catches my eye, about to curse. She swallows. "You should find her," she says with a sigh. "I want to go with you."

I shake my head firmly. "I don't want to take you into something dangerous. He could be baiting me."

"And maybe he's baiting you to leave so I'm here alone." Her eyes widen with panic, then she gasps when someone pounds on the door.

"Rome! Romeo, let me the fuck in."

Leo. I throw the covers up over Vittoria as I head for the door. He's still wearing last night's clothes.

"Where the fuck is she?" He looks like shit.

"Just woke up, how the fuck do I know? Where was her bodyguard?"

That's when I see him, hanging behind Leo in the shadow of the hallway. Leo jerks his head toward me.

"Come here," he growls. "Tell your fuckin' Don why his mother's missing."

Amadeo hangs his head. "Fell asleep, Boss. Think someone drugged my drink."

I clench my fists so I don't hit him. I'll deal with him in private. I don't want to scare Vittoria. I keep my tone tight, my voice calm. "You were fucking drinking when you were on the job?"

He winces and doesn't respond. I'll punish him, but not in front of her. If he wasn't so loyal to the Family, I'd kill him.

"You go with Tavi and Leo, and you scour the

fucking Earth until you find her. When she's safe, you come and tell me. You understand me?"

He nods. "Yessir."

Leo scowls and cuffs him on the back of the head, muttering about fucking millennials and how his generation knew their place. Bullshit they did. Probably makes him feel better, though.

I slam the door. Vittoria's awake, rubbing sleep from her eyes. If my mother wasn't missing, I'd have plans for that naked body of hers.

"So," she says, as if she's been thinking this over. "I'm guessing that your mother's bodyguard failed at his job?" She asks as if trying to understand the order of things around here. She needs to know. I'll tell her everything.

"He did."

"And does he... answer to you?"

I sigh, pulling on a leather jacket. No suit today. "Vittoria." Her eyes meet mine. *"Everyone* answers to me."

A slow smile spreads across her lips. "That's hot."

Fuck, I wish I had time with her. We'll get there.

"So what happens to him now?" She flinches as if she doesn't want to hear the answer. "Do you, like... kill him?"

Not gonna shield her. "I would, if this wasn't his first time failing at the job." I check my gun, not missing the way her eyes watch every move. I slide it into a holster. "I'll beat the fucking shit out of him, though." I flex my fingers, ready to give a goddamn beat down *now.*

When she doesn't respond, I look up at her. The

sun's risen, illuminating her skin, still pink but almost normal. Hardly shows any signs of our session the night before. "He can't do that, Vittoria."

"Oh, I know. It isn't that."

"Then what is it?"

A thoughtful look crosses her face. "It's convenient, isn't it? You want to marry me. I haven't married you yet. Your mom goes missing, and you're called away, when no one's secured your father yet..."

"Yeah." I sigh. I've already thought the same thing. What if he wants me away from her? But blood's thicker than water. I can't give up the hunt for my goddamn mother when the woman who isn't my wife needs me. "If we were married..."

"I know," she finishes quietly. "And I agreed last night."

I look at her wonderingly. I questioned if she'd change her mind when she woke, when she wasn't drunk on sex and adrenaline. She tosses her hair with a teasing look. "I don't go back on my word, Mr. Rossi. I've thought things through. And I have choices, but they're limited."

She's absolutely right.

"I don't have time," I say in a low voice, sitting on the edge of the bed. I pull her to me and drag her across my lap. I just want to touch her. To hold her. I just want to taste her one more time. Her warm body presses up against my clothed one.

"For what?" Her eyes meet mine with curiosity and something else. Excitement?

"To seal that promise. To make you mine. *Now*."

She nuzzles against me like a content little kitten.

"Do what you need to. Leave me with who you trust. Later, we finish this." She swallows hard. "Romeo, in my world we do things differently. We... take our time, I guess you would say." She sighs. "I'm seeing that you play by a very different set of rules in your world."

I nod. "You could say that."

"I'm learning."

I kiss her cheek. Maybe Vittoria could mean more to me than a crown, more to me than the power I want to wield. It's dangerous to fall in love, though. Men like me lose power and threaten everything when they do.

Maybe men like me lose even more when they don't.

I think of my father, the years of infidelity and the coldness between him and my mother. I think of raising children with a woman I don't love.

I'm someone who craves control. How much of this is really in my hands?

"I wish you could come with me," I mutter to myself. I hate the thought of leaving her here. But taking her with me's arguably worse. It's a dangerous fucking move, one I can't risk.

She gets dressed and comes downstairs with me, but my mind's a mile away. She mutters something under her breath.

"What was that?"

"Nothing."

Both of us are in our heads, a world apart from

each other, but trying to bridge that gap with everything we can.

I squeeze her hand as Tavi and Orlando march into the Great Hall, armed and ready to go.

Orlando interrupts. "Rome, we got a lead. Tavi played back the surveillance footage outside Mama's room, and two armed men entered her room around four this morning."

I don't have time to talk to Vittoria anymore. I give her a meaningful look. "We'll talk later."

She only nods.

Loud, raucous barks sound the alarm before anyone else does. My dogs, trained to attack. Vittoria screams as the largest window to the Great Hall shatters into fragments. They're back. I fucking knew it.

"Get down!"

It all happens in a matter of seconds. Shattered glass and high-pitched screams, just before the deafening gunshots.

"*Cazzo!*"

My whole body's over Vittoria's, covering her, while my men spring into action. Leo's on a fucking table. Frantic over the loss of my mother, he doesn't care about the spray of bullets, doesn't even fucking flinch when he's struck.

I look next to see if my sisters are secured, my instincts honed. Gunshots from the east, armored car. Guards outside responded on cue; it had bulletproof glass, but one threw himself bodily to block it. Rosa... Rosa's sprawled under the weight of Mario's arm, her cheek to the floor. Mario's eyes meet mine across the room. I jerk my chin at him.

"Marialena?"

"Jesus fucking Christ," Tavi mutters. I look to where he is. Marialena, feet spread apart, with a fucking *Ruger* in hand. Where'd she get that piece?

"Get her the fuck *down*," I growl to Orlando, who's closest to her, but he doesn't respond.

"Jesus." Tavi's eyes widen in fear. His voice chokes out, "He's hit, Rome."

My blood runs cold as Orlando slumps to the floor.

Santo. Where's Santo?

Our guards got the assailants. The floor of the Great Hall's littered with blood and broken glass, fragments of mugs and scattered pastries. I check on Vittoria.

"You alright?"

She nods shakily. My heartbeat slows, but only for a second.

We don't have Santo, and Orlando's shot.

I get to my feet to survey the damage and call out instructions.

"Tavi, call the doctor. Leo, secure the hostages. Mario, find Santo." I kneel beside Orlando and grab his wrist, my heartbeat hammering until I find a steady pulse. Can't tell where he's hit, looks like more than one place. I whip off my T-shirt and wrap it around his arm, trying to slow the heavy bleeding.

"Stay with me, Orlando." Blood will run like a fucking river for this. I don't know who it is, but we'll know the answer in minutes, and why they came. I've got a list of enemies a mile long. My father might be deranged, a fucking lunatic, but he wouldn't do this, I know he wouldn't.

But he'd cause a diversion, and my mother's gone.

And that's when it hits me. She isn't here. She didn't get shot because she isn't here.

And my father wasn't here the first time we were attacked.

Footsteps pound outside the Great Hall. Doctor Cho, an older man near retirement, and his assistant Lewellyn run in, bags in hand. He falls to his knees beside Orlando and takes his pulse.

"Low pulse, lost lots of blood." The doctor frowns. "We'll have to get him to a hospital. We don't have what we need here, sir."

I nod. "I don't fucking care what you have to do, you save his life."

Doctor Cho only nods. "You know I'll do everything I can, Mr. Rossi."

"Rome!" Marialena stands in the doorway, her gun still in hand.

"And you," I begin, shaking my head. "When the fuck did you learn to shoot? Who gave you permission to fucking *carry*?"

She bites her lip but doesn't respond. I stifle a growl. I feel as if I've lost control of fucking *everything,* but if I don't keep my temper, I'm as bad as my father. He ruled with iron fists and rage. I'll rule better than that.

Mario stands, holding his phone to his ear.

Rosa's with Marialena by Orlando's side. Marialena kneels beside him and places her hand on his head.

"He'll be okay," Doctor Cho says. "He will, I promise."

She angrily swipes at her tears. Rosa's eyes are dry, her lips pressed together. She's seen this and worse, and isn't one to cry when the shit hits the fan.

Leo enters the Great Hall with a blood-soaked fabric napkin held to his shoulder. "Goddamn motherfucking Castellanos, would've bet my nuts on it," he says, gritting his teeth through the pain.

"You got 'em?"

"You bet your fuckin' dick I got 'em."

"Dungeon?"

Leo rolls his eyes and shakes his head. "No, I took 'em to a fuckin' *tea party* first."

"You better watch your goddamn mouth," I say on a growl. "The only reason I don't knock you on your ass is because you're already hurt." I shove him anyway. "Consider yourself warned, brother."

He stumbles a little and winces when he hits his arm, but there's pride in his tone when he says, "Jesus, you'll make a good fuckin' boss."

My phone rings. Mario. I didn't even realize he had left the room. "Yeah?"

"Got Mama, brother. You're not gonna believe this, but I'll fill you in later."

"Good." At this point, there's nothing I won't believe. "I'm sending the girls to you. Keep her and them secured in the war room." My mind's racing with all the pieces of the puzzle that connect, with all that has to happen next, when Leo smacks my arm, hard. Jesus, I'm gonna beat his ass.

"Mama's secured," I tell him. His eyes light up in relief. He's loved her like a sister even when my father hated her. He nods.

"You gonna marry that girl or what? Get this fucking family back on its feet."

Sure as fuck I'm gonna marry her.

I reach for Vittoria. Ready to take her to the chapel right here, right now.

My fingers hit air. I turn to find her.

She's gone.

———

CHAPTER EIGHTEEN

"MERCY BUT MURDERS, pardoning those that kill." Romeo and Juliet

Vittoria

I OPEN my eyes and blink, rubbing my hand along my head.

"You okay?" It's a voice that sounds like Romeo's but... different. Where am I? The last thing I remember, I was shoved to the floor when there was an attack, only this one was way more violent and deadly than the first. Bloodshed, broken glass, and Romeo's rough body over mine...

I don't recognize where I am, but these grounds are huge. With so many rooms and tunnels, I could be anywhere.

There's a man next to me and I can't see his face. "Who's there?"

"Cut the fucking small talk." I hear the sound of a match being struck, then Narciso Rossi's face lights up behind a cigar. Fear strikes my heart. Romeo said he'd kill me.

I look quickly to my left.

"Santo?"

His jaw is set, his hands in fists.

"Believe me when I tell you this is not my choice, Vittoria." He shakes his head. "But I will be good to you."

What?

I'm on a carpet with someone's folded blanket underneath me, in a part of The Castle I haven't seen before, with the lingering scent of something ancient and sacred. Every one of the windows lights up in stained glass with Biblical images. Jesus, kneeling under the weight of a cross, a crowd of angels gathered by a manger, Moses's tablets of commandments.

Incense? I'm in a chapel. Why have I never gone to the chapel before, and what is Santo talking about?

Narciso stands by an altar beside someone else dressed in black. He lights a candle.

"No lights," he orders. I wonder if he thinks they'd find us if there were lights in here. Makes sense. Wherever we are, they'd find us if there were lights.

I look down at my hands when I realize I can't move freely. I'm bound by the wrists and around the ankles. I try to piece this all together. During the commotion of the shoot-out, someone must've knocked me out and taken me. They must have distracted Romeo, too, because I can't believe that he would've let me be taken like this.

"He won't let you get away with this," I say to Narciso.

"As if he has a say? Shut up." I see the manic anger in his eyes, and know he's been plotting this. He never wanted Romeo to get the power to begin with. He knows that he will be fair, and that he wouldn't let Narciso use his bullying tactics. He knows that Romeo won't stand for this.

Narciso grabs a man beside him by the scruff of the neck and pushes him into a semi-circle of dim light near the candle. I blink in surprise. It's the priest from the other night. And then it dawns on me with such force I gasp. He's brought us here so that he can force us to marry.

The priest shakes his head. "This is contrary to God's law. Marriage must be a mutual agreement. It nullifies the actual commitment of the couple if—"

Narciso shakes his head and draws a gun. Cocking it, he puts it to the priest's head.

"Do it."

I'm shaking as Santo takes me by the arm and drags me to the front of the chapel. I'm still bound, so I stumble. He quickly draws a blade. I flinch, preparing for pain on instinct, but he only bends and slices the rope at my ankles.

"Stupid girl," he growls. "I told you I wouldn't hurt you." The angry grip on my arm says otherwise.

I whimper, unsure of what will happen next, my

mind racing with possibilities. I can't see where we're located or what we're next to, with the light so dim.

"What will this accomplish?" I say, my voice shaking. "What are you trying to prove? You won't get away with this. And you know that your family wins if I marry any of them, but Santo isn't one of the brothers."

Santo flinches as if I struck him, and the grip on my arm tightens. "No one asked you for your input."

"Isn't that the problem? No one asked me for anything. I didn't ask to come here. I didn't ask for an inheritance or anything that belongs to any of you. I don't know why I'm the bad guy in this situation."

Narciso glares, his eyes so narrowed I can barely see the pupils. "You didn't do this? Fucking liar. You have no money. You have no friends. You have nothing but what we've given you, and you expect me to believe that you had nothing to do with this? I know who your father was, and I knew your grandfather."

He did?

"Marry them," Narciso growls, his gun pointed at the priest's temple. The priest's hands shake as he opens his prayer book. Santo holds his head high and grips me firmly.

"The abbreviated version, Father."

The priest fumbles over words. One eye's swollen shut, his lip bleeding. Someone roughed him up and made him come here, made him do this. I'm sick to my stomach.

Romeo… where's Romeo? I hated the thought of marrying him, but now the thought of being married to anyone else…

"I won't agree." My voice sounds high and thin in the stone-walled chapel. "Do what you want to me, but we aren't married unless I take those vows, and I will not."

I have to stall. If I can stall, I can get out of here…

Santo shakes his head and winces. "Don't do this, Vittoria," he warns. "I promise, I'll treat you well. I'll treat you like a queen. But I can't stop him…"

The priest plows on as if no one's talking, uttering words that are meant to bind a man and woman together. I look around me frantically, at the flickering candles and brilliant windows, the beautiful, dim interior of the chapel filled with hard wooden benches and memories. I feel as if I've been yanked from the modern world into a time warp, where my rights no longer matter and the word of a monarch rules all.

Narciso shouldn't be that monarch any longer. It's time to knock him from his throne and bring justice to this family. It's time for Romeo to become my husband and me his wife. It's time for me to take the Rossi name and begin a new era.

"I won't," I shout, stomping my foot. Santo grips me harder.

"No, Vittoria," he says. "Don't. You don't know what you're saying. You don't know what you're doing…"

"I will not marry you!" I scream, as the priest's words drone on and Narciso screams in fury, our voices and shouts melding into one horrifying rant. Santo grabs my shoulders and shakes me until my teeth rattle, but when Narciso starts toward me, Santo shoves me behind him, blocking Narciso's blow. He strikes Santo across the cheek, the sound of the wicked slap making me ill.

Narciso shoves Santo to get to me, but Santo stands his ground.

The sound of a woman's voice at the back of the chapel halts him in his tracks.

"No!"

He peers into the darkness. Whoever it is walks slowly, with a heavy sigh I feel in my bones, weary and tired.

"Show your face!" Narciso yells.

"Mia donna, stai zitto." Nonna steps into the light. She folds her arms across her chest. "You. Traitor," she says, matching Narciso's fury. "My husband had wishes. You!"

She wags her finger at him.

"You fault my Romeo go to jail! You fault my husband dead."

"Santo, silence her," he growls. Santo looks to her then me. If he reaches for her, he has to let me go and my legs are no longer bound. Narciso's enraged, unaware of the two choices Santo has. My eyes dart around the room, looking for an escape, when Nonna looks me in the eye.

"Vino, Vittoria." Her eyes dart to the corner of the room, to a door I hadn't seen before.

Vino. Wine. It takes me a second to realize what she means, but when I do, my heart races.

"Now, Santo!" Narciso booms, clearly more intent on hurting Nonna than he is in securing me.

Santo reaches for her, letting me go. I duck in case Narciso tries to get me, and I run.

I hear Narciso's furious scream, a muffled thump, and the deafening shot of a gun. Nothing hits me. I reach for the door, yank it open, and fall.

———

CHAPTER NINETEEN

"AY ME! SAD HOURS SEEM LONG." ~*Romeo and Juliet*

ROMEO

"WHERE IS SHE?" Marialena and Rosa scour The Castle with Tavi and Orlando, but something in my gut tells me she isn't here. *God.*

God!

How could I have let her get taken away? I know my father was behind the attack, and I suspect I know why, but how he managed to pull her straight out from under me... I'm frantic with the need to find her, to secure her. I know he'll hurt her.

But not if I kill him first.

I'll forfeit my throne if I do. It's the most founda- tional principle of our brotherhood, the Rossi Family's unalterable rule: the Underboss can't hurt the Boss. If we allowed that, men could off their bosses to usurp a position of leadership.

But if he had anything to do with this attack, if he created a diversion by attacking his very own family, we'll make an exception. We'll have to. He's gone insane, and lost whatever power his position gives him.

I have to find Vittoria. I have to keep her safe. Fire burns in my gut, fueling the need to find her, to make this right. She came into my life for a reason, and I'm going to make her my wife.

I scour the grounds with my brothers and sisters, looking in every room and hidden tunnel, behind every goddamn door and tapestry. The Castle was designed to hide things, a clever maze within its walls. But as we search, I become more and more frantic. She's not here.

Marialena screams. "Romeo. Romeo! There's a fire in the chapel! Look, Romeo!"

I look out the window of the Great Hall, where I can see just a glimpse of the chapel at the edge of our property. Flames erupt toward the heavens, igniting the night sky.

"Vittoria," I say in a hoarse whisper, fear choking me. I run toward the door that will take me to the chapel, my brothers following at my heels. Sparks fly into the air, the smell of smoke and burning wood thick.

Tavi, faster than all of us, gets there first. "It's locked!" He pounds on it with his fist, then leaps back to assess the windows. Some already cracked and broken. It feels like a symbol of my family's demise, the ancient chapel that connected us to the only chance of redemption falling to ruins.

"Windows are too small," I shout above the roaring sound of the fire. None of us would fit through them. Tavi barrels toward the door behind me, his face set, and when he reaches the door, he puts his whole body through it. If it were any bigger, like the ornate doors of our chapel in Tuscany, he couldn't have done it. But these doors are small, imported from Italy decades ago. They splinter under his weight.

Tavi leaps into the fire-filled chapel.

"She ain't here, Rome!" he screams over his shoulder. He knows why I'm here. She isn't there. The heavens open as rain falls from above, blinding my vision and making the flames of the chapel momentarily flicker before they resume their deadly consumption.

Santo's strapped to the altar, screaming as flames engulf him.

"No!" Tavi screams. "*No!*"

He launches himself bodily at Santo, and smothers him to put the flames out. When I reach them, Santo's screaming, but the flames are dying down, the smell of burnt wood and incense mingling with the smell of burnt human flesh.

"Oh, God. He did this to them."

"Get the doctor, Tavi, *now.*"

"Where is he?" I thunder at Santo. "*Where is he!*"

Santo nods toward the back of the chapel where my Nonna lies, unconscious, a gun only inches from her fingers, and my father lies, bleeding out onto the burgundy carpet runner. His eyes are half-open, blood pooling in the corner of his mouth.

I fall to my knees to escape the noxious fumes.

Where's Vittoria?

"Get them out," I order my brothers. "Get them out of here."

I reach for Santo and drag him toward the exit. He moans, unconscious but fucking alive. I leave him on the front step to the chapel, when it dawns on me.

The chapel, at the furthest end of our property, is connected to the outermost portion of The Castle.

I told her where to go. I told her where to go when she was in trouble, and if she listened to me… if she could get there safely… I know where she is.

"Secure them," I tell Tavi. I look back to the house. Mario's got my sisters and Leo's watching over my mother. It's my job to find Vittoria.

Tavi looks down at Santo, unconscious but alive. I'll take him to the doctor before I fucking interrogate his ass.

Santo. Why do I know in my gut that Santo's behind this? I trusted him. I trusted him as I trust all men of the Rossi brotherhood.

I make sure no one's following me and run for the wine cellar.

Sirens sound, fire engines coming to put out the fire. I don't know who called them, but I don't care. There's only one thing I care about now.

I run down the hallway behind the dining room, past the library and kitchen, past the war room until I get to the secret passage to the wine cellar. My hands shake with nerves as I slip the key into the lock and twist.

The door falls open in the silence, an audible click the only sound.

"Vittoria?"

Nothing but silence. My gut was wrong. She isn't here. Why did I think it would be that simple?

I throw the door all the way open and descend into the wine cellar. It's dark and dank in here, but no one was able to enter except for me.

I don't have my phone or a light, but we keep candles nearby in every room for emergencies, hearkening back to when The Castle was built. I grab the candle from a wall mount and strike a match, illuminating the interior of the windowless room.

"Vittoria?"

Nothing. No one's here. With a sinking feeling in my stomach, I turn to go. She's gone, and I have no idea where to, or how she'll ever get back.

I take one last look around the room and see nothing. But she has to be here. She isn't in the chapel, and she isn't in the house. No vehicles left our property after the attack. She's here. She's somewhere in the hidden recesses of The Castle.

I'm not a praying man and accepted years ago there was no redemption for a man like me, but seeing the chapel consumed in flames and the desperation clawing at my flesh makes me beg for something beyond my own reasoning. "Please," I say, to who or what I don't know. I want a chance to make things right. I want a chance to put this family back where it should be, and marrying Vittoria is step one. *"Please."*

I move the candle from left to right in a final sweep. Something catches my eye. I start, shocked at what I see, a flash of white skin illuminated by the candlelight.

Vittoria's on the floor, sprawled out with her arms askew.

Oh, God. I'll kill whoever hurt her, *kill them.*

When I reach her, she's covered in dust and blood, her hair's disheveled and in her eyes, but I've never seen anything more beautiful in my life.

"Vittoria." I lift her in my arms, and she stirs. She's alive. She's alright, and she's alive.

I kiss her cheeks and pull her to me as voices sound above us. I don't care. I don't care what the fuck happens to anyone else, Vittoria is my only concern.

I close my eyes when I hold her to me. This is the danger of falling in love with a woman. I've taken the vow of Omertà, the vow that will bind me to loyalty from my brothers above all. Sworn in blood to a code of honor, loyalty, and silence, I've vowed to put my family above anyone. But this woman… this woman will undo me.

Vittoria opens her mouth. "Romeo."

She's okay. Oh, God, she's alright.

"How did you get in here?"

She shakes her head. "There was a passage… in the chapel… like a slide almost, some sort of chute. I fell down and hit my head at the bottom, but here I am."

She pushes herself up suddenly. "Romeo! Your Nonna and Santo. He'll kill them!"

I don't need to ask who "he" is.

I want to know what she knows, how conscious she is. "Where are they?"

"The chapel."

"We're taking care of it, baby."

Here in the cocoon of this windowless room, I hold her to me. Here, in the silent recesses of the place I call home, I make a vow.

Too long I've been silent against my father's tyranny. Too long, I've been silent while my father's dictatorship destroyed my family. Too long, I've allowed devastation to rip us apart.

I lift her in my arms and head for the stairs, as she wraps her arms around my neck and fills me in. Her voice is hoarse, affected by smoke and trauma, but it's beautiful to my ears.

"You were all distracted with the attack. I bet you anything your father did this. He wasn't here during the first attack, was he? He wasn't here during the second attack, either."

"Great minds think alike," I say with a wry smile.

"Though fools seldom differ," she finishes. "The entirety of that proverb will keep you humble, sir."

Jesus, I love this woman.

She winces in pain when we reach the doorway. "Shh, baby. We'll find out everything. Don't hurt yourself worse."

"He tried to make me marry Santo!"

What?

Rage storms across my chest.

"The priest started saying the prayers. He beat up the *priest,* Romeo, to coerce him into performing the marriage. What kind of a monster is he?"

The kind that will hunt down anything between him and what he wants.

When we reach the landing, I see the Great Hall's nearly vacant. The front door to The Castle is wide open, my men outside and surrounding the chapel that's engulfed in flames, but the rescue team's arrived. I talk quickly to Leo. Mario's held off law enforcement, allowing only the firefighters in.

"Oh my God, Romeo," Vittoria whispers. "He'd do anything to get what he wanted, wouldn't he?"

"Romeo! *Rome!*" Rosa's frantic voice rises over everyone's. "Help him, Romeo! He'll kill him."

I look to where she points. Tavi's got my father in his grip, a knife to his throat. Tavi could kill him with one twist of his arm, but it's a mortal sin to harm the Boss. He'd die first. My father's come to with a last roar of vengeance, swearing to kill whoever's in his path.

I nod to Tavi. "Ottavio. You have my permission."

I don't miss the flash of pain on his face before he spins, and with a roar of anguish and hatred, knocks our father on his ass. In seconds, he's got him pinned under his knee.

"You win," my father says in a hoarse whisper. "You son of a bitch. You win."

"It was never a competition," I snarl. "You want me to win? I win when we bury you." I want to end it for him, take that gun from the ground and point it at his head. I want to pull the trigger and watch the light go out of his eyes. I want to send him straight from this chapel to hell, where he belongs.

Vittoria's hand is on my arm, holding me back. I try to shrug her off, but she holds fast.

"Don't do it, Romeo. You have every right, but you don't have to. Don't do it."

If I kill him, I lose everything.

"Let him bleed, brother." Tavi stands beside me, a look of disdain on his face while he stares at my father. "He'll bleed out within the hour."

My father screams and fumes and writhes in pain as his blood seeps out of him, while Tavi and I watch. Smoke billows around us.

Vittoria turns away and kneels beside Nonna. She takes her pulse. "She's okay," she whispers. "She'll need a doctor, but I think she's only fainted."

"She shot me," my father says. "Shot me."

"Rome." Mario enters with Father Richard hanging onto him. He's bloodied and bruised and obviously on the verge of passing out. "I'll tell you everything."

We drag my father out to the concrete pavement, away from the eyes of first responders who will try to save him. No one will be allowed to save him now.

———

CHAPTER TWENTY

"BUT SOFT, what light through yonder window breaks? It is the East, and Juliet is the sun." — Romeo

VITTORIA

"I DON'T WANT to see a doctor."

Romeo stands in front of the fireplace, giving me a look that would've had me quaking even a week ago. Now, however, I stand my ground.

"All I've done is what other people tell me to do."

His jaw is set, and his eyes dare me to disobey him. "I don't care if you're injured, *bella.* I will take you across my knee right here, right now, privacy be damned, and after I redden your ass, you'll see the doctor."

And he'll do it, too.

Why did I agree to marry this barbarian?

A corner of his mouth twitches. "You're pretty when you pout, but I won't allow that, either."

"All this *allow*," I say, even as my heart races when he gets closer to me.

It's been four hours since the fire department came and put the fire out in the chapel.

The door to the reception room opens, and his brothers file in.

"Give me the fucking platter, Tav," Orlando says. They're at it again. This time, it's over a silver tray of finger sandwiches. Mario comes in behind them, and my stomach growls at the smell of pizza.

"You two losers can fight over the fuckin' tea party girl food, I'm eating pizza."

"Where'd you get that?" Orlando asks, momentarily distracted from the finger sandwiches. Rosa enters behind him, followed by Marialena.

"None of your business," Mario says, turning his back to him so Orlando doesn't grab the pizza. "If there's any left when I'm done, I might share. Hey!"

Tavi's got Mario by the back of the shirt while Orlando grabs the stack of pizzas.

"Put 'em down," Romeo growls. With a sheepish grin, Orlando obeys.

Rosa curses under her breath in Italian, something about glutinous demons going to hell, but Marialena sits cross-legged on the floor with a piece of pizza in each hand.

"You okay, Vittoria?"

I nod and sit up on the couch, but a stern look from Romeo makes me lie back down. I roll my eyes behind his back, and Marialena grins. She wanted this. I know she did.

"Fill me in, Tav," Romeo says. He sits beside me and pulls my feet onto his lap. He begins to massage them with his strong, rough fingers. It feels like heaven.

Tavi tells all.

Narciso's body has already been brought to the dungeon. I don't know what they'll do next. I don't want to know.

"What about Nonna? She should be seen first." Romeo frowns.

"She's already met with the doctor." Orlando scowls. "And I got her locked in her bedroom so she doesn't try to cook our fucking dinner with a concussion."

"Whoa. That must be serious if it's coming between you and your food." I flush when I realize I might have spoken out of turn, but Marialena's laugh sets off everyone else's. Orlando only shakes his head but smiles.

I put a hand to my head, and Romeo's eyes come to me. "Does it hurt, baby?"

"Yes," I nod. Tears prick my eyes, but not from the pain. I've never had attention paid to me like this before. I've never had anyone care about me.

"What about the other errand?" Romeo's taken a call on his phone and he doesn't meet my eyes. Is he hiding something from me?

"Where?" He nods. "Keep him there. You'll leave him for me to deal with. Better have a fucking pulse when I get there."

"What is it, Romeo?"

He doesn't meet my eyes as he hangs up but works his jaw and shakes his head. I sigh. How am I going to be his wife if he doesn't agree to let me in? "Romeo…"

"Sometimes it's better you don't know things."

"Ha." I laugh mirthlessly. "And that's up to you to decide?"

His eyes light up with the challenge I've thrown him, and his voice goes deeper. "Yeah, Vittoria. It is." He draws in a breath, then lets it out again. "But give it time and you'll know everything."

Romeo raises his voice and everyone goes quiet, tucking into sandwiches and pizza.

"Mama was found with another man. He came to take her away from Papa," he explains. "She wasn't taken as it seemed but left voluntarily."

"But the video footage…"

"Was staged, to make Papa think she was taken."

Oh.

Oh.

I blink in surprise.

"Can't blame her," I mutter before I can stop myself. Marialena snorts. Mario grins at me.

"Vittoria," Romeo says warningly. Then he seems to think twice about his admonition. Bending down, he braces himself on his arm and leans over me. "I'm so glad you're alright." He traces the edge of my jaw with his fingertips. A tingling sensation skates down my chin, down my neck, to my spine. I shiver and close my eyes when he kisses my cheek.

"Marry me, Romeo," I whisper, for his ears only,

when he kisses my other cheek. My body rises to meet his, so eager to touch him, so eager to be touched *by* him, I wish I could make everyone and everything else around us disappear.

"I'll marry you right now, Vittoria. I will make you my wife. I will put my ring on your finger and give you my name. But you know what I expect. No, what I demand."

I do. I nod. I've seen the good, the bad, and the ugly. I can handle it.

"I know," I whisper.

He traces his finger down the side of my cheek, gently, and I can tell he's wrestling with himself. Finally, he nods. "That call just now. I'll tell you what it was about, and then you tell me if your answer stays the same."

"Oh, God, you two, get a room," Tavi says, but Rosa shoves a slice of pizza in his mouth to silence him.

My heartbeat races. What's he going to tell me? I squirm uncomfortably, unsure of what he'll say next. I hold my breath.

"We got a lead on Ashton Bryant. Sent one of my men to secure him." The cool, deadly look of a man who's not afraid of cold-blooded murder makes my mouth dry.

It was the last thing I expected him to say.

"Did you?"

"We did."

He found him.

"You... told them to let you deal with him. You said to make sure he had a pulse."

A muscle twitches in his jaw. "I'll let you know more when I have details, but yeah. He's not dead, not yet, and he'll suffer before he dies."

I'm overwhelmed with the knowledge that my two worlds have collided. Until now, my world before the Rossis and my world after them were two different things. And now...

He found him. He found the man that swindled me and ruined my life. He's going to make him pay.

I'm not sure how I feel about that. Is it right that I'm relieved?

"There's more, Torri." I glare at Mario, but he's giving me a brotherly grin, as if to remind me that if I'm family now I'm subject to his taunts.

"Mario," Romeo warns. "Name's Vittoria."

Mario holds up his hands. "Yeah, yeah, alright. *Vittoria,* we've been looking into why you were here, why you were written into the inheritance. And the truth is, you weren't." I feel strangely cold. I've wondered this myself, but now that we're discussing it, I'm not sure I want to know the details.

Everyone's listening, and I realize then that Leo and Tosca aren't here, and Nonna is missing as well; they've either left or been sent away by Romeo. This right here, sitting in the vast expanse of the reception room, is the next generation.

I nod. I wondered that myself. Why me? I may have an Italian name, but I didn't know this family until recently.

I stare at Mario, trying to comprehend what he's telling me. I don't speak for long minutes, processing. I'm not the only one that does. Romeo is as invested in this as I am, but the look in his eyes tells me this is not the first time he's heard this. He reaches wordlessly for my fingers and interlocks his with mine. I feel as if it's a silent testament of solidarity. We've been through so much, we can get through what comes next.

"When you told Romeo about what happened to you," Mario continues, "we began an investigation. We joined what we knew with what Orlando did, and behind the scenes we've been looking into why you would be written into an inheritance, when it's the first time that's ever happened. Up until this will reading, the inheritance of the Montavio family and anything involving the Rossis has always gone strictly to family. But this time, things were unprecedented. There were other pieces to the puzzle that we had to sort out, such as why my grandfather would bring someone else into this home. And it's pretty simple, really."

"He didn't want your father to have a role anymore," I say softly. "Right?"

"He wanted Romeo to be the boss. The Don."

"We all did," Tavi says softly.

"So what does this all have to do with Ashton? I don't understand."

Romeo continues to stroke his thumb over the top of my hand, but he doesn't look at me this time.

Mario clears his throat. He continues. "You know there was no Ashton. You know the man that pretended to be with you was no real person. You know that he swindled you, but what you don't know is that he was working with our enemies."

"Let's cut to the chase." Romeo's voice pierces through the darkness in the room. All eyes are on him, but he's looking at me. He will not shy away from difficult conversations.

"I'm going to be the one that tells you, Vittoria. Our enemies were in league with a lawyer who fabricated everything, including my grandfather's will. It was an elaborate, detailed plan, but there's a reason why even my mother and grandmother didn't know about it. You were set up. They used you as a pawn."

My voice is hollow. "So the swindling didn't end with Ashton."

He shakes his head. "We believe the plan was for the man who pretended to be Ashton Bryant to set you up to get my grandfather's money, take the throne away from my father, and then to use everything against him."

"So I'm not in the world. That was part of the whole farce."

Romeo blows out a breath and nods. When he speaks his voice is pained. "Yeah, baby. They set it up so they had access to your accounts, and if they could make you inherit the money, they'd take that, too."

"Who is this?"

Romeo looks at Mario. "We're still deciphering that, but we'll find out when we question the man we brought here tonight. The same one you were once engaged to. The man called Ashton worked with my family's rivals."

"They used me."

"They did. As far as we can tell, there is no connection between you and my family, you were only used to separate us. The lawyer's been found to be working with them as well."

"Isn't it a federal offense to tamper with legal documents?"

Romeo's sad smile has a sadistic, chilling edge to it. "Vittoria, he has a lot more to fear than the law."

Of course he does. Oh, God. He double-crossed the Rossi family.

I look at Orlando, the gentle giant with his huge muscles and intimidating frame and see the glint in his eye, the way his fists curl by his sides. I look at Tavi with his ruthless mile-yard stare. He's wearing glasses tonight, and it only makes him look that much more intimidating. I look at Mario, and the usual jovial expression's faded to something dangerous and lethal. Even Rosa's jaw tightens and Marialena's eyes cut to me with a promise of retribution.

"You're one of us, now, Vittoria," Marialena says. "And we protect what's ours."

I'm not one of them, though. I haven't taken my vows to Romeo and have no ties to this family. I'm as penniless as I was before, only now I've been taunted with the promise of so much more. It hurts. It *aches*.

Oblivious to the storm within me, Mario continues.

"Ashton, or the douchebag who called himself Ashton, worked with someone else, and he used my grandfather's death and the fake will as a manipulation tactic."

"How do you know this?" I ask.

Romeo's eyes cut to Mario. "The motherfucker confessed."

Tonight, I saw bloodshed and fire, pain and death. I still haven't recovered from any of it. I shake my head, trying to let it all sift like sand through my fingers, to settle in and make sense, but it doesn't.

Romeo looks sad, and that makes me sad, too.

"Let's get to what matters now, Vittoria. Without the actuality of a will, there's no incentive for you to marry me," Romeo says, and he can't hide the tremor in his voice.

Marialena turns away quickly and swipes at her eyes. She loves her brothers with everything she's got, and I realize with sudden vivid clarity that I do, too. I've never seen her cry, and it pains me to think she is now. Are they crying over what happened? Or are they crying... over *me?*

Rosa speaks up, her voice tremulous. "You may not have six million dollars coming to you, Vittoria," she says with certainty in her voice. She stands, her hands fisted by her sides. "And I will never be the one telling a woman to marry against her better judgment. Believe me, I wouldn't. I couldn't do that to you." She looks at Romeo and then back to me. "But Romeo marrying brings power to this family we haven't seen. It puts the power of authority in

the hands of a man who will actually wield it justly."
My mind is reeling with everything that I'm
processing. "And I can't speak for Romeo, but I can
say without question that we will provide for you,
amply. We can match or better what the fabricated
will promised you."

They want to pay me to marry him?

"But why do you need to marry now?" I ask
Romeo. "If your father... if he dies, then don't you
become the Boss?"

He shakes his head. "In name only until I marry."

"Wow, your family was super traditional."

Mario rolls his eyes. "You have no idea."

They're an organized crime family. By the
world's standards, they are not good people. I have
no place in this family, I have nothing to gain from
this... at least in the eyes of the world.

Rosa continues. "But we will all be good to you,
Vittoria. We would welcome you as a sister among
us. We would provide for you, and you would reap
the benefits of being part of this family."

I blink, startled. "You still want me? Knowing
that what we thought isn't true? Knowing what we
do, you still think I have anything of value to bring
to the Family?"

"Vittoria," Romeo speaks up. "You have everything to bring to this family." He leans forward and
frames my face with his hands. "And I don't want
any more talk. I want to know. Will you marry me?
Will you marry me right now, tonight?"

I'm bewildered by everything that's happened,
but the only thing that's clear to me is that I belong

here. There may have been lies, there may have been betrayal, but there are some things I know with certainty.

One of them is that I love Romeo. The other is that he loves me.

"I have nothing to bring to you." I don't bring an inheritance, I don't bring an established family behind me, I don't bring anything with me but... me.

"I don't wanna hear you say that again," Romeo says. "Don't you ever negate who you are." Marialena sighs and swipes at her eyes again. "You're everything to me."

I nod. "Then... yes. Yes, Romeo. So much *yes.*"

Rosa doesn't miss a beat. "Bring in Father Richard," she cries out to the uniformed staff who wait by the doors. There's still soot on Romeo's face. Tavi is bruised and bloodied. Marialena's hair is a mess, and she only grabs another slice of pizza and grins at me.

I look down at my ripped and tattered clothing, I look down at who I am. And I know who I want to be. I nod. "Let's do this."

It's the least romantic, most pragmatic, fastest wedding in the history of all weddings, defying even a Vegas Elvis chapel wedding to be more efficient than this.

But in the end, I take my vows. In the end, I become Romeo's wife.

———

CHAPTER TWENTY-ONE

"The more I give to thee, The more I have." ~ *Romeo and Juliet*

ROMEO

THE MAN who wronged my wife sits in a windowless, cold dungeon, awaiting justice. He's earned what happens to him next, but I've earned the night with my wife.

I sent her to my bedroom... *our bedroom.*

If I had my way, we'd be in my home in Tuscany, surrounded by flowers, good food, and rivers of wine. Instead, we're in The Castle. But now I am the king of the castle, and she is my bride.

"Get ready for me, sweetheart," I tell Vittoria. "Take a bath. Shave your legs. Wash your hair, and when you're done, put on a robe and lie in bed."

I kiss my way down the length of her body until her skin is pink, and her hips rise to meet me.

"Where are you going?" she asks, a little breathless, but I suspect she already knows.

"I'm putting an end to the life you left. I'm seeking justice for the wrongs done to you." She nods. I brush my thumb over the soft hollow in her cheek and kiss her. "As Don now, my job is to protect you and make sure you're not harmed again."

She doesn't ask any more questions. Good girl.

My brothers wait for me in the dungeon, where the man who hurt my wife sits waiting for me. I remember the night I met her, the night I killed for her.

I killed for her once. I'll do it again. I close the door to the dungeon with a resounding bang.

———

CHAPTER TWENTY-TWO

"THUS WITH A KISS I DIE." ~Romeo and Juliet

VITTORIA

AN HOUR LATER, I'm ready. I lay in bed, waiting for Romeo. My Romeo.

The door opens and he enters, weary, but determined. I don't want to ask what he's done, why his knuckles are lacerated and bloodied.

"Stay there." His word is absolute. I know this now.

"Can I help you?"

"No, *bella.*" He walks to the bathroom and turns the shower on. "My brothers are dealing with the aftermath of everything we've been through, Vittoria. I'm washing off the memory of this night. I want a shower, and then I want to bed my new wife."

It's time for them to rebuild. It's time for them to defer to their new Don.

He turns on the shower, and I lay in bed, thinking. Processing. I think I hear him crying in the shower, but I can't tell for sure. Tears wet my own cheeks.

Tonight, he found out that his mother's found love in the arms of another man. His father's body lies somewhere, lifeless, but I suspect his heart was empty and vacant before tonight. I wonder if they'll give him a proper burial, if they'll ask Father Richard to come.

I hear the water pounding in the shower, but Romeo's quieter now. Some might call him a ruthless monster, and I'd understand that. He's capable of unspeakable things. But I see the man behind the mask, the tortured soul with the weight of the world on his shoulders. And I'm here to help him carry that.

The shower turns off, and a flutter of excitement ripples through me. It's our marriage night, and my husband's coming to join me.

The door to the bathroom opens, and Romeo steps in wearing nothing but a towel. "My God," I whisper. I bite my lip. "It was worth it."

"What was?" he asks. Though he looks weary, there's a new confidence in the way he holds himself, a sturdiness in his step when he walks to me.

"All that brought me here, to you. I mean… well, look at you."

He looks down at himself, and I wonder if he sees what I see. He wears a towel slung low around his waist, concealing almost nothing. I let my gaze travel over his large, broad shoulders, the muscles that ripple beneath scars, and ink that travels from his neck to his arms and abdomen. Words with a message. Ink meant to brand.

He moves his powerful, well-muscled body with surprising grace, but his movements are swift and virile. His long, sturdy legs carry him with an air of command that comes naturally to him and an air of authority he's earned. I look at his powerful, broad chest and sturdy, masculine physique, and my fingers graze my lips.

"What is it, *bella?*"

"Checking for drool," I mutter. He grins, actually *grins,* and his whole beautiful face lights up. I sigh.

"You like what you see, Vittoria?" He bows his head with a touch of modesty. "I'm glad."

He kneels beside me on the bed. "You're mine now. You'll do exactly what I tell you, won't you?"

I shake my head and bite my lip. "Of course not."

A quick look of surprise crosses his features before his gaze darkens. "So that's how it will be."

I nod, my heart thundering in my chest. My pulse races in anticipation of prodding him now that he has nothing at all to stop him from doing whatever he wants to me, whenever he wants to. I've married him. I've stepped foot into the lion's lair, and now he very well may eat me alive, but I've realized something along this journey. I'd rather die his victim than live a colorless life.

I will not consent to blind obedience. It's not who I am. But I willingly took my place as the wife of the Don, and over time, I'll learn what that means.

"I'll have to teach you, you know."

I nod. "I know."

He gives me a warning look. "My word is law, woman."

I nod again. "I know that, too."

"And if you disobey me..."

I drag my fingers to the robe and untie it. The snow-white terry cloth falls to the bed, revealing my naked skin. "You'll punish me," I say in a seductive purr as my fingers graze my nipples.

"You think I won't?" he says in a whisper.

"I'd be disappointed if you didn't," I whisper back.

And then he's on me, my wrists pinned beneath his hands, his hard, heavy body pressed on top of mine. "You've never been whipped," he rasps in my ear. My thighs clench together.

"That sounds scary," I whisper.

"You ought to be terrified."

My eyes flutter closed when he bites my neck then laps the pain away before he suckles. I want it, all of it. I want him to unleash himself on me.

I trust him.

"I can take it," I promise.

"We'll see about that." His cock's hard, pressed between my legs with insistence. My legs part.

"Tonight, I want to fuck you. I want to own that pussy. You'll do what I say and I'll let you come."

"Oh my God. You'd punish me with deprivation?"

"I'd punish you in any way I want."

Gah. I swallow hard, my pulse thundering.

"You're mine, Vittoria. *Mine.*" There's an almost angry insistence to his tone that ratchets my pulse even higher.

I nod, even as I know I don't fully understand what that means, what the implications are. "Any man that touches you loses his fingers. Looks at you with anything but chastity loses his eyes. Do you hear me, woman? Any man that disrespects you loses his tongue. If I find another man's come near you…"

"You'll kill him," I breathe.

"Painfully. Slowly."

I nod again, swallowing as he kisses his way along my jaw. "My brothers will defer to you and treat you with respect. You don't leave my side unless you've got an army of bodyguards in my stead and every living person that comes near you knows you're the queen of this Castle."

I nod, starting to understand, beginning to process it all. It both terrifies and excites me.

I part my legs when he lines his cock up at my entrance. "Nothing comes between us." He thrusts in one savage motion, impaling me. My head falls back as exquisite pleasure floods me. "No condom, no birth control, absolutely fucking *nothing*. You'll take my come, every last drop, and when you leave this room you'll have me still in you, my bite marks on your skin like a brand."

"Is that all? Tell me how you really feel," I breathe.

He smiles against my mouth, but he isn't finished. "You'll have my children. You've taken my ring…" He thrusts again, and my pulse races, my body convulsing with the perfect fullness of him, "… and taken my heart with it."

"I love you, Romeo," I breathe, as he pounds into me, over and over again, his groans mingling with mine, our naked skin like silken wraps, sliding against one another.

"And I love you, Vittoria. Vittoria Rossi," he whispers, as my body succumbs to bliss. "My wife."

I close my eyes and really feel what he says, allow myself to be called *wife*. For some reason, it actually makes me feel like the queen he says I am.

Much later, Romeo makes a phone call and orders food brought up to us on trays. We linger in bed, naked. He ties my hands together, something that excites me and unnerves me all at the same time, but then he feeds me little bites of iced scones and rich pieces of thick bacon, followed by tangy bites of orange and thin slices of ripe apples. I swallow every bite.

He makes me come with my wrists bound, using his fingers and tongue until I'm writhing and deep in the throes of perfect ecstasy. The bound wrists, I know, are only a prelude of what's to come with him. He likes control. I'm learning that I like giving him that.

He releases my wrists only long enough for me to feed *him*. Like his brothers, the man has an appetite. He takes the proffered bites of baked goods, a few bites of an egg sandwich, and sips of coffee as appetizers, then makes love to me until I climax so hard I scream myself hoarse. It feels good. Release, you could say.

I lay next to him in bed tangled in the sheets, the evidence of our lovemaking still sticky on my thighs as I lay against his chest. We'll clean up, but now I like this sort of filthy little vignette.

"Pull your jeans on," he whispers in my ear.

"I haven't showered—"

A sharp crack to my ass silences me. "Put 'em on, babe, or I'll plug your ass to teach you to watch your mouth."

Plug. Your. Ass.

WUT.

"Uh. Okay, so… Mr. Kink, I have no idea what the hell you're even talking about."

His eyes light up with a fiery devilry that tells me I'm screwed.

An hour later I'm wearing a *bejeweled* butt plug and walking as if he's found the internal *switch* to my obedience button. He beckons to me from the dining room, and I walk to him like he's got a remote control to my will in his hand, only it's solidly wedged between my ass cheeks.

Every step feels like foreplay, helped out by the fact that he christened each ass cheek with his belt before he slid the plug in. Said something about making me wet and making things glide more easily, but don't they make lube for that? I think he just likes to do what he wants with me.

I'm not complaining.

I know he has a lot to tend to today. We've been through so much, and we haven't come to the end of this battle. In some ways, I suppose it's only just the beginning. He's on the phone when I reach him in the dining room.

"Cain. Romeo Rossi. Need a favor, man."

He tugs me onto his lap, and I become so keenly aware of the plug in my ass I don't hear another word he says. I have a vague notion that Cain has something to do with Marialena's friend, and that Romeo's calling in a favor.

I don't question him. I'm already seeing there are intricacies and ins and outs to things I don't under-stand, that he and his family live by maxims I don't yet know.

We don't go downstairs the next day. He takes his phone calls sitting at his desk with me, naked, straddling his lap. He orders our meals to be brought up to us, and I eat more than I have in my entire life. With my belly full I nap, sated by our intense lovemaking. And when the evening dark-ness begins to settle, he gets a wicked glint in his eyes.

"You know I like control," he says, his voice raspy. I nod. A slow, wicked smile crosses his face. "Go to the walk-in closet and see what I have in there for you."

Still naked, sore from the epic lovemaking, and a

little drowsy from the nap I just woke up from, I do what he says.

I open the door, and gasp. He's had all my clothes brought here, but it's only the beginning. Shelves upon shelves of shoes, boots, sandals, sneakers. Rows upon rows of dresses, sweaters, tops and bottoms. But that's not what makes me gasp. Small knobs are fastened along one wall and he has various tools and toys displayed. I wonder for the first time if I've bitten off more than I can chew.

"Vittoria, come here." I feel as if I'm walking on needles, waiting for him to instruct me to bring one of those wicked-looking tools to him. I'm already drunk from the sex that we've had all day long, and I'm not sure what he'll make me do next.

I can't get away from him even if I wanted to, but the physical restraint makes everything seem more intense. He walks to the closet and returns with a few things I don't recognize. A blindfold, a stick of some sort, and a small little leather thing. He fastens my ankles to the stick, spreading my legs wide. I feel as if I've been trussed up for a sacrifice.

"What's on your mind?" he asks, working some tool in his hand. I love the look of concentration he gets, the way he focuses on me like there's nothing in the world that matters. And the deliberate, calculated pain he administers in small doses escalates in every nerve in my body so that they sing in a euphoric symphony.

So I tell him. "I feel as if you're going to sacrifice me on some kind of altar."

"Sacrifice?" He shakes his head, bends, and pinches my ass cheek.

"Ow!"

"Didn't you hear a word I said? I'm giving you to *no one*." He unravels a soft leather strap.

"Nuh uh." My pulse quickens.

"No?" His voice is hard, demanding. "You're telling me no?"

"I am," I say loftily, using every ounce of courage I own. "And what are you gonna do about it?"

He lifts a leather belt and comes to the bed as if I've just given him a gift.

————

CHAPTER TWENTY-THREE

"That all the world will be in love with night..."~Romeo and Juliet

ROMEO

I WAKE beside the most beautiful woman I've ever seen. The early morning light illuminates her skin, but I like to think it's the all-night lovemaking that paints her cheeks that soft, pale blush. The scent of coffee lingers in the air, cinnamon and bread and bacon.

"Is this our honeymoon? I can deal with this. Forget traveling," she murmurs, her eyes still closed but a smile playing on her lips. "All I need to do is make love to my husband and eat the food your staff makes."

"You'll have both of those things for the rest of

your life." I roll over and kiss her cheek, already hard just watching her lie here next to me. She rolls over to meet me halfway, and slides her hand to my cock. Her fingers wrap around me, and she begins to stroke while shooting me a wicked grin.

"My, my," she whispers. "Your stamina's impressive, Romeo."

I kiss her cheek as I nestle my face in the hollow of her neck.

After we settle peace back into The Castle, some of us will go back to our homes in various places in Massachusetts. Tavi to his place in Boston near the North End, Orlando to Tuscany to oversee the vineyards and winery, Mario to wherever the hell his harem will follow him, and Santo... I still need to deal with Santo.

He tried to marry Vittoria, but my sources confirm he was blackmailed by my father. We had to deal with the aftermath of the attack, and I wanted a few days with Vittoria before I dealt with him, so I had him stationed at a safe house in South Boston until today.

Today, we deal.

After a morning languishing about in bed, we rouse ourselves and get ready for the day. Nonna meets us in the dining room with a platter of Vittoria's favorite pastries, sfogliatella, flaky pastry filled with ricotta and candied fruit.

"My God, you'll fatten me up," Vittoria says, but that doesn't stop her from taking two of them.

Nonna smiles. "Too thin!" she says, waving her fist in the air. "Too thin. Your grandfather, he like," she says, gesturing to the pastries before waddling out of the room.

Vittoria looks at me, her eyes wide, the sfogliatella halfway to her mouth. She blinks in surprise at me. "Did she say my grandfather?'

"She did." Motherfucker. "Nonna!"

Nonna looks over her shoulder inquisitively. "Si?"

"You knew her grandfather?"

"Si," she says with a nod before the door shuts behind her.

"*Nonna!*"

She comes back to us with a labored sigh. "Much to cook, Romeo, what is it?"

"We didn't know that. How did you know her grandfather? It's important."

"In the war, her grandfather and my husband. Saved life. Good friends until he died." She blows out a breath. "Now I go?"

"My grandfather knew your grandfather... my grandfather saved your grandfather's life?"

"Which means... that without him, I wouldn't be here," I say. Wow. It's hard to wrap my brain around, but I'm glad that I know this now. It makes Vittoria that much more special to me.

I wonder what else Nonna has up her sleeve.

"Nonna!"

She curses in Italian behind the door before she slams it open. "*Si.*"

"You know anything about Santo?"

She sighs. "Si. Of course. My husband no like Santo, no blood line. Doesn't trust him. Says he will betray in the end." She shakes her head, her thick accent coloring her words. "Your father used him. He took Vittoria in that chapel but I there." She pounds her chest. "I see. Santo no want to hurt her. Santo afraid of father." She shakes her head and her typically harsh tone softens. "Be kind to Santo, Romeo. Your father..." her voice trails off. "He no good to him."

I frown, processing all of this.

"Now I go," Nonna says, glaring at me.

"Anything else I need to know before you do?" Other than Mama, she's probably the only one I have no control over.

She smiles. "The pots have ears, Romeo. They listen." Singing a little ballad, she goes back to the kitchen.

"Should bug the kitchen," I mutter.

"I dunno, I kinda like the way she tells it, though," Vittoria says.

I run a hand across my brow and pinch the bridge of my nose.

I have much to do.

She holds my hand and laces her fingers with mine. "What's on your mind, Romeo?"

"So much to do. I have to interrogate Santo, and I don't want to use our usual methods. I just want to ask him questions, give him the benefit of the doubt." He's taken the vow of Omertà like all of us, and I can't imagine he'd betray us. "But he tried to marry you..."

She nods, likely suspects he'll answer to me for that. But I'm weary. So fucking weary. I never liked violence, but this was my lot in life. I've taken the throne as king of this castle, and my duties are heavy.

"And your mother…" Vittoria works her lip. "The night she left…"

"She was with her lover, and no, we don't know who that is yet." Could prove problematic, or it could prove useful. "And if the Castellanos are after us…"

Vittoria nods. "A whole other can of worms."

"Yeah."

My mind goes back to twenty years earlier, when I was just a boy. A boy who wanted a smoke by the quarry… My family's buried so many secrets, it's only a matter of time before the skeletons surface.

Vittoria stands, walks to me, then straddles my lap. She rests her head on my shoulder.

"You carry a lot, Romeo. So much, don't you?"

I nod. I close my eyes and hold her to me. I relish the warmth of her body and her soft, feminine scent. I breathe her in then breathe her out. I run my fingers through her hair and try to think about how much I love her, how much I need her, but it's overwhelming to me.

"You don't have to carry it alone anymore."

"Thank you."

We hold each other in the quiet. She rests her head on me and we don't say another word. Sometimes, words don't capture the essence of a moment.

EPILOGUE

"*Give me my sin again.*" ~*Romeo and Juliet*

VITTORIA

ONE YEAR later

"WHERE. ARE. YOU."

I know that tone of voice, and I know I'm in trouble. I also know that this is exactly what I wanted and what he needs right now.

Life in the Rossi family's on speed, *always.*

Orlando's been arrested, Tavi's getting married in an arranged marriage next week to a woman none of us have ever met, and my period's late. The Family has grown, healed. Tosca's home, a semi-retired matriarch of the family, since Romeo's assumed the position as patriarch, and she doesn't talk about the affair she once had. I do wonder if she holds a candle, though.

Santo was demoted, after proving Narciso blackmailed him, but he's working hard to get himself back in Romeo's good graces. I keep my distance from him.

And Rosa and Marialena have helped me with all of this, explaining how to handle things as they come and Tosca, in her own way, has as well. We've been trying now for months to get pregnant, with no luck, and it's important to him. I'm more willing to let things happen in their own time, but Romeo's stressed under the weight of it all.

I know exactly how to bring him comfort. Give him a reason to seize control, and my hotheaded, dominant, boss of a husband will be back in the right frame of mind in no time.

I dip my toes in the hot springs, one of my favorite things to do in Tuscany. Saturnia is a spa town in Tuscany, and the hot springs are open all year long. He doesn't like me coming alone, which I have not done, but I don't think now's the time to tell him I've got two bodyguards in tow.

"Hot springs, honey," I say nonchalantly. "Relax."

"Relax?" he growls. "*Relax*? I come here to find you and you're nowhere to be found? I texted you twelve times, *twelve times*, Vittoria, and you didn't respond to me." He's seething. Uh oh. My ass clenches.

"I'm sorry."

"You fucking will be."

My heart taps a beat in my chest, the dance of dominance and submission a dangerous one that Romeo loves and I'm still learning the steps to.

When I get home, he's waiting for me, dressed in a three-piece suit that he hasn't even shrugged out of yet. I helped him pick it out. Pinstripe navy, to bring out the color of his eyes.

"Hi, honey," I say cheerily, pushing past the way my heart hammers so hard in my chest I can hardly hear myself speak for the pounding in my ears.

"Don't fucking 'honey' me," he says, every bit the dangerous king of the underworld I married. "Strip." His eyes rake down my body, eying the bikini I'm wearing. I had a cover-up on at the springs and this bikini's only for his eyes, but he doesn't need to know that. "That's what you fucking wore to the springs?"

He doesn't like me to wear anything that would draw unwanted attention to me.

I shrug.

"Vittoria," he growls, his eyes narrowing dangerously. He crooks a finger at me. "You have three seconds."

I tip my head to the side. "Yeah? Or what?"

"Or *what*?" He curses in a string of Italian so dirty my cheeks blush.

"You'll have to go to confession for that, sir."

He lifts the folded belt in his lap and snaps it. My sex quivers.

"And so will you, sweetheart. Right here. Over my lap." I see the tension around his shoulders ease a bit when I lower myself over his lap. His knees pressed up against my belly, I sigh, even as I brace for the punishment he'll give me.

A hardheaded man like him needs an outlet. His outlet is *me.*

I'll tell him the truth, all of it, after he's whipped my ass and made me climax. I'll cuddle up to his chest and tell him all the things, and he'll run his fingers through my hair and hold me, because this is how we work.

This is how we live.

This is how we love.

————

FROM THE AUTHOR: Thank you for reading Oath of Silence! *I hope you've enjoyed this book!*

Would you like to read a bonus epilogue? Who wants to see...a Rossi family wedding? Go here: https://Book-Hip.com/RFTTTZA

IF YOU'RE ready to read more in the Rossi family saga, read on for a preview!

————

OATH OF OBEDIENCE
    Chapter One
    Orlando

I WAKE up at the crack of dawn. No one tells me what to do, most especially the roll call asshole who clangs an alarm at six in the morning. So my eyes snap open at five, every morning.

My roommate snores gently, but it don't bother me. I grew up with so many brothers and sisters, you just sort of ignore noises over time. They fade in the background like so much else. There's a small window in here, a cell I earned for good behavior. The other cells are windowless, when you're not locked into solitary.

I push myself out of bed, slide down the bunk, and hit the floor. Nothing like waking the body up with a morning plank. I drop into plank position, forearms on the floor, abs tight, welcoming the burn in my muscles. Give myself thirty seconds to rest the abs before I'm up again. I'm panting and sweating by the time I'm done. I stand, stretch, then hit the floor for push-ups.

"When I get out of this hell hole, remind me to have you on speed dial, bro," Dario says, rolling over. He props himself up on one elbow and smiles, the flash of white against pink lips the only thing I see in the dark.

"Oh yeah? You startin' up a fuckin' bromance?" I say, panting, in between reps.

Dario chuckles and talks through a yawn. "Fuck that. You know if I wanted a bromance, would've hit on you when I was fresh outta the damn shower, not all sweaty and shit."

I smile but don't reply, my breath coming in short gasps, my muscles straining with the effort of push-ups. Last I checked, I hit a deuce and a half on the health office scale. Not easy to fucking push-up two hundred fifty pounds, especially before I've had my coffee. You make due in a small cell, though. I've worked my body hard since I've been in here, and I won't stop.

Roll call comes and goes. I take the utilitarian shower we're allowed before the payphone comes by, wheeled on a cart.

"Rossi. You're up."

The corrections officer shoves the call cart to me. I hear a murmur of voices the next cell over and somebody mutters my name. Gotta be a new guy. Everyone else knows who the fuck I am.

"Don't need a call today," I tell him, turning my back on it before I grab the makeshift pull-up bar for another set of reps. He clears his throat. I ignore him.

"Nah, man. Incoming. Might make that call today if I were you," he says.

I push up, and feel the lengthening of muscles in my abs and back and welcome it.

"Oh yeah?"

"Yeah."

He runs a hand through his hair, and I drop to the floor. I give him a sharp look. He knows something.

He takes a step back.

Good. Haven't lost my fuckin' touch in here. It's better for me when a look works as well as a fist.

The officer's young, thin, and ready to shit his pants. Never understood why guys like him didn't pick another fucking job. Why corrections officer? Why voluntarily push yourself into a prison with inmates that scare you shitless?

I take the phone, and he flinches. I sigh. "Bronson. Leave, man. Go cook some fuckin' books, will ya? They pay better than this hell hole, and you'd sleep better at night." I shake my head and pick up the phone. Dario chuckles behind me.

I get a little knot in my throat when I hear Romeo. He's been in Tuscany on business until last night. I've missed my older brother's voice.

"Got a surprise for you, Orlando."

I release a breath and run my fingers through my short cropped hair. "Yeah? WHat's that?"

"Now if I tell you, wouldn't be a surprise, would it?"

I smile, warming at the sound of his voice, the familiarity of talking with him. Fuck but I miss my family. "Guess not."

"Be on the lookout, man. Around lunchtime."

"Alright, if you say so."

He chuckles, and I hear the whisper of a female voice in the background. Vittoria, his wife.

"Tell Vittoria I say hello." I only knew her a year before I was taken into custody, and that was a goddamn year ago. "Any bambinos coming yet, man?"

He sighs. "Not yet," he says in a low voice. "Ain't for lack of trying."

I groan. "Rub it in, why don't you?" Still, I feel sorry for him. Rossi family tradition tells us that children are a king's crowned jewels, and that life is incomplete without little ones running around underfoot. Some might even say the Rossi family views children as a commodity, and it's why my mother had so many. I have other views, though. I think we helped her not feel so lonely. Hell, maybe we still do.

Jesus I miss them, all of them, even pain-in-the-ass Mario and bossy Rosa. Marialena I miss most of all. My baby sister and I were always close and have grown even closer after my father's passing.

We chat a bit longer before I hang up the phone, curious what he's got planned for me. Money, maybe, so I can pick shit up in the canteen. New books, even better. Already plowed through every damn thing he's sent and most of the books that interest me on the prison's library shelves. It won't be food, which sucks, since I'd give fucking anything for a plate of Nonna's pasta or Mama's panzerotti. And it sure as fuck won't be a goddamn conjugal visit lined up for me, thanks to Boston's puritanical ways.

I slug down breakfast like medicine, tasteless oatmeal and burnt sausage, drink the swill they call coffee, and toss down an orange for the hell of it. Suppose if they used oranges to fight scurvy back in the day when traveling by ship, couldn't hurt behind bars.

I do another workout after breakfast and check on deliveries. Nothing from Romeo. When I come back, nearby cellmates are yelling out chess moves. We can't play actual chess here, so the more astute yell out moves for a mental game.

"My bishop takes your bishop," Dario says, giving me a wink when I get back.

"You winning?"

"When am I not winning, man?" he asks. True.

I stand for the fourth damn roll call, wondering if Romeo was just blowing smoke up my ass. That's not who he is, though. Romeo's word is law, damn near carved into tablets like the commandments from Sinai.

I'm thinking. Mulling shit over. Finally, I clear my throat.

"Dario." I keep my voice low so no one hears. "You know who I am, brother?"

He sobers and nods. "I do, man." His eyes shoot to the skulls inked on my knuckles, before looking at the rose on my forearm. "I do." There's fear in his eyes I didn't expect, and it dawns on me that he might think I'm threatening him. Wouldn't be the first time I bared my forearm as a claim to the Rossi brotherhood. There are times when it's helps to reference your status as an established brother of high rank in the most powerful organized crime ring in New England.

I continue to keep my voice slow. "When you get out of here," I say in a little whisper. "You come and find me. Do you know where to find me?"

He nods and swallows audibly. "I do."

"The fucking car theft landed you here. You come see me and I'll give you a better job than that."

We're always recruiting new men to our brotherhood, always swearing men in with vows of allegiance, obedience, fidelity and honor. The original core of our ring are related by blood, but when we find someone worthy of the oath of Omertà, we're not above recruiting. And I know this man to be loyal, hard-working, and fucking ruthless.

It's time to hit the shower. I follow behind Dario, but when we get there, the usual guards are gone. My stomach clenches, my instincts primed. *Shit.*

Dario meets my eyes in a silent vote of confidence, and I give him a nod. Not a touch of fear in his gaze.

My eyes quickly linger on the scarred floors, marred by sharpened shanks. The shower is one of the most notorious places for a beat down.

Someone overheard our conversation. Should've fucking known it.

"Orlando!" Dario shouts. I duck when I see him look over my shoulder, on instinct, and a fist flies through the air where my head just was. Adrenaline courses through me, excitement weaving its way through my limbs.

The brothers in my ring of men have been trained in many things. Interrogation, money laundering, intimidation tactics, among other things.

Me? I've been trained to fight.

I duck one blow, only to take one of the side. I elbow my attacker without a second thought, and feel my elbow crack ribs. Dario has my second attacker in a headlock, but the third barrels at me full force, knocking the wind out of me. When I'm heaving for breath, Dario held to my side in a headlock, my attacker walks around me.

"You think because you're a Rossi, your shit don't stink?"

He circles me with a blade. I don't respond. There's no response to someone taunting me except to wipe this concrete floor with his face. I flex my fingers.

I don't have time to get away. He lunges for me, but I quickly dodge. His head rams into my solar plexus, winding me. I'm knocked on my ass. But I'm so furious, I come up swinging. He drives at me, slices along my arm. And then one quick move I grab his wrist and go to snap it.

Dario shouts, "Orlando, no! You're out of here man. They're jealous. They don't want you out."

I knock one out cold and don't give him the beating he deserves. Dario sits on the second. The third I restrain with my own bare hands. Son of a bitch.

I have him at my mercy. I could beat the shit out of him. I could fucking kill him. At the thought, an image of the last man I beat, his head smashed against the concrete pavement outside of a dive bar in Southie, flashes in my mind. I'm serving time for involuntary manslaughter. I meant to give him a beating, teach him a lesson for badmouthing The Family. I didn't know he was gonna hit his fucking head. Didn't know it would kill him.

And I don't want the blood of another man on my hands.

It's why my father hated me.

The alarm sounds, too late. Planned.

Guards come in, prepared to cuff and restrain. Dario speaks up. "Orlando was attacked, and he did nothing. Check the footage. These guys came after him because they're jealous."

Goddamn it. If they fucked anything up…

A guard comes with a set of keys and shakes his head. "You're lucky you've got a friend in here," he says, shaking his head. "I'm here to let you out."

I blink. "Let me out?"

"Yeah, brother. And if you'd beat those other guys, if you were guilty at all…" his voice trails off.

Dario grins at me. He called it.

"Remember, Dario," I tell him as I'm led out in cuffs. "Remember what I said."

"I will, brother," he says, nodding with a sad smile. He clears his throat and calls the next move out loud and clear. "Check mate."

———

USA Today bestselling author Jane Henry pens stern but loving alpha heroes, feisty heroines, and emotion-driven happily-ever-afters. She writes what she loves to read: kink with a tender touch. Jane is a hopeless romantic who lives on the East Coast with a houseful of children and her very own Prince Charming.

You can find Jane here:

My newsletter:
https://landing.mailerlite.com/webforms/land-ing/l2a8h4
My Facebook reader group:
http://facebook.com/groups/275445129563714
http://janehenryromance.com

BB bookbub.com/profile/jane-henry
f facebook.com/janehenryromance
O instagram.com/janehenryauthor
a amazon.com/Jane-Henry/e/B01BYAQYYK

Manufactured by Amazon.ca
Bolton, ON

22312330R00173